The Togakushi Legend Murders

The Togakushi Legend Murders

Yasuo Uchida

Translated by
David J. Selis

戸隠伝説殺人事件

Charles E. Tuttle Company
Rutland, Vermont & Tokyo, Japan

Published by the Charles E. Tuttle Company, Inc.
of Rutland, Vermont & Tokyo, Japan
with editorial offices at
1-2-6 Suido, Bunkyo-ku, Tokyo 112

© 1994 by Charles E. Tuttle Publishing Co., Inc.

LCC Card No. 93-61515
ISBN 0-8048-1928-9

First edition, 1994

Printed in Singapore

Contents

Prologue

The bolt came loose with a noise so loud it frightened him. Apparently, though, it was lost in the wind, because he heard no sign of any movement in the house. Since sundown, the wind had been strong enough to sway the larger branches of the trees. The whole mountainside had come astir, and an occasional gust of wind roared like a howling beast past the eaves. It was a south wind, out of season for the end of November. The old people of the village said such a wind could bode no good. But for him, it came at just the right time.

Slowly, very slowly, he opened the heavy sliding door, then crept up the step into the hallway, his face so close to the ground that he might as well have been sniffing for scents. Lying on the floor, he closed the door. Making sure there was still no noise in the house, he finally stood up and headed for the room he wanted.

He was a little lame in the right leg. During military training the year before last, the gun of a new recruit had gone off accidentally, sending a bullet through his right thigh. At the time, he could have killed the man, but when he realized that the injury had gotten him out of further military service, he could have thanked him. Actually, it didn't hurt much any more, and although he couldn't run, at least he didn't have much trouble walking. In the presence of others, however, he was very careful to exaggerate his limp, and at every change of season, he complained to everyone he met of the pain, and cursed his ill fortune. Whenever he met families of soldiers at the front, of course, he always told them that he couldn't wait to get into battle himself. If only his leg would heal, he would add, chewing his lip.

Nearly all the young men of the village had been drafted. Even those with families, as long as they were young and healthy, were receiving their red slips one after another. The only ones yet left were those who were extremely lucky, or those like him, who were physically unsound. And no matter how lucky a man might be, the red slip was sure to come sooner or later. But he had made his own luck, and as long as he kept on acting, he would be safe.

As the tide of war turned against the country, the sad notifications of those killed in battle were pouring in. Some families had already lost all their breadwinners. He had been going around visiting such families, consoling the widows, and helping out with any work requiring strength. Men's hands had become scarce in the village, and in spite of his disability, his services had become invaluable everywhere. He had always been a careful and diligent worker anyway, and his somewhat guilty conscience had pushed him to work even harder.

Needless to say, no matter how good the intentions of a young man, it was not really desirable for him to enter the home of a young widow or a daughter come of age. In the present state of things, however, society could not afford the luxury of such gossip, so it was tacitly understood that everyone would look the other way. Actually, he couldn't say what his intentions had been. Maybe it was just what happened when a man and woman were thrown together like that. It had happened to him with not just one widow, but three. And he—not particularly attractive to women until then—had gone into such ecstasy as to believe that any village woman worthy of the name could be his for the asking. Why, then, had he been forever wearing himself out for others? More and more, he had felt a compulsion to take a girl of marriageable age for himself, a compulsion so strong that he had actually tried to do it, thereby getting himself into very serious trouble. The girl's father had nearly killed him, and he had escaped only by making an abject apology.

With the spread of rumors of that encounter, even the widows who had been giving him their favors became wary of their reputations and would no longer let him come near them. And now, having thus tasted sex and being unbearably hungry for more, the only way he could see to get it was to steal into a house under cover of night and make a woman his. Such a custom had long since disappeared from the village, but he knew that it had once existed, and he had resolved to follow it.

Stealing through the hallway, he did worry that he was setting his sights terribly high, but he had persuaded himself that if he was going to do it at all, he might as well do it big. Taki had always been like a goddess to him. A marriage to her was something worth risking his life for. Besides, the only other people in the house were an old servant couple, Keijiro and his wife, so even if something did go wrong, he would not be likely to encounter such an ugly scene as had occurred last time.

✳ ✳ ✳

Descendants of a long line of old-time diviners, the Tendoh family held a special position among the hereditary families of Shinto priests who tended the Togakushi Shrines. Taki was the Tendohs' only daughter, a girl of extraordinary beauty even in early childhood, whose fame had spread to places as far distant as Tokyo through visitors to the shrine and students of Shintoism. As a little girl dancing in her shrine-maiden's outfit, she had always enthralled her audiences.

As she grew up, her looks had ceased to be the only thing extraordinary about her. Time and again, she had seemed possessed, in words and conduct. Science could not explain her behavior, leaving it to individual opinion whether she was merely insane, or whether she was truly possessed by spirits. But belief in spiritual possession was in the nature of the Togakushi region, and she quickly became known among the villagers and Shintoists as a girl of very special powers.

Fearing what those powers might become when they matured, however, Taki's parents had not welcomed their daughter's singular predisposition, so when she graduated from grade school in the spring of her fourteenth year, they had sent her to Tokyo—on the pretext that she was going there to learn manners—to be entrusted to the care of the family of a viscount, who was their close friend and an enthusiastic worshipper at the Togakushi shrines.

She had returned to Togakushi three years later, along with the viscount's son, who was being sent to stay with the Tendohs in hopes of effecting a cure for his tuberculosis through a change of climate. It had been given out that Taki was to act as his nurse, but those close to the Tendohs could see that the two young people were strongly attached.

That had been in the summer of the year before last, and

since then, the Tendoh household had been visited by misfortune. At the end of last year, Taki's parents had both died within a short time of each other of malignant influenza compounded by pneumonia, there being no way to get the proper medicines to fight the diseases. Then, at the end of the summer of this year, with the war situation worsening and even students rapidly being drafted, the viscount's son had finally been called back to Tokyo, leaving the stately Tendoh home inhabited only by Taki, about to turn nineteen, and the elderly servant couple, both over sixty.

* * *

The intruder had thus persuaded himself that there was nothing to fear—except perhaps Taki herself. He was not sure that he would not lose his nerve when he came face to face with her, whom he had always considered totally out of his reach. The respected Tendoh family, with its long line of Shinto priests, had a history dating back to the Muromachi period, and what was he but the son of miserable peasants? To be sure, he had been born with a good head on his shoulders and had attracted a fair amount of attention to himself in school, serving as class leader and all that, but graduation had left him still just the son of peasants. By no stretch of the imagination was he a suitable match for a girl of her class. In a peaceful world with a stable society, he would never have been trying such a preposterous trick. But times were different now, maybe so different that he might even succeed. If he did, he would be taking the heiress of the Tendoh family for his bride. Carnal desire and greed were making him bold as well as desperate.

Having helped out at the end of every year with the traditional housecleaning, he was thoroughly familiar with the rooms Taki used. The first double sliding door past the turn of the hallway was the entrance to her bedroom, but just before he got to the turn, he heard her coming out. Hastily, he took cover behind a large cabinet. The sliding door opened and a dim light threw her shadow across the floor. Holding a candlestick, she stepped out into the hall. He almost said something at the sight of her in her shrine-maiden's dancing costume of white tunic and crimson pantaloons, red lips vibrant in a pale face illuminated by the flickering candle. When she closed the door behind her, her face looked even more a vision in the candlelight, and though he wondered what she could be up to at this time of night, he was overcome by her otherworldly beauty.

Quietly, she opened the big sliding closet door across the hallway. The closet appeared to be stuffed with instruments of Shinto rituals. Taking hold of a big cross-tied box on the far right, she lifted it without seeming effort, which surprised him, because it looked quite heavy. Setting it down in the hallway, she stepped into the closet. He couldn't imagine what she was doing, and he was even more surprised when she closed the door behind her, leaving the hallway dark again, except for a dim light visible under the door. Soon, even that disappeared.

For a while he just stood there, expecting her to come out again any second. But she didn't. He stood motionless for five or ten minutes. Then he thought he heard voices, hushed whispers that seemed to come from far away, but he could tell they were young, much too young to be those of Keijiro and his wife.

Pretty soon, he recognized one of the voices as Taki's, but he still could not identify the other. He found enough courage to go over to the closet door, press his ear against it, and listen hard. Now he clearly heard laughter, hers and someone else's, fainter. He opened the door and entered the closet. Taki was not there, but the voices became much clearer. Then he heard her, in a passionate voice, say the name "Tomohiro."

It was that fellow! Tomohiro was the name of the viscount's son—Tomohiro Tachibana. The intruder felt the blood rush to his head. While helping in the garden, he had often seen Tachibana pass by on the veranda. He could see the pale oval face, the face of a boy with an elite upbringing. Taki was always following close behind, with no concern for the eyes of a mere hired hand like himself. He had hardly existed for either of them, but the effeminate boy from Tokyo was robbing him of his goddess, and he could not bear the humiliation and jealousy.

As he cursed to himself about the viscount's son enjoying Taki's favors, probably in a secret room behind the closet, he suddenly remembered that Tachibana shouldn't be there at all. He had received his draft notice and was supposed to have returned to Tokyo! But who else could it be? The intruder groped frantically along the wall. There had to be a device somewhere for moving it! Finally, by mere chance, he touched something and felt a slight motion, seemingly of the entire wall in front of him sliding to the left a bit. With great caution, he pushed it further, until suddenly he was blinded by a bright light shining through the opening. When his eyes adjusted, what he saw made him dizzy.

The area of the room was only about three mats, but still, having worked in that house practically every day, he didn't see how he could have failed to notice it, small as it was. He could not imagine how the space had been designed to hide such a discrepancy.

Against the opposite wall, a girl and boy were locked in an embrace. On a thick silk pallet, the boy was lying on his back and the girl was face down on top of him, her crimson pantaloons discarded near her feet. Her white tunic mostly covered them, but he could tell from the protruding hands and feet and a glimpse of the girl's back that they were naked.

There was no mistake. The girl was Taki and the boy was indeed the viscount's son. The intruder saw her sit up astride him and cry out for joy, upon which the boy raised himself and embraced her madly. The tunic fell from their shoulders, revealing practically their whole bodies under the light of an electric bulb.

✳ ✳ ✳

The south wind had stopped blowing, and the day passed pleasantly with no wind at all. Keijiro and his wife spent all day in the garden cleaning up dry leaves and twigs.

"Can I help with anything?" offered Tachibana.

"Don't be ridiculous!" replied Keijiro, glaring at him. "You're taking a chance just coming out onto the veranda. You'd better get back inside."

"Oh, it's all right. Nobody will see me," laughed Tachibana. Confident he was safe, he didn't mind having a little fun with the old man. He had been hiding here for three months, and all the tranquillity was beginning to bore him. He could no longer believe the eyes of the authorities might find him all the way out in this lonely village deep in the mountains. Just once, several men from the Nagano City Police had come and searched every corner of the house, but they had completely missed the secret room. It had already been two months since that search, and Tachibana was sure that the army and the military police must have forgotten all about him.

"Tomohiro! You shouldn't be here!" exclaimed Taki in a shrill voice behind him.

"Oh! You scared me!" He made a show of jumping. When he turned around, however, her look really frightened him, though it did not express anger, but rather fear.

"Okay, okay," said Tachibana, making a joke of it as he withdrew into the room. Taki quickly slid the door shut and came up to face him.

"Why can't you understand how worried we are about you?" she said, crying. Taki was subject to sharp and violent swings of emotion.

"There's nothing to worry about. I know what I'm doing."

"Then will you please stop going out onto the veranda? It frightens me terribly."

"Okay, since you feel that strongly about it. But you sure are a worrier, you know," Tachibana laughed.

Taki didn't even smile. She just stood there looking at him for a moment, then suddenly fell to her knees and began to topple over forward.

"You'll hurt yourself!" he cried, dropping to the floor and catching her in his lap, where he put his arm around her. She clung to his neck, her face close to his, crying wordlessly. She would not tell him what was wrong. She had done many strange things, but he had never seen her like this before. He spoke to her as he would to a small child. "Now why don't you just tell me what's making you so sad? If you won't tell me, how can I do anything about it?"

"When you go, it will be all over for me," she managed in fragments, beginning to sob convulsively.

"Me? Go? Where? Where is it you think I'm going?" he asked gently, rocking her in his lap.

She began to shake her head in time to the rocking. He knew this was her way of saying that she didn't know. The fear that had overcome her was a vague one. With hardly bearable pity, he held her close. "I'm not going anywhere," he said. "I'm always going to be with you."

But Taki's fear was beyond the reach of Tachibana's protestations of everlasting affection. Apparently frightened by some sort of premonition, she seemed to be sinking deeper and deeper into melancholy. Tachibana had been seeing that melancholy ever since he received word from his father in Tokyo that the red draft slip had come for him.

At the time, unable to believe the authorities would have sent a red slip to him, the eldest son and heir of a viscount, a college student, and one presently taking a cure for tuberculosis besides, he had thought there must be some mistake. Although he told Taki cheerfully that he would be back in no time, she had warned him emphatically not to go and had given him a lot of trouble. Tearing himself away from her and going to Tokyo, he had found a hard reality awaiting him. His draft deferment had been canceled, and his father the viscount, apparently on extremely bad terms with the military, had apologized to him with a look of fear that Tachibana had never seen before, and which frightened him to the core. He was sure that if he were ever sent to the battlefield, he would die before an enemy bullet ever hit him.

But Tachibana did not want to die, and his father's fainthearted look told him it was all right to run. The elder Tachibana must have known what that would mean for the rest of the family, but thought it preferable to having his whole family line cut off. "This war can't last much longer," he said finally, avoiding the expression of any personal feeling before turning abruptly and walking away.

Having gotten the message that he should not throw away his life, Tachibana had run. The day before he was supposed to report, he had taken the morning train from

Ueno and arrived in Nagano that evening. Avoiding the
bus, he had headed for Togakushi along the winding path
that led from behind the Zenko Temple to the old road.
Hurrying through the night on an empty stomach without
a stop at either of the two teahouses along the way, solely
concerned with getting to his destination, he had reached
the Tendoh house in the dead of night, and been startled to
find Taki waiting for him beside the door. Keijiro and his
wife were up as well, happily preparing a bath for him.

"Taki was sure you would be here, and here you are!
Now don't you worry about a thing. We're all ready to
protect you," said Keijiro, alluding to the secret room. He
and his wife were crying for joy, unconcerned that Tachibana
was betraying his country.

That night, Tachibana had slept with Taki for the first
time, at her instigation. She had come into the secret room
behind the closet in her shrine-maiden's dancing costume
and put something that looked like dried weeds into an
incense burner. When he asked her what it was, she had
answered only that it was hemp, as she put her head
coquettishly against his chest. The bluish smoke rising
over the incense burner had filled him with a miraculous
feeling of exaltation, such that all his fears and troubles
and self-hatred gave way to an expansive feeling that the
only people in the world were himself and Taki. His time of
joy and fulfillment passed in a dream, and before long, he
had fallen into a deep sleep.

And now, three months later, Taki had another such
premonition. He could reason it away, but seeing how
unhappy she was, he could not rid himself of the uneasy
feeling that she might be right. As evening approached, her
state became really alarming. At supper, she did not touch
her food, but kept looking around her restlessly, throwing
her arms around him from time to time. Infected by her

fear, Keijiro and his wife were both nervous and kept getting up to make sure all the doors were locked.

After sunset, the north wind began to blow, and the evening cold belied the comfortable warmth of the day. Taki made Tachibana retire early to the secret room, staying right beside him all the time, too rigid to speak and crying incessantly. She could not tell him what was frightening her. She knew only that something evil was approaching.

Around nine, they heard the sound of a car coming up the slope and stopping in front of the house. She held her breath, and he could feel her clinging ever harder to him. Voices came from the entryway, Keijiro asking who was there, and a very loud voice answering. Tachibana did not recognize the name given, but he was relieved to realize that he did know the voice. Keijiro must have been just as relieved, because he released the lock and opened the door.

Simultaneously with Keijiro's scream, they heard an unfamiliar, angry voice, followed by the rude clump of street shoes approaching down the hallway. "There!" said the first voice, and they heard the closet door open. Something fell, and then the wall was yanked open in front of them. A young military officer stood there, gripping his saber. Seeing his military police armband, Tachibana knew all was over.

"Oho! You've been living quite a life here, I see!" said the officer, barging straight into the room, casting a lecherous look at Taki in her shrine-maiden's costume. "Well, you can't make fools of the army like that." He glanced back at the NCO behind him, then turned toward Tachibana and shouted, "Get up!"

Tachibana stood up slowly, pulling his robe closed across his chest, Taki cowering at his feet. With no warning, the officer slammed Tachibana with his fist, knocking him back against the wall. With difficulty, Tachibana regained his footing.

"Handcuff him!" ordered the officer.

The NCO yanked Tachibana's hands behind him and put handcuffs on so tight they dug into his skin. Then the officer hit him again, this time full in the face, knocking him flat. His head hit the wall as he fell, and he began to lose consciousness. Though aware his nose was bleeding, strangely enough, he felt no pain at all. He heard Taki scream.

"Hey, get those funny clothes off the girl," said the officer with a leer.

"Huh?" said the NCO, hesitating.

"Hop to it!" shouted the officer.

The NCO put his hands on Taki. Tachibana tried to cry out, but his voice wouldn't work. The crimson pantaloons and white tunic were ripped off.

"All of them!" rasped the officer.

"Yes, sir!" said the NCO, his eyes getting bloodshot like the officer's. He slapped Taki's cheeks as she tried desperately to resist, distracted with fear, her eyes vacant and moving aimlessly, her whole body twitching. Dimly seeing her exposed breasts, Tachibana finally managed to raise himself, open his mouth, and shout, whereupon the officer shoved the muzzle of his gun into it. With the excruciating pain of broken front teeth, he sprawled backwards.

"You do it first," said the officer with a lewd laugh. "I don't mind."

"No, no, after you, Lieutenant."

"Don't be silly! Go ahead!"

"No, I'll go last."

Totally limp against the wall, Tachibana heard the misplaced courtesies from far away. The last thing he heard was the officer saying, "Now take this, you son of a bitch," as he kicked him in the pit of the stomach with his military boot. Tachibana's already foggy vision went blank.

✳ ✳ ✳

On August 20, 1945, the Hoko Shrine village suffered the most disastrous fire in its history.

Seeing the flames lick upward, Haru Kusumoto knew immediately that it was going to be a big one. The summer's drought had been endless. Not only had there not been any rain for the past month, there hadn't even been any clouds worthy of the name. The dry south wind coming across the Zenkoji Plain had been blowing up the slope all day every day, until it had taken every last drop of moisture out of the soil.

Situated on an incline at the southern edge of the Togakushi Plateau, the village centered on ten-odd households of Shinto priests who tended the Hoko Shrine, one of the three main shrines of Togakushi. The approach to the peak where the shrine stood was a straight road up a long steep slope lined on both sides with the magnificent thatched-roof houses of the priests, around which were scattered the houses and shops of the villagers. At the top of the slope, the road made a wide detour to the right around the base of the peak and continued on toward the village around the Middle Shrine.

Standing on the very summit of the peak, the Hoko Shrine was reached by a precipitous stone staircase from the top of the slope. Togakushi had once been a mecca for ascetics practicing their religious austerities, and this staircase was one of the remnants of that past. Standing at the bottom and looking far up the stairs between the giant cedars, most people dreaded the thought of climbing them.

Even some of the local people, not to mention many unaccustomed worshippers from afar, avoided the main approach up the stairs in favor of the gentler "Women's Slope" to the left.

But it was not until she became pregnant with her first child, her daughter Natsue, that Haru Kusumoto had begun to use the Women's Slope. Until then, ever since she was old enough, she had always used the long staircase in both directions. Even now, she was still in the habit of breezing down it.

Leaving the shrine office, Haru looked back from the top of the stairs to see Natsue still watching her from the passageway that ran from the office to the shrine stage like the gallery used in Noh drama. Leaning against the railing, Natsue spread out her arms and gave the long sleeves of her shrine-maiden's dancing costume a big shake. It was the cute mannerism of a child, but looking at her from this distance, Haru realized that her daughter was growing up. Give her just six months or a year.

In addition to the regular rituals, for a suitable donation the dancers and musicians of the Hoko Shrine could be employed at any time, as they were this day, to make special offerings for individual parishioners or groups. Until shortly before, warlike prayers for victory and good fortune in battle had been in the overwhelming majority, but with the official surrender, these had given way completely to prayers for the safe return of soldiers from foreign campaigns, and routine peacetime prayers for a good harvest and family safety.

Only Shinto priests and their families could be shrine dancers. It was the obligation of every little girl born into a Shinto priest's family, as soon as she reached school age, to serve several shifts a week dancing on the stage as a shrine maiden. She was relieved of the obligation only when she reached puberty, a menstruating woman being the greatest taboo in a Shinto ritual.

Looking back, most women had fond memories of the days they had spent dancing on the shrine stage, but for some little girls, it could be a very trying experience. A shy child like Natsue, for instance, would never get used to the stage no matter how long she spent on it. On a day when it was her turn to serve, she was always in a bad mood, from the time she got up. It was Haru's job to coax her into her costume and get her to the shrine office, from which point her husband Nagaharu, a Shinto priest, took over.

Waving back at Natsue, Haru turned to go down the steps, and it was then that she saw the flames. The lines of cedars, said to be hundreds of years old, rose toward the sky on either side of the staircase. In the green of the branches which hung over the stairs from left and right, there remained a thin strip of open space directly above, and through that space, from the vicinity of the farmers' houses at the bottom of the slope far off in the distance, she saw a column of smoke and flame shooting up almost like a signal flare.

It was later determined that the fire had started in a barn, the result of three little children accidentally setting fire to the hemp-stalk wall while playing with matches. Of the principal products of Togakushi, the best known by far was buckwheat, but next came hemp, which flourished because the soil was conducive to the growth of long fibers of high quality. The stalks were a by-product that remained after the outer skin was peeled off for fiber, and when dried they burned very well and could be used for such things as fuel for the big fires built as a send-off for the spirits at the end of the celebration of their annual visit. Unfortunately, the local farmers also used the stalks to make the inner thatching for the walls and roofs of their barns, because they provided the needed ventilation and were the cheapest thing available. But in the event of a fire, there was no material worse.

Consuming the hemp-stalk wall in an instant, the fire leaped quickly to some brushwood piled up in the barn and then to the thatched roof, from which it soared skyward with an appalling shower of sparks. Except for the post office and the school, almost every building had a thatched roof, every one dry as a withered shepherd's purse. The fire jumped first to the house of the barn owner, and about the time that house was enveloped in flames, blue smoke was beginning to rise from the roofs of surrounding houses.

Any number of unfortunate circumstances compounded the disaster. Next to the drought itself, there was the fact that the fire had started at the lower edge of the village, and was thus blown up the slope by the dry south wind from the valley. Lunch was over and all hands had just gone off again to the fields. The drought had completely dried up the water supply for firefighting. In normal weather, the stands of cedar would have served to impede the flames, but the tips of their sprigs had dried to the color of straw, and far from serving as a check, they flared up like giant torches as soon as the resin was heated to combustion point by the fiery hot wind.

Nagaharu Kusumoto, who came running at his wife's call, stood there at the top of the stairs and groaned. He was still in the costume of the god Tajikarao, in which role he was always cast because of his strong build. Based on the myth of the Rock Door of the Heavens, the performance at the Hoko Shrine consisted of such parts as the goddess Uzume's dance, with Tajikarao's opening of the Rock Door as a climax, and the Dance of Urayasu, performed by shrine maidens. Other priests came running out after Nagaharu. Mitsuyoshi Otomo, who had been playing the role of Uzume, came out in a white flaxen tunic over a crimson pleated skirt. His gentle face instantly began to twitch. Of all the priests there, his house appeared closest to the fire, although the view was obstructed by the cedars, making it hard to determine the exact location from which the smoke was rising.

"Oh my God! I've got to get down there," said Mitsuyoshi, dropping his skirt on the ground and rushing down the steps.

"Father Otomo," called Haru after him, suddenly re-membering, "Would you check Taki's place, too, please?"

"Okay," called Mitsuyoshi, too busy watching his foot-steps to turn or even nod his head, leaving Haru wondering if he had really heard.

Toward the end of the year before, the military police had come to Taki Tendoh's house and taken away the viscount's son, who had been harbored there. Haru had heard from Keijiro and his wife that the men had raped Taki. Several days later, Taki, Keijiro, and his wife had been arrested, this time by the civilian police. Three months after that, Taki had been released alone and sent home, four months pregnant, and insane. Since then, she had been taken care of by Haru and her mother.

"I wonder what this is going to do to Taki," said Haru to her husband, standing beside her. Taki was due this month, and Haru was afraid the shock might cause her to give birth on the spot. She didn't know what they would do if that happened.

But Nagaharu did not seem to hear her. "Why aren't they ringing the fire bell?" he shouted.

"Isn't that fire pretty close to the fire tower?" someone shouted back.

"Then maybe they can't get the firefighting pump out," shouted someone else.

Everyone was apprehensive, imagining what was going to happen to the place if they were forced to just let the fire burn itself out.

"Anyway, all of you had better get home," said Nagaharu. "Haru, you take Natsue and get down there quick."

"What are you going to do?" she asked.

"Warn the villagers with the drum. Without the bell, people in the fields and mountains may not know there's a fire yet." He started at a run toward the shrine.

At the shrine stage, the religious group gathered to witness the dance offering they were supposed to get for their donation stirred in surprise as Tajikarao burst on stage and began to beat the drum with a discordant rhythm. Hurried along by the sound, Haru, with Natsue by the hand, went down the Women's Slope. Still in her shrine-maiden's costume, Natsue had trouble keeping her cuffs from getting tangled as she tried to keep up with her mother. On top of that, she was still holding the bell she had been using in the dance, and it was ringing busily with every step she took. This annoyed Haru, but she couldn't tell Natsue to throw it away. Moving along to the mingling of drum and bell, she was greatly surprised to find herself imagining that she was back dancing on stage in the days of her childhood.

The Kusumoto house was right at the base of the peak, so Nagaharu could afford to let the other priests go down first, because his house was farthest away from the fire. Haru's mother, Nobu, was standing outside the yew hedge wondering what to do. "It's a big one!" she exclaimed, relieved to see Haru. She pointed all around toward the bottom of the slope. In the time it had taken

Haru to get down from the peak, the smoke had spread considerably.

"Where did it start?" asked Haru.

"Who knows? The patrolman from the Middle Shrine was here a few minutes ago, and he says he got word that the fire had even got into the post office."

"Even the post office? That means it must be all over the bottom of the slope."

"I guess so. Dry as it is, who can tell how far it will burn?" Suddenly Nobu realized someone was missing. "Where's Nagaharu?"

"He's beating the drum, because the firebell didn't ring."

"Oh he is, is he?" Nobu looked up at the peak. She was used to the sound of the drum, but right now it only made her mad. "At a time like this, he ought to be down here with us. What are we supposed to do without him?" she said, scowling. Nagaharu was an adopted son-in-law. The Kusumotos had produced only women for the last two generations, and he and Haru had yet to produce a son.

"I wonder how Taki's doing?" worried Haru. The smoke did not look like it was too far from the Tendoh house. "I'm going to go have a look."

"This is no time for you to be doing that!"

"I'll be right back. Would you mind getting Natsue changed out of her costume?" said Haru over her shoulder as she rushed off.

As Haru came around the curve at the top of the slope, the whole scene of the fire came into view. The level area at the bottom was already a sea of flames, and even outside that area, the fire had spread to ten or more houses. It seemed to be moving faster along the houses to the east than it was north up the slope with its many trees, and there was already a lot of smoke pouring from the windows of the school building, about a hundred meters from the heart of the flames. If the school caught, the fire would spread much further in one leap. Haru imagined the scene as she ran along with shaky knees.

The handcart with the pump being brought down from the Middle Shrine village rattled loudly past her. The firemen in their livery coats were mostly middle-aged or older, and their hoarse shouts to mark time as they pulled the pump hardly inspired confidence. Out of the blue smoke into which they were headed came small groups of people fleeing up the slope with only the clothes on their backs. The fire must have spread too quickly for them to save a thing. They hurried along as fast as they could, covered with soot, children howling and adults raving.

As Haru reached the Otomo house, the family was trying to get its belongings out. Two houses away, the farmer's roof had caught fire, and they could feel the heat on their cheeks with every gust of wind.

"It's no use. We've got no water," said Mitsuyoshi, carrying an oblong chest, nodding toward the pond in his garden. A little stagnant water was barely visible on the bottom, and the newts were turned red bellies upward.

"Did you check on Taki?"

"Yes, but she wasn't there. She must have already fled."

Placing the chest on the cart, Mitsuyoshi hurried back into the house. Out of it came his wife, moving slowly with her palsied mother-in-law leaning on her shoulder. The younger woman grinned at Haru. What the grin might mean, Haru could not guess. The older one, her bloodshot eyes fixed on the sky, kept mumbling about the wrath of the gods. She had suffered a collapse from the shock of the defeat, and since then had taken it into her head that the gods were sure to punish Japan for its unconditional surrender.

Mitsuyoshi had said that Taki was not there, but Haru

decided to check anyway. Taki's house was just a block away on the other side of the street, and it would be only a matter of time before the fire reached it. Haru could already hear the rustle of sparks falling on the tops of the cedars, oaks, and chestnut trees above her.

Entering the house, she found the air unexpectedly cool. It was dark inside, and her eyes took some time to adjust. She called Taki's name any number of times from the entryway. The houses of all Shinto priests were big, intended as they were to provide accommodations for religious groups, but the Tendoh house was conspicuously larger than most, and Haru could not be sure that her voice would carry to every corner of it. It was no time for ceremony, and she did not bother to take off her shoes. Going to the back, she looked into the bedroom. Taki was not there. Haru called out at the top of her voice, then strained her ears for an answer. Finally, she heard a faint moaning.

Taki was in the garden at the back, crawling on the ground on all fours, her face smeared with mud.

"What are you doing, Taki?" scolded Haru.

"It's coming out . . . it's coming out . . ." Taki howled at the sky like a wolf, her hand pressed against her lower abdomen, as if she were trying to hold back a bowel movement. Her belt was undone and the front of her unlined kimono was dragging on the ground, her breasts and her gigantic belly half exposed.

"What's coming out, Taki? Do you mean the baby's being born?" asked Haru, rushing over and quickly tying Taki's belt.

"It's coming out, it's coming out," Taki kept on, bobbing her head up and down. Each time her head went down, her tears dripped onto the ground. Fear and pain were once again distracting this unfortunate girl.

Haru had to do something, but what? "Taki, you wait here. I'm going to get my mother." She started to go.

"Don't go! Oh, please, don't go," cried Taki desperately.

"But . . ." As Haru turned to look at her, Taki fell flat on her back, her legs toward Haru, and the bottom of her kimono fell open. Before Haru could avert her eyes from the embarrassing sight, what she saw made her gasp. From between Taki's spread thighs, a blood-smeared spherical mass was pushing its way out. It was unmistakably the baby's head. All over Taki's white thighs and buttocks were dribbles of slime that looked like the trails of slugs, and trickles of blood were running everywhere.

She would die like this, thought Haru, rushing into the house in a daze. She fumbled all over the place in the darkness until she had managed to find two cushions, a pair of scissors for cutting the umbilical cord, and some thread, then she went back to the garden.

The baby's shoulders were already visible. Taki's arms and legs were stiff, and she was groaning intermittently, apparently with the effort of trying to push the baby out. Haru placed the cushions under Taki's buttocks. The baby came out slowly above them. With an agility she would not have believed possible of herself, Haru took hold of it and laid it gently on the cushions.

In the distance, she heard the roar of the fire.

Poison Plain

 From the Rokumu Slope behind the Zenko Temple, the winding road up the mountain gained altitude steadily. Making a wide detour around Mount Omine, it came out all at once on the Iizuna Plateau, from which point it became a level road called the Birdline, with many straightaways, cutting through a forest of larches toward the Togakushi Mountains. Ahead of them, Togakushi West Peak was already showing its mysterious face.

Tachibana had heard that this "Birdline" had been constructed along practically all of the route once followed by the so-called Old Road, which had served as an approach for worshippers to the Togakushi Shrines, and he was now whizzing along comfortably in a car on the same route up which he had fled thirty-eight years ago. Since the fall of 1964, when the Birdline was completed, Togakushi had ceased to be isolated by the surrounding mountains.

"This is the first time you've been to Togakushi, isn't it, Professor Tachibana?" asked Shimizu, who was sitting next to him.

"Uh, I was here for just a little while many years ago."

"Were you really? As a matter of fact, I thought that was a look of fond reminiscence on your face. Well then, I don't need to tell you about the place, do I?"

With a rueful smile, Tachibana realized that he must indeed have been looking sentimental.

"Anyway, you certainly are a real life-saver, agreeing to come along like this," said Shimizu for the tenth time. "When Shiraishi told me he couldn't make it after all, I was really in a spot. A clumsy oaf like myself certainly wouldn't have been welcome there alone. You'll make a much better impression. This should get us a lot of good will. Should make the sponsors pretty happy, too."

"You make me sound like a male geisha," laughed Tachibana.

"Oh no, please don't take it like that. It's your reputation that I'm counting on. It was because of that that I asked you to join me. I'm not kidding you."

"I don't mind."

"Of course, like it or not, there come times when not only the administrators, but the professors as well do have to play male geisha." But it was obvious from Shimizu's smile that he didn't dislike it too much.

T— University, where Tomohiro Tachibana taught, was at the top of the second rank of private universities, but it had established affiliated high schools all over the country and put so much effort into seeing that they all had good baseball teams that the joke was going around that its high schools would soon be taking over the nationwide high school baseball tournaments. The university had become better known for baseball than for learning.

Shimizu, the university president, held a Doctor of Science degree from Imperial University and was a scientist of undisputed reputation, but he had found his true calling as an administrator. He showed great skill in negotiation with outside organizations, and when it came to getting his own professors to do something, he was an excellent persuader. There was something about the man that made it impossible to dislike him.

Having wanted to establish an affiliated high school in Nagano City for a long time, he had jumped at the chance to scratch the back of a member of the education subcommittee of the lower house of the Diet elected from the First District of Nagano, a man named Shishido. Hearing that Shishido wanted to build a golf course somewhere in the area, Shimizu had offered his cooperation in return for assistance in obtaining permission to build the school. Now he was hurriedly responding to Shishido's rush invitation to the first meeting of the organization to promote the golf project, a meeting which was actually a party to entertain local people of influence, from whom Shishido was expecting considerable opposition.

Tachibana had been dragged along in spite of his protest that he did not even play golf. "You can't know whether you might enjoy it or not unless you pick up a club and give it a try," Shimizu had said, unconcerned. "And anyway, the enemy should be satisfied if we just put in an appearance."

Shimizu had made it sound like a picnic, an invitation that would not bear refusal. But before they arrived, Tachibana had thought the meeting was to be held somewhere in Nagano City, and evidently Shimizu had made the same assumption. It was only in the car sent to meet them at Nagano Station that they learned they were going to Togakushi. Shimizu had been quite pleased, but if Tachibana had known, he would most likely have refused the invitation, whatever the consequences. Togakushi held altogether too many bitter memories for him.

He had visited Togakushi once more, after the war, in the summer of 1947. His tuberculosis had gotten worse on the Southern Front, where it had been compounded by malaria, but just when he began to think he was finished, the war ended. After this narrow escape from death, he was late being repatriated and had to spend a long time in the hospital even after that. But as soon as he was able to get around, he insisted on going to Togakushi. He was ordered by the doctor, of course, to stay put, but he was not to be stopped, and in the end he left the hospital without the doctor's permission.

In the two and a half years since he had seen it, though, the Hoko Shrine village had changed completely. Looking up in the direction of the shrine from the bus stop at the bottom of the slope, he could not believe his eyes. The rows of priests' houses were gone without a trace, and in their stead was nothing more than a scattering of poor, barracks-type huts. He rushed frantically up the slope, only to find that the Tendoh house was gone with the rest. Of that imposing structure with the secret room in which he had hidden, not a pillar was left, only the bare, dark-red scorched foundation. That was the cruelest stroke of all.

A woman in traditional work pantaloons had come out of the hut across the street pushing a bicycle, and Tachibana ran quickly over to her. When she turned around, her face looked familiar. He remembered her as the daughter-in-law of the Otomo household, whom he had occasionally seen from a window. But she didn't recognize him. That was natural enough, since he had seldom gone out, and had stayed hidden all the while he was evading the draft.

"Excuse me," he said, "could you help me?"

"Yes?" she said.

"The house that used to be here, the Tendoh house, what happened to it?"

"The Tendoh house?" She gave him an enquiring look. "You don't know about the fire, then?"

"Fire?"

"Yes. The big fire the year the war ended. The whole neighborhood burned down."

"There was a big fire?"

"Yes." The woman's look asked what else there was to say.

"What happened to the people in the Tendoh house?"

"You mean, to Taki?"

"Well, uh, yes . . . there was someone named Taki, and uh . . ." mumbled Tachibana vaguely, before he realized that he was being so cowardly as to try to conceal his identity. Angry at himself, he spoke up. "Yes, that's right. The young lady named Taki and the elderly couple who lived there."

"You want to know where they are now?"

"If you don't mind."

The woman looked troubled. "I'm not sure, but I heard they died."

"You mean, in the fire?"

"No, no, not in the fire."

"Then when, and where?"

"I'm really not sure."

"But you do know what happened to them after the fire, don't you?" Annoyed that she wouldn't give him a straight answer, Tachibana raised his voice.

"Who are you, sir?" she asked, looking up at him.

It was Tachibana's turn to try to avoid a straight answer. "Well, I stayed here once, and I haven't been back to Togakushi for a long time, so I . . ."

"Well then, it's better that you don't know. I'm very sorry, sir."

With a deep bow, he hurried off, imagining he saw the light of recognition in her eyes. Tachibana the returned soldier, who had lived through all the humiliations of war, was a mere shadow of the student of two or three years earlier, but he feared the shadow might be recognizable.

He went straight up the slope to the top and began slowly climbing the stairs to the shrine, noticing along the way that the village had not been totally destroyed. The two or three houses closest to the peak had survived, as if under the shrine god's protection. And he found some solace in the fact that the giant cedars on both sides of the staircase remained.

A drum sounded to signal the beginning of a dance offering, recalling for him the summer of his first year of junior high school, the morning after his first arrival in Togakushi to stay with the Tendohs, when the sound of the drum had for some reason frightened him. Now, so many years later, each beat filled him with inexpressible emotion.

He reached the top of the stairs just as the shrine maidens were preparing to come on stage. Four young girls in white tunics over crimson pantaloons, wearing gold crowns and shaking sacred bells in each hand, came across the boardwalk and around the veranda. When they had performed their ritual worship in front of the shrine and taken their places at the corners of the stage, a flute began to play a peaceful tune. The drum beat out a monotonous rhythm and the girls shook their bells in time to it, as they spread their long sleeves and began a serene dance.

He had stopped, his eyes fixed on the stage, thoughts crossing time and space to see Taki once more as a child on that same stage. She had been far more graceful and beautiful than any of the other dancers. No one could compete with her for beauty as a dancer. The dance was usually monotonous, but it never seemed so when she was performing it. The other three dancers had always seemed merely to be following her lead. Taki herself would be in a sort of trance. She had once told Tachibana that she forgot everything when she was dancing.

And now he had been told she was dead. In spite of himself, he began to cry, and the shrine maidens on the stage became but a haze.

More than thirty years had passed since that last visit. Tachibana had thought that what had happened to him at Togakushi had been locked tight away in the recesses of his consciousness, along with his war memories. In the mid 1950s he had gotten his position at the university, and in 1957 he had begun a calm, uneventful marriage. He had gone neither against the trends of the times nor with them, but had spent his whole life in mediocrity. He and his wife had never had any children, probably because of the malaria he had contracted, and she had died just before their silver wedding anniversary.

Shortly before her death, she had expressed pity for him, but when he asked her why, her response had been only a faint smile. After her funeral, he had recalled the incident and wondered why it had never occurred to him before that perhaps she had known—while pretending not to—that a part of his heart was elsewhere.

* * *

The golf-course meeting was held at the largest hotel in Togakushi, the Koshimizu Plateau Hotel, a smart, three-story, North-European style building facing West Peak across the Togakushi Plateau, splendidly located with the Togakushi Ski Slope on Mt. Kenashi right behind it.

The promoters spent from 3 P.M. to about 4:30 P.M. explaining their aims. Then came a reception starting shortly after five. July had just begun, and there were not yet many visitors to the Togakushi Plateau. Toward dusk, it began to look like rain, but there were no complaints about the weather. Guests who had disparaged the hotel as a place way off in the mountains at which they could not expect a decent meal were more than satisfied by the feast of top-quality beef dishes, as well as fresh crab and shrimp from the Sea of Japan.

Shimizu introduced Tachibana to one local person of influence after another. Tachibana exchanged perfunctory greetings with all of them. But one person bothered him a little, a man introduced as the head of the Takeda Firm. Glancing at his face as they exchanged cards, Tachibana had the feeling they had met before, though the name, Kisuke Takeda, did not ring a bell. He was a man of strong features and solid build, a little over sixty, with his scalp visible through thinning hair, neatly parted on the side.

Something must have struck Takeda as well, because he looked strangely at Tachibana, and his hand seemed to be shaking as he received the card. But his greeting itself was perfunctory, which seemed to indicate that he did not, after all, think they had met. At the time, Tachibana thought they must have been mistaking each other for someone else, or had perhaps just met somewhere in passing. But later he found himself unable to forget Takeda. Something about the man kept on bothering him. From time to time during the party, he glanced at Takeda, often to find that Takeda was looking at him. When their eyes met, both of them would quickly look aside. But after several such incidents, Takeda suddenly disappeared from the party.

"Is something the matter?" asked Shimizu, coming over to fill Tachibana's wine glass. "You don't look like you're having a good time."

"Oh yes, I am," replied Tachibana, putting on a smile. "By the way, who exactly is that gentleman, Kisuke Takeda?"

"I say, you do have an awfully good eye, don't you? That

fellow is right at the center of the financial world of northern Nagano Prefecture. He's got especially strong ties to Representative Shishido. Fact is, Shishido is reluctant to show himself at the head of this golf course business, so he's using Takeda as a sort of front. They say this Takeda has a lot of power behind the scenes in Nagano politics. We'd better get him on our side, too."

"I see," said Tachibana absentmindedly, gazing in the direction in which Takeda had disappeared.

2 The rain which began in the middle of the night of July 3rd continued until just before dawn on the 7th, when the mysterious peaks of Togakushi were once again sharply outlined against the blue sky.

At about nine that morning, five co-eds got off a bus at the Imai bus stop. They had come from Nagoya the day before last, and had been staying at a tourist house in Kinasa, shut in by the rain. Now they were finally out to take the hike they had been waiting for, though they had been told that the mountain trail might still be impassable. They wanted at least to get far enough to see the Demoness Maple's Cave.

After walking for twenty minutes from Imai, they came to the Ashitagahara information sign, located on a rise that gave a good view of the scattered houses of upland farmers. The sign said that the Demoness Maple had use to come here every morning because it reminded her of her native Kyoto. Another twenty minutes or so beyond that, walking uphill along a narrow farm road, they reached the Arakura Campground, on a pleasant plateau surrounded by white birch and larch trees. Normally it would have been covered with tents and lively with crowds of young people, but they had all been chased away by the three straight days of rain. After a brief rest in the office at the campground entrance, the five girls started out for the Demoness Maple's Cave. Just two-hundred meters along the trail was a sign which told them that this place was known as "Poison Plain" because it was here that the Demoness Maple had served poisoned saké to the enemy general, Taira no Koremochi.

"Plain, huh? Must be talking about you, Miyuki," said the girl first in line, making a malicious pun as she started out again. She took one step and fell down with a little scream.

"See? Say things like that and you get what's coming to you," said the leader, coming over to help her up.

"Over there, over there," whispered the girl, pointing at something as she reached for the hand offered.

Just twenty or thirty meters ahead of them, against the base of a thick tree, a man was sprawled as if dead drunk, in a sitting position on the bare ground. He was dressed in a well-tailored summer suit, but it had gotten all wet and hadn't had time to dry out.

The leader gasped. One by one, the other girls froze in their tracks as they reached the spot. Taking strength in numbers, though, they did not flee.

"He's dead, isn't he?" whispered one of them.

"He can't be!"

"Ssh, he'll hear you!"

But the man could not hear them. His hearing, along with all of his other senses, had long since ceased to function.

"He is dead!" declared the leader, her voice hushed.

The girl on the ground pulled herself slowly to her feet, her legs very weak.

"Don't run!" appealed the leader feebly, as one of the

girls started to do so. But the rest of them panicked and followed suit. The girl who had just gotten up fell again as soon as she started down the slope. Her comrades left her sitting there covered with mud, cursing through her tears at their retreating backs.

Contacted from the campground office, the local patrolman rushed there. Reassured by the sight of him, the girls managed to collect themselves after their headlong flight and lead him and the two men from the office back to the scene. Even the mud-smeared girl, who had finally come in, sulking, joined the others at the last moment, afraid to be left alone.

The patrolman requisitioned all the rope in the office and asked the other two men to carry it. Some distance before they reached the body, he stopped everyone, then went on alone, his billy club at the ready. Having made sure the man against the tree could do him no harm, he bent over for a closer look.

The suit was certainly out of place for the scene. Though a soaked mess, it and the tie both were obviously very expensive. The man looked like he had been all dressed up for a night on the town. He appeared to be about sixty. His head was sunk on his chest and his thinning hair was hanging down over his forehead. His face, the nape of his neck, the backs of his hands—all exposed skin was blotched with death, and the odor of decay was already about him. It was obvious that he had been dead for some time.

The patrolman came back to the others and cordoned off the area by looping the rope around the surrounding trees. Leaving the two men from the campground on guard, he took the girls back to the office.

Nagano prefectural police headquarters received the first report at 10:20 A.M. Inspector Takemura was about to get into the car with his usual driver, Kinoshita, when he was stopped by Miyazaki, his superior, the head of Investigative Section One.

"Takemura, you ride with me, will you?"

"Oh? Are you going too, sir?" Takemura thought it strange that the head of Section One himself should be going out on the first report of the discovery of a body. Something must be up, he figured, but he got in beside Miyazaki without asking what.

As soon as they started, Miyazaki got on the radio to Nagano Central Station, in whose jurisdiction the body had been discovered. "Get this to all investigators headed for the scene in Imai, Togakushi Township. When they get there, they are not to approach the body, but are to see to it that the area is not disturbed. Under no circumstances is anyone to do anything until Inspector Takemura and I arrive."

The bewildered Takemura finally asked, "Something up?"

"Yeah." Miyazaki's long, narrow face became even longer and narrower as he pursed his lips and wrinkled his forehead in a deep frown before continuing. "You see, this body that's been found in Togakushi, there's a possibility that he may be a VIP."

"A VIP? Who?"

"We're only going by his age and the clothes he's wearing, but there's probably no mistake."

"Oh?"

"We think it's Kisuke Takeda."

"Takeda!" exclaimed Takemura. "You mean, *the* Kisuke Takeda?"

Even Takemura, unfamiliar as he was with politics and finance, had heard of Takeda, one of the top two or three businessmen in the northern part of the prefecture, a man who was sure to have his hand in any big real estate deal

there. Takemura recalled hearing that Takeda had recently
been involved in the promotion of a golf course near the
Togakushi Ski Slope, and he supposed also that the man
must be active behind the scenes in politics.

"Then there's been a missing persons search request out
for Takeda?" continued Takemura.

"Yes, unofficially."

"But we haven't heard a thing about it where I am."

"That's because the chief decided that only the department heads and me and the head of Section Two needed to
know. Of course, it looks like the head of Section Two had
to put several people on it to begin making private inquiries."

"Which means, in other words, that we're going to have
to work with Section Two on the murder, I take it?"

"Now let's not get ahead of ourselves! We don't know
yet that it is a murder," said Miyazaki hastily.

＊　＊　＊

It was on the morning of July 5th that the prefectural
police had been informed of Kisuke Takeda's apparent
disappearance. At home that day, Chief Shoichi Nagakura
had received a telephone call from Governor Masagi,
requesting that he pay a visit to the governor's mansion on
his way to work, on a matter of the greatest urgency. The
subdued voice had sounded quite unlike that of the normally frank, unaffected governor. Guessing it would take a
while, Nagakura had a scheduled conference put off an
hour.

He had hardly expected to find Representative Hirofumi
Shishido at the governor's mansion. Shishido was a member of the ruling party, but not someone Nagakura thought
much of. He was the very picture of a man one respected
out of fear alone, a man not only publicly active in politics,

but rumored to wield considerable power behind the scenes as well.

"Ah, Chief Nagakura, terribly sorry to have called you out so early in the morning." It was Shishido, all smiles as he stood up with extended hand, who greeted Nagakura in the reception room. For Shishido, that was hardly imaginable behavior, and Nagakura was on instant guard.

"Then this matter concerns Representative Shishido?" asked Nagakura, looking past Shishido to Governor Masagi just behind him.

"No, it doesn't, really," replied Masagi, "but Representative Shishido thought it would be better if we got you here."

Masagi would be seventy-two this year. Now past the middle of his fourth term, he was a mainstay of prefectural politics, widely supported by conservatives and liberals alike. Blessed by nature with an elegant head of silver hair, a strong, well-tanned face, and a tall muscular build, he added to those charms a reputation as a man of integrity, who could be counted on to be fair to everyone.

Shishido, on the other hand, was a man of such a different stamp that Nagakura could not imagine what he was doing there. Although he could not have been much past sixty, he looked as old as Masagi actually was. Of short build, with a considerably receded hairline and deep wrinkles at the corners of his eyes, he spoke suavely, but there lurked about him something so ominous that even his smile was chilling. He was a man quite capable of parting from someone with a smile and then making contemptuous threats behind the person's back.

"Actually, you see, I just heard about this myself last night," said Shishido softly, leaning forward as Nagakura sat down on the sofa, "but it seems that Kisuke Takeda has been missing since the night before last."

"Takeda? Missing?" said Nagakura hesitantly, wondering about the other man standing behind Shishido. "And this gentleman is . . . ?"

"Oh, don't worry about him. This is Izawa, Mr. Takeda's secretary. It was he who told me the news. Oh yes, Izawa, I guess it would be better if you told the Chief all about it yourself," said Shishido, giving his chair facing Nagakura up to Izawa and sitting himself down deep in the sofa beside Nagakura.

Nagakura could tell that Izawa was extremely tense, apparently not just because he was in the presence of three big shots, but with genuine concern about his employer's disappearance.

"Er, uh, where should I begin?" asked Izawa. As Takeda's secretary, he had to be a capable man, but his voice was shaking pitifully.

"Well, just tell me everything in order from the beginning," said Nagakura. "When did Mr. Takeda disappear, and where did he disappear from?"

"He hasn't been seen or heard from since he left the Koshimizu Plateau Hotel in Togakushi around 7 P.M. on the evening of the 3rd."

"You were in Togakushi with him, then?"

"Yes, for a meeting and party from three that afternoon, to get preparations started for the construction of the Togakushi Plateau Golf Club. The first hour and a half or so was spent in presenting the aims of the builders and the plan for the layout of the course. Then, after a short break, a dinner party began a little after five. Some time after it began, though, Mr. Takeda said he wasn't feeling too well and was going to his room. I went with him as far as his door, but he said he would be all right and I should return to the party. I confirmed the next morning's schedule with him briefly, and then joined the party again. That must have been a little after six. That's the last time I saw him."

"Did anyone else see him after that?"

"Yes, the desk clerk said he saw him leaving the hotel a little before seven, so I guess the desk clerk must have been the last person to see him."

"Did he go out alone?"

"Yes, apparently."

"Do you have any idea where he might have been going?"

"None at all, I'm afraid."

"Had he said anything about going out?"

"No, not a thing."

"So when did you realize that something was wrong— that he had disappeared, I mean?"

"He was supposed to come down to the restaurant at eight the next morning. When he didn't, I waited thirty minutes and then phoned his room, because he had an appointment that required leaving the hotel by 8:50 at the latest. But he didn't answer the phone, and that's when I began to think that something must be wrong. Of course, it never occurred to me then that he could have just disappeared. I was afraid he might have been taken so ill that he collapsed, so I hurried up to his room, but it was empty."

"What did you do for a key? Wasn't the door locked?"

"No, it wasn't. His key was lying on the table."

"Then that means he must have left the hotel without bothering to lock his door, right?"

"Yes, but all he ever kept in a hotel room were personal effects. Anything else, like papers and so on, he always left with me in an attaché case. He never kept anything with him that he couldn't put in his pockets, so I don't think he would have worried about locking the door."

"I see. Go on, please."

"After that, I asked the desk clerk whether he had gone out, and I was told that he had been seen going out the night before, but not coming in again. So I had to assume that he had spent the night elsewhere, and all I could do was wait for him. But he never came back." Izawa finished with head bowed, as if in apology.

"And that's the story," said Shishido unhappily. "I wouldn't have thought anything could be seriously wrong myself, but Izawa tells me nothing like this has ever happened before, and he's terribly worried. So I thought it best we consult the police, and Governor Masagi agrees."

"By 'seriously wrong,' may I take it you are referring to the possibility that Mr. Takeda may have been the victim of some kind of crime, Representative Shishido?"

"Er, uh, well, I wouldn't like to put it quite so directly myself, but yes, I guess you can take it that way."

"Do you know of anything in Mr. Takeda's affairs that would suggest that possibility?" asked Nagakura, turning back to Izawa.

"No, I don't. Nothing at all."

"If that's the case, we can act on that assumption. For instance, he might have been involved in a traffic accident. But if there are any indications whatsoever, then we will have to consider the possibility of a premeditated crime. Now how about it?"

Izawa was ill at ease, the perspiration beginning to appear on his forehead. "Well, uh, I still can't think of . . ."

"I'm sure there are some things that Izawa just doesn't know about his employer," interposed Shishido with a smile, to relieve the tension. "I'm afraid Mr. Takeda was no saint, and when you're in business, you can't help but make a few enemies. Some people just take things the wrong way, so it's always possible that somebody had a grudge of some sort."

"Then do you know of any particular possibilities, Representative Shishido?"

"Me? No, no, if Izawa can't think of any, how would I know? I've been acquainted with Mr. Takeda for a long time, but I really don't know that much about him."

"I see." Nagakura sat up straight. "Well, I'll send out orders right away for a search all over the prefecture."

"I'm afraid that won't do, Chief Nagakura," said Governor Masagi. "Representative Shishido thinks the investigation should be kept secret for the time being, and I agree with him. After all, it's hardly been two days, and what if Mr. Takeda suddenly turns up after we've made a big thing of it? Besides, I do think we'd better be awfully careful, just in case he's been kidnapped for ransom, you know."

"You think there is that possibility?" Nagakura frowned, gazing up at the ceiling with his keen eyes. Turned forty-six this year, he had been one of the most promising members of his graduating class at Kyoto University. In a sense, his stint as chief of the Nagano prefectural police was a test, on the results of which his future career would depend.

Unlike the self-governing regions of Tokyo, Osaka, and Kanagawa, with all their big cities, Nagano Prefecture may be thought to be simply a peaceful region blessed with natural beauty and made for tourism, but there are in fact quite a few difficulties involved in its administration. For one thing, there is the great area it covers, fourth in size behind Hokkaido, Iwate, and Fukushima. Moreover, there are differences in the living conditions in the three distinct areas of the northern, central, and southern parts of the prefecture, differences which sometimes give rise to conflict.

In addition, no other prefecture is contiguous to so many others—eight of them, in fact: Niigata, Gunma, Saitama, Yamanashi, Shizuoka, Aichi, Gifu, and

Toyama. Thus anyone using a car to commit a crime can cause the police a lot of trouble. Three years ago, for instance, there had been a series of kidnap-murders of female office workers, masterminded by a woman, in which the kidnappings had taken place and the bodies had been left in various places in the three prefectures of Toyama, Nagano, and Gifu, necessitating a widespread investigation with which sectional rivalries had seriously interfered.

With all of the tourists flowing in, the majority there for mountain climbing, there is a never-ending string of mountaineering accidents to be dealt with, too. Nagakura's predecessor, who had suffered through the series of kidnap-murders, had been quite right in telling him, after turning over his duties, that this was an uncommonly troublesome place.

Nagakura thoroughly agreed. And this case would involve one of the most prominent people in the prefecture. He had a premonition that it was going to turn into a big mess. "I don't think there's much chance that he could have been kidnapped for ransom," he said, half to convince himself. "If he had been, we should have been contacted by the kidnappers by now."

"I suppose not," agreed Masagi, "but if not, then what could have happened to him?"

"Well, what bothers me is that he left the hotel of his own accord. If his disappearance is somehow connected with his departure from the hotel, or else, if perhaps he engineered it himself, then . . ."

"What do you mean?" broke in Izawa, offended. "Are you suggesting that he's absconded with something?"

"No, I didn't say that. But what if he just got tired of work and decided to take off somewhere for a rest for two or three days without telling anyone?"

"I can assure you that Mr. Takeda would never have done a thing like that."

"That's right. He wouldn't," agreed Shishido. "He just isn't the kind of person who would do such an irresponsible thing."

"Then I'm afraid the police will have to assume the worst," said Nagakura, in as casual a tone as possible, which nevertheless caused Izawa to begin trembling. Shishido shook his head most unhappily.

After leaving the governor's mansion and returning to the police station, Nagakura immediately summoned his top-ranking officers and explained the situation to them, ordering a secret investigation to be conducted by Section Two, and instructing his men to be prepared for the worst. At the meeting, he had made a point of telling Miyazaki that if they should be unfortunate enough to discover the worst, he should be sure to put his very best man in charge of the on-site investigation.

 "And that's why I want you on this case," said Miyazaki, trying to make it sound like he was doing Takemura a favor.

"Oh," said Takemura, pulling a long face.

"What's this? You look like you don't much want it."

"I don't. I don't know the first thing about business or politics."

"You can leave that end of it to Section Two. But you're my ace detective, and I've been keeping you on hold for this, because I need somebody who can hustle."

Now that he thought about it, Takemura realized that he and his men would normally have been assigned to the couple of cases that had come up in the last day or two, but instead they had been twiddling their thumbs over a little desk work on some old cases. He could tell by Miyazaki's tone that he did not want Section Two to solve this one first. To be beaten out by Section Two on a murder case would put Miyazaki in an awkward position. An administrator had to worry about a lot of things, and Takemura could sympathize with him.

"Okay, I'll do my best," said Takemura, this time with a little enthusiasm.

* * *

The river which flows south along the west side of Nagano City to its confluence with the Sai near Kawanakajima has the beautiful name of Susobana, and the river itself is still beautiful too, with fantastic crags jutting out everywhere along its course, and seasonal changes still visible in the folds of mountains along its western shore. This is in spite of the arched dam completed across its upper reaches in 1969 and the large-scale housing developments appearing in the mountains along its western shore, resulting in a decreased flow and poorer quality water.

At the northern edge of Nagano City, the river makes a sharp turn to the west and extends in a practically straight line toward the Togakushi Mountains, where lies its source.

The police car with Miyazaki and Takemura followed the national highway upstream from this bend for about fifteen kilometers, the river flowing faster and the valley getting deeper all the way, to the confluence with the Kusu River flowing in from the north. From this point, scattered farmhouses were visible on the surrounding hills. Now called Tochihara and located in Togakushi Township, it was once known as Shigarami Village, supposedly taking its name from the *shigarami,* or weir, that legend has it the demoness Maple built there to keep out the enemy forces.

Leaving the national highway at Tochihara and heading north for about two kilometers to the village of Imai, they reached the scene at 11 A.M. The path up the mountain had been closed, and a crowd of investigators, early-bird reporters, and curious spectators were gathered at the barricade.

The reporters peered into their car as it pulled up, amidst such comments as "Hey, the head of Section One is here himself!" "And Inspector Takemura too!" "Must be somebody important dead up there!" Takemura had to give them credit for their intuition.

An area of radius fifty meters from the site had been roped off, and uniformed and plain-clothes police were waiting outside it. From among them, Chief of Detectives Tsuneda of Nagano Central Station approached.

"You got here fast," said Tsuneda. "We just arrived ourselves. Do you want the CID men to begin right away?"

"Yes, but could you have them first open a path to the body, so we can get over there to identify it?" requested Miyazaki.

"Sure."

Tsuneda set his men immediately to checking a path to the body for footprints and such. The work went unexpectedly fast, because there was practically nothing worth looking at. The whole area was forest, with weeds covering the ground, and there were signs of trampling, but nothing like an identifiable footprint.

"It's no good," said Inspector Kojima of CID, going in and motioning to them to follow. Kojima was a veteran, referred to by the venerable title of "old," and with his white hair and the wrinkles at the corners of his eyes, he did indeed look like he had quite a few years on him, but the truth was that he was in his middle forties. Takemura had known him since the case of the dismembered corpse three years ago, and in spite of the difference in their ages, the two were quite congenial.

Avoiding the plaster that had been poured here and there, the group walked over to the body. Miyazaki kneeled down beside it for a good look.

"There's no mistake," he said with a sigh.

"It's Takeda?" asked Takemura.

"That's right. Kisuke Takeda," replied Miyazaki without turning around.

"Kisuke Takeda? You mean, *the* Takeda!" said Tsuneda and Kojima practically as one, looking at each other. Now they understood why Miyazaki was there in person.

"Okay, get started with your inspection. I've got to report in," said Miyazaki, rushing down the slope.

Shortly thereafter, the medical examiner arrived. "He's been dead for three or four days," judged the experienced doctor right off, after pressing the purple-spotted skin.

"That would mean he was dead by July 4th, right?" said Takemura.

"Mhm. Taking into consideration the temperature and humidity in these parts, that should be about right, but we won't know any more until after the autopsy."

"I don't see any external injuries. What did he die of?"

"Poison," said the doctor without hesitation. "It's a little hard to tell because he's so wet, but I'm pretty sure it must have been cyanide."

Suicide or murder, the body could hardly have been there for three or four days, so someone must have left it there. Wondering why anyone would have taken that trouble, Takemura looked around. The only building nearby was the campground office. The older of the two men who worked there was waiting beside the rope, probably at police request. Moving a little away from the body, Takemura beckoned to him.

This man was a permanent employee of the Togakushi Township government, and the other was a college student working for the summer. Both were natives of Togakushi, and the younger man was expecting eventually to fill a permanent position, too, when one became vacant.

Naturally, the man waiting was nervous, but he looked to Takemura like a normally outgoing person. Giving him a cigarette and lighting it for him with a match, Takemura opened with, "Is this campground always so quiet?"

"Oh no, it's usually very crowded in season, but we haven't had any campers since the day before yesterday because of all the rain."

"Have the two of you been in the office all the time?"

"Yes, we live there. We're on duty around the clock."

"And you didn't know there was a dead body over there?"

"No, we had no idea, until the girls told us."

"But that place is on the trail up the mountain, isn't it? I should think anyone climbing the mountain would have seen the body right off."

"Probably so. In fact, it wouldn't have had to be someone going up the mountain. We take a look around the campground from time to time ourselves, and if the body had been there when we did, we couldn't have missed it."

"When's the last time you took a look around?"

"I think it was around two yesterday afternoon. We only checked to make sure no campers had come in, and then we went right back to the office. But if that body had been there, I'm sure we'd have seen it."

"Since the road passes right in front of the office, I guess you would have noticed if anyone had gone by, wouldn't you?"

"Well, when there are a lot of campers and mountain climbers, we don't take note of every single one, but on a leisurely day like yesterday, I think we would have noticed. But I wouldn't guarantee it. Of course, no matter what chance there might be that we could have missed it, I can't believe that anybody who knew this office was here would have wanted to carry something like that past it. I mean, how could he be sure we wouldn't see it?"

"How about at night?"

"At night? Well, I guess we might have missed it then. But it gets pitch dark around here, and it was especially dark last night. It could have been done with a flashlight, but we would probably have seen the light."

"But the fact is, you didn't see anything, so I guess you must have been sound asleep."

"I guess so. Then you think the body was brought here last night?" said the campground attendant, with an uneasy shake of the head. "But why would anybody have wanted to bring it out here?" The same doubt had occurred to him as to Takemura.

Miyazaki returned. The chief of detectives at headquarters had ordered another meeting of administrators. "He doesn't want it let out that we've identified the body until we get back. It sounds like he got that request from above," Miyazaki told Takemura.

"They're interfering with our investigation!" grumbled Takemura, disgusted. "We *have* identified him. What's with these financiers and politicians?"

"Take it easy, now! They must have their reasons. There are probably a lot of things they have to take care of before the information gets around."

Miyazaki made a very brief, formal announcement to the reporters at the campground office. "The victim has not been identified. The body is that of a male, about sixty, who appears to be of the senior executive type. We believe he has been dead for three or four days. Cause of death was apparently poisoning, but we won't know anything for sure until we get the results of the autopsy."

He barely had time to take a breath before being swamped with questions.

"Then is there a strong possibility of murder?"

"We can't say yet whether it was murder or suicide."

"But this is a pretty strange place for someone to be found dead."

"You're right, of course. That's why we're here."

"Aren't you evading the question, sir? Tell us, is there a strong suspicion of murder, or not?"

"You can tell your readers that we are investigating the possibilities of suicide and murder both."

"Our editors will have our heads for an article like that!"

There was a burst of laughter. Realizing that they were not going to pin Miyazaki down any further, the reporters turned their attention to the girls who had discovered the body, and then went off to send in their articles. Miyazaki relaxed a little, knowing that at this point they would have to treat the case like any other discovery of a body, and it would make no more than a little stuffing for the evening papers.

After Miyazaki had accompanied the body down the hill, investigation of the vicinity began in earnest. More than one hundred men, some with dogs, went into the bamboo-grass brush still soaked with rain and dew to look for clues. For any case, the initial search was always the most important, and the one to which the most energy was devoted. It was also the most primitive, there being no other way to do it than by using a human sea of investigators.

Detectives from Section One were dispatched to question residents of the surrounding villages. The road leading to the Arakura Campground was from the village of Imai at the bottom of the hill. There were fields along the way, but the closest house was one kilometer away. The road was unpaved and wide enough for only one car. Since the men in the office had not heard a car, it was assumed that someone must have parked some distance away, then carried the body into the campground on foot. It was estimated that no matter how hard it might have been raining, the car could not have come closer than three hundred meters without being heard. That would mean that someone must have carried the body, already smelling of decay, a considerable distance, which in itself would make the case a bizarre one.

Nothing important was being found near the scene of the discovery, and neither were the detectives having much luck with their questioning of residents in the surrounding villages. They were unable to find anyone who had heard a car, even though it must have been the middle of the night, and of course there was no such thing as an eyewitness. Leaving the remaining search to his men, Takemura headed for the Koshimizu Plateau Hotel with Kinoshita, his regular driver.

At about that time, Chief Nagakura was holding a most unusual press conference at the Nagano Central Station. Since press notifications had been carefully prepared and sent around beforehand, practically all of the mass media were there, along with four television cameras.

With Nagakura were his chief of detectives, Tsukamoto, the head of Investigative Section One, Miyazaki, and Kisuke Takeda's secretary, Izawa. A lot of reporters recognized Izawa, but none of them had any idea why he was there, which created considerable curiosity right from the start. When they finally learned the identity of the body, even hardened reporters were appalled by the news of Kisuke Takeda's unnatural death.

Takeda was, by title, the president of the Takeda Firm, on the surface a small company of twelve employees with a main office in Nagano City, a branch office in Matsumoto City, and assets worth twenty million yen. It was supposed to be dealing in real estate, metals, and some other business, but even the tax people couldn't keep track of all its dealings. It was affiliated with five other incorporated companies at various locations, each independent, with its own president, but all shadowy. In a word, most were probably ghost companies. Hardly any of them did any regular business of note, but often one would suddenly pop up in some real estate deal worth ten or twenty billion yen. Popular opinion had it that all of them were fronts for the Takeda Firm, but nobody could put his finger on the exact connection, and there were other, even more mysterious companies continually being created and dissolved.

Kisuke Takeda had done a skillful job of operating an organization whose dealings were impossible to trace. It was said that he could do as he liked anywhere in Nagano Prefecture, but that was about all that anyone not close to him could say. Everyone was aware, however, that he had been a real power behind the political and financial scenes of Nagano Prefecture, and that his death would result in some major changes. One did not have to be particularly knowledgeable to realize that Takeda's murder would break open a beehive.

Chief Nagakura described the facts of the case to the assembled reporters: Kisuke Takeda had been missing since July 3rd; his body had been found this morning in the Arakura Campground outside Imai in Togakushi; cause of death was cyanide poisoning; there was some suspicion of murder, and so on. The chief made a point of extending his sympathy to the bereaved and promising every possible effort toward a rapid solution of the case. As soon as he finished, he was swamped with questions, but he quickly turned over the floor to Miyazaki, who was to bear the brunt of the questioning.

Miyazaki was an old fox at this, and if the truth be known, he rather enjoyed it. The reporters were mainly concerned with finding out just how strong was the possibility of murder, and if it was murder, where were the police directing their suspicions, and did they have any particular suspect yet? Also, what sort of motives were they considering? Since Chief Nagakura had so far avoided a clear declaration that the case was being investigated as a murder, however, Miyazaki had a good excuse for avoiding discussion of any theories based on that premise. As a result, there was no real substance to the exchange between him and the reporters. The only juicy information they got was that Inspector Iwao Takemura had been put in charge of the case, and their cheers for the master detective were half in desperation.

"If you're sending Takemura up against it, doesn't that mean it must be a pretty difficult case?" came the tricky question. Since the case of the dismembered corpse, Takemura had fast been making a reputation for himself. The raincoat that had become his trademark had even led to his being called the "Columbo of the Japanese Alps," a name which fit his appearance perfectly. One of the reasons for his popularity was that he had not tried to improve that appearance even after receiving a double promotion, raising him to the rank of inspector in one leap.

"Well, no help for it," grumbled one of the reporters. "We'll just have to make tomorrow morning's headline 'Takemura On The Case.'"

4 "Togakushi Shrines" is the collective name given to three independent shrines, the Hoko Shrine, the Middle Shrine, and the Inner Shrine, each dedicated to a different god. The Birdline toll road, which runs out of Nagano City across the Iizuna Plateau, comes out on an ordinary road just short of the Hoko Shrine. About one kilometer further up that road is the Middle Shrine, whose surrounding village used to mark the extent of settlement in Togakushi. The area beyond, as its name Koshimizu-ga-Hara or Water-Crossing Plain implies, used to be covered with bamboo shrubs and swampy areas of skunk cabbage. But backed by craggy West Peak of the Togakushi Mountains, the entire stretch is blessed with beauty all year round, making it not only ideal for sanitoriums and mountain villas, but also giving it potential for large resorts. Thus, in recent years, the stretch of plateau beyond the Middle Shrine and up to the Inner Shrine has been rapidly developed with villas.

In spite of the nationwide craze for the development of such resorts, however, the Togakushi Plateau—except for its paved roads and ski lift—has not been subjected to any remarkably large-scale development. Thus it retains the strong image of a secluded country place, and that in itself makes it thoroughly attractive to big investors.

As Takemura and Kinoshita drove by the Middle Shrine, they saw from their cream-colored compact several tour busses and a considerable number of private cars parked in the square in front. The Togakushi Plateau, quiet for a while, would rapidly be getting lively again, and there were a lot of local young people hard at work cutting the bamboo brush beside the road. A little way out of the

Middle Shrine village, Kinoshita turned right, shortly after which they passed through the stretch of villas and then saw the white building of the Koshimizu Plateau Hotel at the bottom of the ski slope.

When Takemura showed his badge, the desk clerk paled. Although it was obvious from his manner that the police had been expected, they were nevertheless kept waiting for nearly an hour in the coffee shop on the first floor. Kinoshita, young and impatient, kept getting up to go press the clerk, but each time the clerk asked them to wait just another moment.

Around them in the coffee shop were three groups of noisy students. Perhaps it was a feeling of freedom that made them so loud as to spoil the quiet so hard to come by.

"I wonder where those kids get the money to play around with," said Kinoshita in disgust. "I suppose they must have sponged it off their parents, but I don't see why their parents stand for it."

"Now, now," laughed Takemura, "you're jealous."

"No I'm not. I just feel sorry for their parents. They worked hard for that money."

"Maybe their parents don't mind. They might be happy to have the kids enjoying themselves."

"You think so? That might be all right if the kids did as much for their parents as the parents do for their kids, but filial piety is out of style nowadays."

"Oh, I don't know about that. I hear you've got a reputation for being a filial son."

"I try. But my parents didn't do all that much for me. I mean, the parents of these kids aren't likely to get much in return. That's what they don't understand, the fools!" Kinoshita was really angry, and not just because he was tired of waiting.

He was a good man, thought Takemura, with a pleased

smile. Twenty-four years old and dressed in a windbreaker over a long-sleeved sport shirt, Kinoshita quite resembled the other, more modern youths in the place, but hearing him talk about old-time filial piety made Takemura decide that the closed society of the police must do something good for a young man.

Takemura himself was even more of an anachronism. Having no formulated ethics, no religion, and no concept of ideology, he had not chosen a police career out of any strong desire to guard the Establishment or for any lofty ideal of protecting the public peace and welfare. He had done so out of a need to eat.

He had graduated near the top of his high school class, but family circumstances had forced him to give up the idea of going on to college. Together with his teachers' regrets, however, had come the suggestion that his excellent high school record would open up the path to success with the police. Influenced as well by the same TV detective dramas that influence most boys who eventually join the police, he had taken the suggestion, and found in a year or two that he had undergone an undeniable and remarkable change, and been given a purpose in life.

The police organization has incalculable effects in the molding of individuals. After the superficial mold is removed, though, personal ability, effort, and more than anything else, special aptitudes count most. In particular, a good detective needs deductive powers and imagination. Iwao Takemura, a man blessed with just those talents, was meant for the job. When he found himself on a challenging case, his excitement was like that of a hyena licking his chops before some delicious prey. He would forget everything else, not satisfied until he had seen it through to the bitter end. It was not infrequently that enthusiasm led him to ignore his position as inspector. That job was supposed to be mainly managerial, but he continued to operate the way he had always done, behaving like a staff detective—sometimes an eccentric one.

A raise and a very nice place to live had come with his double promotion, but this had not made him conceited. He did not own a car, nor would he even buy a new raincoat. At the height of summer, of course, he didn't carry his raincoat, but he did refuse to give up his rumpled white shirt and tie. He had taken just one look at the sport shirt and string tie his wife Yoko had bought him—"just for midsummer," she had said—and stuffed them into a drawer. "You really ought to try wearing something different once in a while," pleaded Yoko, who had been pleased with her purchase. But Takemura had evaded the issue with, "Don't be ridiculous. A man can't go around wearing any old thing just because his wife tells him to."

* * *

It wasn't so very hot, but when the hotel manager finally showed up, his face was covered with perspiration.

"I'm terribly sorry to have kept you waiting so long," he said, bowing and scraping. "I'm Takano, the manager."

"Well, you must have had quite a time preparing for this meeting," replied Takemura, unable to resist the sarcasm. "I'm sure you were very worried about Mr. Takeda."

"Er, uh . . . oh yes, yes, you're right, of course," mumbled Takano, flabbergasted. He was a short man of about fifty with a pleasant, round face, which expressed clearly his total loyalty to his job.

"We need to ask some questions concerning Kisuke Takeda's death. I wonder if you'd mind calling the desk clerk who was the last person to see him?"

Takano hurried out and came back with a young man

named Aibara, a tall, slim, handsome fellow. He sat down quite properly, facing Takemura.

"According to your statement, it was a little before 7 P.M. that you saw Kisuke Takeda going out. Is that correct?"

"Yes, that's correct."

"Was there anyone else at the desk with you at that time?"

"No. There was somebody in the office behind the desk, but as a rule, unless we're serving guests, we usually keep only one person on the desk at a time."

"All right then, since you were the only one to see him go out, I want you to consider your answer very carefully: are you absolutely sure that it was Kisuke Takeda you saw?"

"Yes, absolutely."

"Did you know Mr. Takeda on sight?"

"Oh yes. He had stayed here several times since this spring, and besides, I had heard that he was a big stockholder in the hotel."

"Oh really?" Takemura looked at the manager for confirmation.

"Yes," confirmed Takano, "Mr. Takeda owned a lot of stock in our parent company, the Kawanakashima Tourism Development Corporation."

"Then I don't guess you could have mistaken him for anyone else. Okay. Now, did you notice anything at all peculiar about him as he went out?"

"No, nothing in particular. I bowed to him as usual, but I didn't notice anything strange."

"Did you see what he did when he got outside?"

"No, I'm afraid not. But I did hear afterwards that the driver of the vehicle we use to pick people up and take them to the station had seen a gentleman walking west along the road in front of the hotel. He saw him from a distance, but he was reasonably sure it was Mr. Takeda."

"But not certain?"

"No. It was a dark cloudy night, and the driver only caught a glimpse of him from a distance while taking a break. He said he wasn't certain."

"But the time checks, is that correct?"

"Yes, just about."

"You say the man was walking west. Could you be more specific?"

"Well, as you know, our hotel is more or less at a dead end, and the main road going away from here heads southwest toward the Middle Shrine. But there's another little road, an unpaved forest road running due west from in front of the hotel. About three hundred meters from here, it crosses an old road called the Echigo Road, and another three hundred meters beyond that, it comes out on the new road, right at the entrance to the Inner Shrine, where there's a parking lot and a restaurant. But this forest road is covered with loose gravel and not many people use it even during the day, so the driver remembers thinking how strange it was someone should be using it at night."

"If it was Mr. Takeda he saw, do you have any idea where he could have been going?"

"Well, er . . ." The desk clerk looked at the manager in embarrassment. The manager blinked his eyes rapidly, signaling him to be careful how he answered.

Disgusted, Takemura hurried the young clerk for an answer. "Come on, now. It can't be that big a problem! Just tell me what comes to mind."

"Well, I guess he must have been going out for a stroll."

"Oh, sure. But when he didn't come back, didn't it occur to you that he was gone too long for a stroll?"

"Yes."

"And what did you think of then?"

"What did I think of? Well, I don't really . . ."

"Just tell me whatever occurred to you at the time. For instance, did you think he might have been going out to meet someone, or something like that?"

"Yes, that's what I thought."

"Then, had he done the same sort of thing when he was staying here before? Going out alone like that?"

"Yes, I believe he had."

"About how many times?"

"Maybe two or three, I think."

"Could it have been more than that?"

"I guess so."

"Had he ever stayed away all night before?"

"No, never. He always came back the same evening."

"You seem awfully sure of that, but I've been told that Mr. Takeda was in the habit of leaving his key in the room. If that was the case, how could the desk clerk be sure he had returned?"

"Because he had to pass the front desk on his way in, and we would most likely see him."

"Most likely? You mean you could have missed him?"

"Well, that's possible, if the clerk had to leave the desk for some reason. But in the morning, there are always two people on the desk to handle check-outs, so if he had come in from outside then, he could hardly have passed by without being seen."

"In other words, if he tried to come in the next morning, his evil deeds would come out, eh?" said Takemura with a conspiratorial grin.

"Yes, they would that," said the young clerk, finally relaxing.

"Thank you," said Takemura. "Well, I hope you'll forgive me for pressing you so hard with questions, but that's my job, I'm afraid."

"Oh, don't apologize! I happen to be a mystery fan. I love mystery novels and TV mysteries, and I've always wanted to see a real detective at work!"

"Oh really? How nice! My wife likes mysteries, too. When that TV program, 'The Mystery,' comes on, she doesn't even know I'm there."

"'The Mystery?' Why, I never miss one of those!"

"You don't? Then did you see last week's story, 'The Tragedy of the Red and Black?'"

"Oh yes, of course! That was a good one, wasn't it? It had quite a twist to it. My friend and I were trying to guess who the murderer was, but we never did figure it out. But I'll bet you did, didn't you, Inspector?"

"No, no, I didn't figure it out either," laughed Takemura, while Kinoshita stood by wondering what was so funny to everyone.

Having finished with the desk clerk, Takemura asked the manager, Takano, to show him Takeda's room. As he started to follow Takano up the stairs, however, Takemura suddenly stopped. "Doesn't the hotel have an elevator?" he asked.

"No, I'm terribly sorry, I'm afraid it doesn't," said Takano, a man too easily embarrassed. He came back down the two or three steps he had ascended, bobbing his head in apology. "This area is designated as a scenic zone, and regulations prohibit buildings that stand more than ten meters high. If we installed an elevator, we'd have to have a room for the mechanism above the third floor, and that would put us over the limit."

"I see. Well, it's better for the health, anyway."

Takemura went up the stairs carefully, step by step,

looking down at his feet. The staircase was wooden, the plain woodwork exposed in keeping with the North European style of the place. As soon as they reached the third floor, he turned back and went down the stairs again, leaving Kinoshita and Takano standing at the top looking puzzled. When Takemura came back, Takano told him Kisuke Takeda had always stayed in the same third-floor suite. Apparently it was hardly ever given to ordinary guests.

"The hotel was completed the year the great alpine events were held at the ski slope here, and the very first guest in this suite was the Imperial Prince," boasted Takano, as he opened the door.

The suite consisted of two adjoining Western-style rooms, the outer a parlor and the inner a bedroom. For a big hotel in Tokyo, that would not be rare, but it was quite something for these parts. There was plush carpeting, thick cloth wall covering, a rather tawdry chandelier, and a parlor suite that was probably Danish. Takemura walked around the room making sighing sounds, putting his face close to everything, as if trying to taste and smell it.

There were two three-quarter-width double beds in the bedroom, which Takemura found considerably more tasteful than the living room. He opened the door just to the right of the entrance to the bedroom and found a spacious vanity with washbasin, and adjacent to it a toilet and a bathroom. Just add a kitchen and it would make a considerably finer place to live than his own.

"I wonder if I could see the person who cleaned this room the next day?" asked Takemura, turning to the manager.

"Just a moment, please," replied Takano, picking up the phone. In hardly any time at all, a man in his forties appeared, and Takano introduced him as a Mr. Ohta, the person in charge of cleaning.

Ohta, a man of even smaller build than Takano, looked the strictly honest and steadfast type.

"Did you check this room the morning after Mr. Takeda was here?" asked Takemura.

"Yes. This is a special room, so I always clean it myself."

"Oh good. That will make this faster. Now then, may I assume that Mr. Takeda had not used the bed or bathroom?"

"Oh no. He had used them."

"He had?" Takemura's expression stiffened, as did Kinoshita's. "Then you mean he had taken a bath and laid down?"

"Yes, I think so. The bathtub and a towel were wet, and the bar of soap had been used. And the sheets and pillow looked like they had been lain on, and the robe had been worn."

"Which would mean that Mr. Takeda had taken a bath, then put on the robe and taken a rest on the bed, right?"

"Yes, that's what it looked like."

"But we were told that he returned to his room a little after six and went out again a little before seven. That's only thirty or forty minutes. An awfully short time to have gotten undressed, put on a bathrobe, taken a nap, and even a bath, don't you think?"

"Yes, you're right, of course, but since that is what he actually did . . ." Ohta looked a little upset. Short time or not, a fact was a fact, and he obviously couldn't see the point in questioning it.

"By the way, has anyone used these rooms since Mr. Takeda was here?"

"No, nobody."

"Okay. Mr. Takano, I'm sorry about this, but could I ask

you to see that the rooms are not used for a little while? We'll have some men from CID here in the next day or two."

Pulling a pair of gloves out of his pocket and putting them on, Takemura opened the drawer of the desk against the living room wall. It contained stationery with the hotel letterhead, picture postcards, a brochure, a hotel information folder, and so on. Holding the blank letter paper up to the light, he could see faint impressions of writing.

"Mind if I borrow this?" he asked, handing the paper to Kinoshita. "By the way, was the room next to this one occupied that evening?"

"Yes, it must have been. We were full up with people connected with the golf course. Those from Nagano City went home that evening, but most of those from farther away spent the night in Togakushi. There were so many that we couldn't put all of them up ourselves, and we had to find rooms at other hotels in the vicinity, so I hardly think we could have had any vacancies."

"In that case, I'll ask you to give me the name and address of the occupant of that room when we go downstairs." Takemura kept his hands busy as he spoke, opening the big thick cover of the information folder. It began with the usual stipulations about conditions of stay, followed by information about hotel facilities, a diagram of emergency escape routes, a description of the restaurant and coffee shop, ski information, and so on—the usual content.

"Wow, this looks delicious!" he exclaimed gluttonously, his mouth really watering as he looked at the picture of a meal on the restaurant menu. "Is the meal on this cart for one person?"

"No, I believe it's for two."

"I should hope so! It doesn't look like one person could

eat all that, does it? Still, even for two, that's quite a meal! I suppose this is a picture of one of these stews over here?"

"Well, I don't know if we could really call it a stew or not. Actually, it's a fondue. There's melted cheese in that pot, and the meat and vegetables and shrimp and everything on these skewers are dipped in it to cook. I don't know whether you'd call it boiling or deep-frying, but anyway, that's how it's eaten."

"Oh, so this is what they call fondue! I'd heard of it, but I never saw it before. Then, it's served on a cart, like this? Hey, that's great! I'll have to bring my wife here one day to try it. But I'll bet it's expensive, isn't it?"

"Well, yes, I'd say a meal the size of the one in this picture would be quite expensive, but of course, this is only a sample. I'm sure we could prepare something to fit your budget."

"Really? A sample? I suppose it would have to be. It really looks terrific! There's shrimp and scallops, and good beef, and I guess the wine is imported?"

"Yes, it is," replied the manager, his smile wearing somewhat thin. This detective was certainly taking his time. Even Kinoshita was looking a little tired.

"Wait a minute, though," said Takemura, inclining his head. "If you use this cart for room service, how do you get it up here? You'd have an awful time getting it up the stairs, like a portable shrine, wouldn't you?"

"Oh, there's no problem there. We have a dumbwaiter to bring the cart up, meal and all, from the kitchen."

"Oh, you do? Well, that's a relief. That means you can bring it up still aboil. Well, it sure does look delicious."

"It's just about dinnertime. Would you like to try some? We'd be happy to prepare it for you."

"No, no, don't worry about us. We were planning to stop at the Middle Shrine for some homemade buckwheat noodles on the way back. But I would appreciate it if you could show me that dumbwaiter."

Takemura's interest had jumped to something else. Kinoshita, always with him, should have been used to it, but he still sometimes wondered how some of the things the Inspector chose to stick his head into were possibly going to be of any use to him.

When they left the room, Takemura's attention fixed on the emergency door at the end of the corridor. "I suppose that door can be opened at a touch even at night?"

"Yes, from inside."

"Then anyone who wanted to could just slip out in the middle of the night?"

"No, not so easily. When the door is opened, a buzzer sounds in the office behind the front desk."

"Oh really? You think of everything, don't you? Then nobody can get out without paying his bill." Takemura sounded quite like he was planning to try it himself.

They went back along the corridor toward the stairs. In a recess to the right just past the stairwell were drink machines. Beyond them was a small area marked off with a sign that read "Employees Only Beyond This Point," where there was an opening in the wall for the dumbwaiter, which looked about half the size of an elevator in width and height, with a door that opened and closed vertically.

"Could you show me how this works?" asked Takemura, excited.

"Well then, why don't we try it with that?" said Takano, pointing to a big laundry cart. He looked rather like a showman as he pushed the button to summon the dumbwaiter. "When it's in use, this lamp lights up and the dumbwaiter won't respond to the button elsewhere."

When Takano pushed the button, the "In Use" lamp lit up simultaneously with the sound of a motor starting somewhere below. In a surprisingly short time, the motor stopped, and the door opened. The compartment behind the door was a little over a meter deep. Takano pushed the cart in. There were buttons inside for each of the three floors. He pressed the button marked "1" and started walking away immediately.

"Now we've got to go down and take out the cart," he said. Right beside them was a crude staircase for employees only. Takano started down it at a rather rapid pace.

"Wouldn't it be easier just to ride down with it?" suggested Takemura.

"That's against the law. I hear somebody once got killed in Chiba Prefecture or somewhere, riding on a food-service dumbwaiter."

When they reached the first floor, the laundry cart was already waiting for them behind the open dumbwaiter door.

"Gee, that's convenient!" exclaimed Takemura, impressed, turning to Kinoshita for agreement. "Don't you think so?"

"Yeah," mumbled Kinoshita.

✳ ✳ ✳

When they left the hotel, the sun was already low, and the evening breeze felt almost chilly. The mysterious West Peak looked purple in the remaining light, towering over the plateau that seemed like an expanse of sea. One could imagine that gods, or more likely evil spirits lived there.

"Drive down that road, will you?" Takemura told Kinoshita after they got into the car. He was pointing to the gravel road that headed west, the one someone resembling Kisuke Takeda had been seen walking down. "Take it slowly."

Takemura looked all around him as the car moved

slowly along, with the sound of gravel shooting out from under the tires. "There's nothing at all out here, is there?" he said.

Ahead of them to the right was a wasteland covered with bamboo brush, out of which grew an occasional low tree. To the left was a luxuriant forest of beech, oak, and larch, through which could be seen flickering lights that Takemura guessed must be coming from the villas. As the desk clerk had told them, they soon came to an intersection with another gravel road like the one they were on.

"This must be the old road," said Takemura.

Down the road to the left, buildings that looked like villas were dimly visible in the dusk. Crossing that road, they soon came out on a big, open area where a paved road cut through, and there was a parking lot the size of an athletic field for cars and busses of visitors to the Inner Shrine. With the sun down, the lot was unoccupied, and the only people around were those working inside the restaurant. Directly across the paved road stood a large shrine gate, beyond which the worshippers' approach disappeared into the distance between rows of giant cedar in the direction of West Peak.

"Wait here a minute, will you?" said Takemura, getting out of the car and heading toward the approach. Beyond the shrine gate, it quickly got dark. Just a short distance along the approach, he felt like he was in another world. The roots of the ancient cedar trees seemed to coil like snakes under his feet, and he almost tripped several times. He had not gone a hundred meters before he gave in to the urge to turn back, with an unconsciously quickened pace. He felt like something was coming after him.

Back at the road, he walked toward the restaurant, Kinoshita following slowly behind in the car. The restaurant was just closing up, and when Takemura entered, a middle-aged man and woman who appeared to be husband and wife looked at him rather disgruntled. He showed them his badge.

"On the night of the 3rd, around 7:00 P.M., did you by any chance see a gentleman of about sixty around here?" asked Takemura.

"No, we didn't." The abrupt reply came from the woman. "We close by 7:00."

Glancing at his watch, Takemura saw that it was indeed almost 7:00 now. Feeling unwelcome, he left the restaurant and returned to the car.

"Well, are you ready for those buckwheat noodles now?" asked Kinoshita impatiently.

"Would you drive back along the road we just came on, please?" said Takemura, without pity.

Takemura had Kinoshita drive back along the gravel road as far as the old road, where this time they turned right, toward the villas. The sky was still quite light, but darkness surrounded them under the trees. They passed one villa after another, submerged in the gray shadows. About half the signs at the gates contained the names of individuals, and half those of companies.

It didn't seem like they had gone very far before they came out on the main road connecting the Middle Shrine and the Koshimizu Plateau Hotel.

"You want me to drive back through it again?" asked Kinoshita, resigned.

"Yes, please."

Kinoshita turned around and headed back along the gravel road again. As before, they met not a soul. The evening dusk was thickening every minute. Near the end of the stretch of villas, approaching a large plot on the left with quite a big villa toward the back of it, they saw a woman running out from the direction of the villa, arm raised, apparently calling to them.

"Hey, stop here a minute," said Takemura. He waited for the woman with his head out the window.

She came up out of breath. "Excuse me, are you Mr. Yamaguchi?" she asked, leaning forward. Close up, she was quite pretty. Though surely something over thirty, she had the artless smile of a little girl.

"No, I'm afraid not," said Takemura.

"Oh." The woman was embarrassed. "I'm sorry. I thought I saw your car come by before, and I was afraid some of our guests might be having trouble finding us." She looked suddenly tired.

"Sorry to have made you come out like that," said Takemura. "Do you live in that villa?"

"Yes, as caretaker. It's a company recreation villa."

"You live there alone?"

"Oh no. With my husband and two children. I couldn't possibly take care of that place alone," she laughed, in a way that reminded Takemura of his wife, Yoko.

"Do you often run out to meet people like this?"

"Yes. You can see how hard this place would be to find. So when we're expecting someone for the first time, I often wait out here beside the road."

"How about last Saturday, the 3rd, about this time?"

"Last Saturday? Yes, I was waiting out here for a little while around seven."

"You were? Really?" said Takemura eagerly. "Then do you mind my asking if you saw a gentleman of around sixty at about that time?"

"Yes, as a matter of fact, I did."

Without thinking, Takemura sprang out of the door. "Did you really?"

"Yes, it was just as the guest's car drove up, and I got a

good look at the man in the light of the headlights. He was right up there, walking this way. I think he was about sixty, and he was dressed like a gentleman."

"Could you show me exactly where he was?" Takemura ran up the road about thirty meters and turned around. "Was it about here?"

"Uh, I believe it was just a little further. Yes, that's right, just about there."

Takemura came back happily rubbing his hands together. "Now, what did this gentleman look like?"

"I don't remember exactly, but I'd say he looked like some sort of department head or maybe company head. He was wearing a suit and tie. We don't see many people dressed like that around here." Suddenly realizing how Takemura was dressed, she quickly added, "Oh, I don't mean it's bad to be dressed that way."

A guffaw was heard from Kinoshita, inside the car.

"No offense. Anyway, that helped you remember him, right?" said Takemura, in high spirits. "Now, tell me, which way did he go?"

"Well, right after that, I led the guest's car that way, up to the house. I was running, so I didn't see where he went. Er, excuse me, but are you a policeman?"

"Oh, yes. I'm sorry, I forgot. Takemura's the name. Nagano prefectural police."

"Then the gentleman you're talking about must be the man who was murdered on Poison Plain, right?"

"Exactly. That's a very good guess."

"I thought so. That place, Poison Plain, is connected with the legend of the Demoness Maple. Do you know the legend?"

"Yes, some of it."

"Then did you know that place is where the Demoness Maple served poisoned saké to Taira no Koremochi?"

"Why no, I didn't. So that's where the name Poison Plain comes from, is it?"

"That's right. Actually, you see, I'm a member of a circle that studies the legends and folk tales of Togakushi. When I heard on the news that someone had been found poisoned on Poison Plain, I had this awful feeling. I don't think that was any coincidence. No, I'll bet it was the Curse of the Demoness."

In the evening darkness, the woman's own eyes glittered like those of a demoness. Apparently she loved such stories. For Takemura, however, it was nothing to laugh about. His curiosity was aroused. "I see," he said. "That's very interesting."

But just then, a car came grinding along the gravel.

"Oh, that must be our guests!" said the woman, turning toward the headlights, raising her hand, and moving quickly away from Takemura. The car did turn out to be the one she had been waiting for, and amidst a noisy exchange of greetings, she began to lead it toward the villa.

"Thank you," Takemura called out as she started off. "Just as a precaution, could I have your name?"

"Junko Murata," she called back. Takemura didn't have time to ask her how it was written.

Maple-Viewing Girl

 The search of Poison Plain picked up virtually nothing. Not a thing of any help had been left at the scene, nor were there any eyewitnesses, anyone who had heard the sound of a car, nor any worthwhile information about suspicious characters seen in the area. Whenever the police checked out the rare piece of information that did come in, they always found that it was a case of mistaken perception, or that it had nothing to do with the crime. Even the dogs could find nothing, probably because the rain that had been falling until dawn that day had washed away all scents.

It was particularly strange that no one had even heard the sound of a car. Eyewitnesses or no, it was still hard to understand how, in such a quiet village as Imai, not a single person could have heard the sound of a car in the middle of the night, a car that would have had to negotiate quite a number of upward slopes.

At the investigators' conference on the morning of the second day after discovery of the body, Takemura assigned four men to question residents of the villas on the Koshimizu

Plateau. Feeling that the key to the mystery lay there, he selected three veterans for the job and put them under the command of the trusted Sergeant Yoshii.

"We can assume that Kisuke Takeda must have visited or stayed overnight at one of those villas on the night of July 3rd. Furthermore, there is a strong possibility that he was murdered there, so I want you to be very thorough," he emphasized. "If you need more support, ask for it."

He also had the Poison Plain questioning teams expand their operations to cover several possible routes between the Koshimizu Plateau and Poison Plain, but he did not expect too much there.

Although Takeda's disappearance had turned into a murder case, Investigative Section Two was still on the job. In contrast to Section One, which concentrated on the crime itself, Section Two worked on the political and financial aspects—an operation for which Section One was not well equipped—trying to pick up information about activities that might provide a motive. In such a situation, it was inevitable that a sense of competition should develop between the two sections, and the nervous Miyazaki kept pushing his men feverishly.

Convinced that Section Two was on entirely the wrong track, Takemura regarded the pushing as no more than a small annoyance. "This murder was not committed for political or financial motives, I tell you. It was something deeper than that," he said, trying to calm Miyazaki down.

Miyazaki had a lot of confidence in Takemura, but not enough to leave it at that. "Really? What makes you think so?" he asked.

"My intuition," said Takemura with an easy laugh, "my intuition."

That did not quite seem to satisfy Miyazaki, but with the matter more or less settled for the time being, Takemura left investigation headquarters with Kinoshita, turning over all his desk work to a veteran assistant inspector named Katahira. It had always been Takemura's habit, once the overall direction of an investigation had been settled, to take one man and go out and check around himself.

* * *

Kisuke Takeda's residence was a palatial mansion that stood out even in the high-class residential area of Nagano City where it was located. Takemura recalled hearing that it was the finest house in any city in the prefecture. The brick-patterned concrete wall with tile coping that surrounded the grounds enclosed practically an entire block. A magnificent gateway with an intimidating iron gate confronted the visitor. Between the gate and the drive-up entrance to the mansion was an area the size of a traffic circle planted with three fir trees. The gigantic mansion itself was now overrun with people.

After the autopsy, Takeda's body had been quietly returned home in the middle of the night. It was rumored that the intention of the police to deliver it in the morning had been blown away in one thunderous cry from the widow. "Do you think I'm going to let you make a spectacle of it for all to see?" she was reported to have screamed at Chief Nagakura of the Nagano prefectural police. The story had gotten around about how Nagakura, younger than his head of detectives, had had to calm the older man down as he fumed that the woman did not have to be given her own way.

Whatever the rumors, the fact was that Takeda's body had been delivered to his mansion a little after midnight. The delivery had been witnessed by a single reporter from a local paper who happened to have been staked out there, and as a result, his paper had gotten a big scoop to brandish in the morning edition.

The house was buried in wreaths, inside and out. There must have been over a hundred, with more arriving every minute. But the cars outnumbered the wreaths. Ones that couldn't get in through the gate were parked on both sides of the street, and traffic police were trying to restore order and keep more cars from entering the street.

As Kinoshita tried to move forward, a traffic officer came running up waving to him to stop, probably assuming that the puny little domestic-make car belonged to some youngster in the neighborhood. But seeing Takemura sitting next to the driver, he quickly saluted and apologized.

"You've become something of a celebrity, Inspector," said Kinoshita, half-teasing, but delighted with the situation.

The traffic officer found them a good parking place. Flashbulbs flickered as sharp-eyed cameramen caught sight of Takemura. But his celebrity status was not great enough for the waves of people in black mourning clothes, packed inside the gate, to make way for him.

"Can I go in like this?" said Kinoshita, worried about his casual dress.

"I don't see why not. We're not here to mourn," said Takemura, walking briskly up to the reception table. In doing so, he passed a long line of mourners waiting to register, and the young man in charge looked at him with a suggestion of disapproval.

"Police," said Takemura, showing his badge. "We'd like to see Mrs. Takeda."

Noticeably upset, the man turned to whisper to an older man next to him. The older man turned to the man next to him, and that man looked at Takemura and then came over to him.

"My name is Izawa. I'm Mr. Takeda's secretary," he introduced himself with a bow. "Would you come this way, please?"

He led them into a garden to the left of the house, to a white marble table surrounded by four ceramic stools. More composed than the first two men, he invited them to take seats and sat down with them.

"I was told you would be paying a visit, Inspector," said Izawa, formally presenting his card, "but I'm afraid I wasn't expecting you so soon. You can see with all this commotion that we're not really equipped to give you a proper reception."

"That's perfectly all right. I wasn't expecting one. I'm only here to get some simple information. It's best to do this sort of thing as soon as possible."

"I see. Well, then, I'll be glad to tell you all I can now, but I wonder if I could ask you to forgo your questioning of Mrs. Takeda for today?"

"Well, I suppose that might be all right. I guess it's you who were more familiar with Mr. Takeda's business any-way. But would it be all right if we just see her for a moment, after we finish here?"

Izawa thought about that. "Well, after we finish, I can ask her if she minds."

"Fine," said Takemura, going right to his questioning. First he asked about the connections between Izawa and Kisuke Takeda. Izawa, a distant relative of Takeda's wife, had worked for another company for three years after graduation from a private university in Tokyo. Then he had joined the Takeda Firm, where he soon became secretary to the boss. It came out that, at the time, Takeda already had two other secretaries, but Izawa was soon promoted above them to the position of top secretary—apparently because he was Mrs. Takeda's relative. He had occupied that position for the past ten years, was now thirty-eight years old, and single.

"What, you're not married?" asked Takemura.

"No, I'm afraid I've never been blessed with the chance."

"You mean, because you've had to be with the boss all the time?"

"I'm afraid so," said Izawa with a strained smile. "Except, of course, at night, when I'm sleeping."

"I see. And yet, on the evening of the 3rd, Mr. Takeda went out without a word to you, right?"

"Yes. I was careless."

"Careless? You mean, you let him give you the slip?"

"Er, no, that's not what I . . ." said Izawa, losing some of his composure. "I mean, if I had been with him, this wouldn't have happened."

"No, I suppose not. But why would he have gone out secretly without telling you?"

"Most likely out of consideration for me. To give me a little time to relax, I imagine."

"On the other hand, maybe it was to give himself a little time to relax," remarked Takemura, not without sarcasm.

"What? Ridiculous! That's impossible!" said Izawa, giving him a dirty look.

"No, I don't think it's impossible. Actually, we have information that Mr. Takeda had gone out alone several times in the past from the Koshimizu Plateau Hotel."

"That's a lie!"

"No it's not. Apparently he'd done it two or three times, at least. So you didn't know anything about it, Mr. Izawa?"

"Of course not! It's impossible, I tell you!"

"But it's a fact that he did go out on the evening of the

3rd, isn't it? So how can you be so sure that he hadn't done it before?"

Izawa was silent. Apparently he really had not known anything about it.

"How many times had Mr. Takeda been to Togakushi this year?" continued Takemura.

"Five or six, since the beginning of May."

"For what purpose?"

"To meet with people handling the golf course project."

"Did he always stay overnight?"

"Yes."

"Togakushi isn't so far from Nagano. Did he really need to do that?"

"Oh, he could have returned of course, if he had wanted to. But after he finished dinner with the local people, it was always late. Besides, frankly, I think he just wanted to relax."

"If it were me and I wanted to relax, I think I'd rather go home. Or is it that Mr. Takeda didn't feel at home with his wife? What about that?"

"Er, no, I wouldn't think that was it," answered Izawa vaguely.

"By the way, may I assume that Mr. Takeda used a private car to go to Togakushi?"

"Yes, that's right."

"Did you drive it?"

"Sometimes I did, and sometimes somebody else did. I was the one who was driving last time."

"Did he always stay at the Koshimizu Plateau Hotel?"

"Yes. He owned part of it."

"So the manager told me. Then, did you always stay there with him?"

"Yes, I always stayed in the same place with him wherever we went. In different rooms, of course."

"What time did Mr. Takeda usually retire?"

"Pretty late, usually. Even when he wasn't doing anything special, he didn't go to his bedroom before ten or eleven, and he once told me he was in the habit of reading for a while before going to sleep, so I imagine he must have gone to sleep around midnight. Except of course, when he had work to do, or visitors."

"What about when he was at the Koshimizu Plateau Hotel?"

"Oh, he used to go to his room early when he was there, so I don't know what time he would actually go to sleep."

"How early?"

"Well, he almost always went up right after dinner, so I guess it must have been around seven."

"Really? That certainly is early, isn't it? Then it does sound like his trips to Togakushi must have meant some breathing space for him, doesn't it?"

"Perhaps so," said Izawa, without much confidence. "I'm afraid I'm really not sure."

"By the way, I don't know anything about politics or finance, so I'm just going to ask you this straight out, and I'd appreciate a frank answer. I'm sure that Kisuke Takeda must have had enemies of all sorts, but do you know of any person or any group who might have wanted to get rid of him badly enough to kill him?" Takemura kept his eyes fixed on Izawa as he spoke.

Izawa's eyes wandered for a while, then he shook his head weakly. "I can't think of any, but the fact is he was killed, so I guess there must have been some such enemy that I didn't know about."

"Who would benefit from his death?"

"That's a difficult question, too. He had plenty of business rivals. Or maybe there was somebody whose head he was holding something over. I wouldn't have known about something like that."

"If we were to mention some names, what about his wife?"

"That's absurd!" said Izawa, with a hasty look around him. "How would she benefit from his death? He's the one who's brought her family, the Takedas, to its present prosperity with all of his work."

"What do you mean?"

"Oh, didn't you know? He was adopted into his wife's family. The story is that in the period of confusion after the war, when the Takeda family was beginning to fail, he helped the last head of the company out of a pinch. I was only a baby then, of course, but I've heard the story."

"I see. So he won their confidence and got adopted," nodded Takemura. "Okay, what about Representative Shishido?"

"Oof, you do pick some names! But I can tell you this: Representative Shishido was a sworn friend of Mr. Takeda's. The plan to build this Togakushi Golf Course was originally his. Mr. Takeda wasn't interested and tried to refuse, but Representative Shishido kept after him till he finally went along with it. So I think you could say that the person most hurt by Mr. Takeda's death is Representative Shishido."

"Was there any local opposition to the building of the golf course?"

"Some. But the golf course was only in the planning stages, and there wasn't any strong protest movement against it."

"Then what about Mr. Takeda's employees, beginning with you, Mr. Izawa? Is there anyone among them who had a grudge against him? For example, the man whose place you were given as head secretary? I shouldn't think he would have been too pleased by that."

"No such thing! Being head secretary isn't all that great. There's a lot to it that's inconvenient for a married man, so it's more suited to a bachelor like me. Besides, the man I replaced didn't take any loss in salary."

"Then what about his relations with women? I don't think it would have been strange if a man in his position had had a mistress or a lover."

"Well he didn't, nobody at all. Oh, he was fawned over by geishas, and he may have had an occasional fling with a club hostess, but I'm sure at least that there was no woman who could have felt strongly enough to kill him."

"I see." Arms folded, Takemura fell into thought.

Izawa kept glancing at his watch. "Inspector, if you have further questions, I wonder if you'd mind saving them for some other day? I would appreciate it if we could stop here for today."

"Okay, I suppose we can do that. Now, if I could see Mrs. Takeda for just a moment?"

"Do you really have to?"

"Yes, I'm afraid I do. She was the person closest to the victim, you know. Actually, she should have been questioned yesterday, but we were asked to put it off for a day because she has some kind of heart trouble. I know it must be awfully hard on her, but it's just got to be done."

"I see. All right, I'll ask her if it's convenient."

"Convenient or not, I'm afraid I do have to see her now. I can save detailed questions for later, but I at least have to talk to her for a minute today."

"Do you? Then wait here please," said Izawa with a long face, getting up and walking off.

Gathering the man was afraid of Mrs. Takeda, Takemura grew irritated. If even the police tried to stay away from her, that wasn't surprising, but Takemura always got mad when he saw political influence interfering with an investigation. Take the case of the politician who had committed suicide in Hokkaido. At first the doctor and even the Hokkaido police had yielded to pressure from members of the Diet and announced that he had died of illness. When Takemura thought about how much that kind of kowtowing to authority spoiled the police organization and its individual officers, and how much distrust it caused among the public, he could not help feeling resentful.

It must have taken Izawa quite some time to persuade Mrs. Takeda, but finally he reappeared, looking exhausted. "She says she'll see you. Follow me."

He led them along a winding path farther into the garden to the left, to a broad veranda facing a small artificial hill. There the old lady was seated on a rattan chair, in a neat mourning dress, looking very stately. Her face showed no sign of the misfortune she had suffered, and her silver hair was splendidly curled. Her silver-rimmed glasses suited her perfectly.

"I've brought them," said Izawa, leading them to the edge of the veranda.

Standing there, Takemura could not help feeling like a criminal dragged before the judge. "I'm Takemura, prefectural police," he said, "and this is Officer Kinoshita."

She bowed her head slightly. "Ah, yes, thank you for coming. Superintendent Nagakura told me he would be sending a superior detective. He must have meant you. I do hope you will do a good job."

"Thank you. We will make every effort to find your husband's killer as quickly as possible. Toward that end, there are a number of questions I must ask you, and I do hope I may count on your full cooperation."

"Of course. But I leave everything to Mr. Izawa, so I'm sure he can tell you everything you need to know."

"But as Mr. Takeda's wife, you must have known of some private aspects of his life that Mr. Izawa wouldn't be able to tell me about."

"No," declared Mrs. Takeda, with considerable tension in her voice, "there is nothing special that I can tell you about my husband."

"How about this: would your husband have had any reason to commit suicide?"

"How dare you!" said the old lady, rising abruptly to her feet and glaring at this police inspector invading her garden. "My husband could have had no reason for suicide, and I suggest that you stop wasting time and get down to the business of finding his killer."

She took two or three steps away, then turned and pointed to the table. "Izawa, there's a letter from the detective agency there. It doesn't seem to be anything important, but if it will be of any help to the inspector, you may show it to him. Now, if you will excuse me." With a glance at Takemura out of the corner of her eye, she disappeared into the house without giving him a chance to say a word.

Takemura looked at Kinoshita with a wry smile.

"That's quite a woman!" said Kinoshita in admiration.

"I'm terribly sorry," said Izawa, embarrassed.

"That's all right. Let's have a look at that letter," said Takemura, impatiently.

The envelope had already been opened. Takemura and Kinoshita looked on as Izawa removed and spread out the contents. The envelope was addressed to Kisuke Takeda, from a private detective agency in Tokyo. The contents were a very simple personal history of a man named Tomohiro Tachibana: born 1922, birth registered in To-

kyo, present address also in Tokyo; a Ph.D. in literature
and now a professor at T— University, a private university;
eminent in classical literature, particularly in the discovery
of and research on books of romantic narrative.

"What is this?" asked Takemura.

"I'm afraid I don't know. I've never seen the name
Tomohiro Tachibana before," said Izawa, his head in-
clined. Apparently he was telling the truth. "But I can't
imagine he had anything to do with Mr. Takeda's business."

"When Mr. Takeda used a detective agency for something, was he accustomed to handling the matter himself?"

"No, he always left it to me. As far as I know, he'd never
done it himself before."

"If the man was born in 1922, Mr. Takeda probably
wasn't having him investigated as a prospective marriage
partner for anyone. Could Tachibana have been looking
for another job after retirement, do you think?"

"Perhaps. But Mr. Takeda would normally have left a
matter like that to me." Izawa thought about it for a while
without coming up with any ideas. Finally it was decided
that the document should be left for a time in the hands of
the police.

As Izawa was showing Takemura and Kinoshita out,
they passed three Buddhist priests coming in. The wake
was that night, and the funeral would later be held at the
Zenko Temple. It was to be a magnificent service.

"Kisuke Takeda must've been awfully powerful," said
Kinoshita with a deep breath, looking around at the rows
of wreaths.

"Actually, this reflects the prestige of the Takeda family
more than it does Mr. Takeda's power," said Izawa, somewhat boastfully. "The family is supposed to have been
prominent since the Muromachi period, you know. Mr.

Takeda may be gone, but Mrs. Takeda holds some considerable power of her own."

* * *

When they got back to headquarters, the report was in from CID about the stationery Takemura had found in Kisuke Takeda's room at the Koshimizu Plateau Hotel. The name Tomohiro Tachibana had been written with a ball-point pen on the sheet of paper above the one Takemura had picked up, which would appear to mean that Takeda had contacted the detective agency from the hotel to request an investigation of Tachibana. But why such a hurry, and why had he not left it to Izawa?

Takemura called the hotel to ask whether there had been a man named Tomohiro Tachibana among the guests at the party on July 3rd.

"Yes, we did have the honor of accommodating a guest by that name," answered Takano, the manager, with his exaggerated politeness.

Tachibana had apparently come from Tokyo to attend the party as an endorser of the golf course project. Such an investigation might have been requested if there had been something suspicious about his identity, but the request would most likely have been made by the golf course committee or by Takeda's secretary, Izawa. It would have been strange for Takeda to contact the detective agency himself.

Had Takeda wanted Tachibana investigated for personal reasons instead? If so, why? Did Tachibana have something to do with Takeda's murder?

2 Tomohiro Tachibana's residence in the Nishikata neighborhood of Bunkyo Ward was on a rise in Hongo near Tokyo University, on a quiet street which had been inhabited by scholars and men of culture since the Meiji era.

The Tachibanas were an old family which had lived on that site ever since the Meiji Restoration of 1868, but not being able to pay the inheritance tax when his father died, Tomohiro had sold part of the land and submissively agreed to let a real estate agency tear down the decrepit old house and replace it with a three-story condominium apartment building, in which—as was the fashion of the times— he had been provided an apartment of supposedly equivalent value. As a result, there were very few people left who knew of the former illustriousness of the Tachibana family.

Tachibana had celebrated his sixtieth birthday this year. His wife had died without leaving him a child. His one relative in the world, a younger sister, had married into a large family connected with big business, which reeked so much of riches that he did not get along with them. His sister, however, had been fundamentally suited for such a life, and had been so thoroughly assimilated into the family that a considerable distance had developed between her and Tachibana.

* * *

After the doorbell rang for the second time, Tachibana finally remembered that his wife was no longer there to answer it. It was already two months since she had passed away, but the habits of a lifetime still caused him sometimes to forget and wait for her to do the things she had always done for him.

"Coming!" he called, making it sound cheerful as he got up. There was no special hurry about the work spread out on the table, so he wouldn't mind having a guest right now, whoever it might be.

When he opened the door, two strangers with sullen expressions were standing there.

"Are you Tomohiro Tachibana?" asked one of them, a man of thirty-five or thirty-six, dark complexioned and of undistinguished mien. He was looking Tachibana straight in the eye. The other man was much younger and seemed rather self-effacing. He appeared to be the older man's subordinate.

"Yes, I'm Tachibana. What is it?"

"Police," said the first man, showing his badge and presenting his card at the same time. The card read, "Iwao Takemura, Inspector, Nagano prefectural police headquarters, Investigative Section One." The younger man introduced himself as Kinoshita.

"Police?" Tachibana stood there at a loss, with Takemura's card in his hand.

"We'd like to ask you a few questions," said Takemura. "Do you mind if we come in?"

"Oh, no, please, come in." Tachibana led them into the living room. "I'm a widower, so I'm afraid I can't receive you properly, but can I offer you a beer or something?"

"No, we're on duty, but thank you anyway," replied Takemura.

The fact was, however, that they had spent a long time under the burning sky, asking directions at every corner, and something cold to drink would really have hit the spot. Kinoshita inadvertently licked his lips, and Tachibana, sizing up the situation, got two cans each of beer and juice from the refrigerator and set them on the table, so that both men could choose whichever drink they liked.

"Then, thank you, I guess we will have something," said Takemura. With a warning look at Kinoshita that he had better choose the same, Takemura picked up a can of juice and began to drink it with relish. Kinoshita did the same, but he was so thirsty that he guzzled his juice in one gulp. It dribbled out of the corners of his mouth, and he hastily got out his handkerchief to wipe his chin.

"Professor Tachibana, do you know a man named Kisuke Takeda?" Takemura began.

"Takeda?" Tachibana glanced at Takemura. Takemura was looking at him hard with keen eyes. "Yes, I believe I did meet a man by that name a few days ago at a party in Togakushi. Are you here about him?"

"Yes, that's right. Then you do know him?"

"Well, I've met him, at least. He was introduced to me as one of the promoters of that golf course they want to build. We exchanged cards. But we didn't have any conversation to speak of."

"Was that the first time you had ever met him, in Togakushi?"

"Yes, that's right. But I'm afraid I find this rather peculiar. What is this Mr. Takeda supposed to have to do with me?"

"Then apparently you don't know. You see, Kisuke Takeda is dead. I mean, he was murdered."

"Oh? Murdered?" Tachibana looked at Takemura in surprise. "How horrible! But I'm afraid I still don't see what it has to do with me."

"The fact is that yesterday a letter was delivered to Mr. Takeda's home from a private detective agency in Tokyo. It contained a personal history of yourself, Professor."

"Of me?"

"That's right."

"Then this Mr. Takeda must have had some need to have me investigated. What need?"

"That we don't know. Can't you help us, Professor?"

"No, I'm afraid I can't. My first guess would be that I was being investigated for membership in the golf club, but I was only invited to that party as a last minute replacement, so I was just along for the ride. Nor had I given any indication that I wanted to join the club. Besides, the golf course itself was still no sure thing. They couldn't have been soliciting members yet."

"No, Mr. Takeda was having you investigated for some personal reason. I mean, it doesn't appear to have had anything to do with the golf course."

"A personal reason? Now that puts me at even more of a loss. Unless our president had privately asked him to help find a second wife for me!" With a laugh, Tachibana took a cigarette from the pack on the table and offered his guests a smoke as well. As he did so, his eyes met Takemura's. Takemura seemed to be trying to see into his mind.

"No, thank you," said Takemura.

Tachibana abruptly withdrew the cigarettes and averted his eyes, with an expression of frank hostility that he had not shown to that point. "Whatever reason this Takeda was having me investigated for, I'm not very happy about it. And that it should have made me the target of a police investigation makes it one hell of a big nuisance. Well, anyhow, when and where was the man killed?"

"He died in the middle of the night of July 3rd. More precisely, it is estimated that he died within several hours either way of 2 A.M. on the 4th. But his body wasn't discovered until the 7th, so it's difficult to be exact."

"The night of the 3rd would have been just after the

party, right? I was staying at the Koshimizu Plateau Hotel. Wasn't he staying there too?"

"He was supposed to be. But he left the hotel that evening and never returned. He was missing until his body was found on the 7th."

"Where was it found?"

"In a very peculiar place. On the southwest edge of Togakushi, at a campground called Arakura. One section of it is known as Poison Plain. In ancient times, a demoness named Maple is supposed to have lived there . . ."

"Yes, I know. You're talking about the maple-viewing story. The origin of that place name comes from the poison saké that Maple is supposed to have served there to Taira no Koremochi."

"Oh, you know. That's right. Well, anyway, that's where the body was discovered. On Poison Plain."

"I see. Well now, if the cause of death were poisoning, that would really make a good story, wouldn't it?" laughed Tachibana.

Takemura's expression became even more grim. "As a matter of fact, the cause of death *was* poisoning. Cyanide poisoning."

"Good grief!"

The two detectives kept their eyes on Tachibana, trying to tell whether or not his surprise was genuine.

"That's weird!" said Tachibana. "I suppose it was merely a coincidence?"

"We don't know," said Takemura. "But I, for one, am guessing that the murderer had some special purpose in leaving the body where he did. If he hadn't, he would hardly have needed to go to the trouble of taking it all the way out there."

"Is it really such an inconvenient place?"

"Inconvenient? Well, it's in the mountains."

"Then, couldn't the murderer have been trying to hide the body?"

"No, it doesn't look like it. The body had been left out in the open where it could easily be seen. There would have been any number of better places to hide it. Tell me, Professor Tachibana, where were you during the middle of the night of July 3rd?"

"What?" exclaimed Tachibana, with a contemptuous look of disgust at Takemura. "Are you asking for my alibi?"

"Just a formality."

"Still, I must say I am surprised. Oh well, I suppose you've got to do your job. Let's see now. I was at the Koshimizu Plateau Hotel all night. Is that good enough for you?"

"Is there anyone who can verify that?"

"Well, the president of the university where I teach was staying in the next room, but I don't guess that would do for an alibi, would it? Which means I'm stuck," laughed Tachibana, poking a little fun at the detectives.

✳   ✳   ✳

Just after the detectives left, Fusae Nakayama came in. "I just passed two gentlemen I've never seen before on the stairs," she said. "Did you have visitors?"

"Oh yes, those were detectives."

"Detectives? Is something wrong?"

"They were here to question me."

"You, Professor? Why, you must be joking!"

"Not at all. It seems I'm suspected of murder."

"What kind of idiocy is that? That's terrible!"

"Terrible or not, it's true. You remember I went to

Togakushi a few days ago? Well, it seems that a man staying in the same hotel that night was murdered."

"Good heavens! Is that a fact? But why do they suspect you, Professor?"

"Well, don't I look like an evil man to you?"

"Nonsense! You look like a man who wouldn't hurt a fly!"

"Then maybe they suspect me because I look too innocent."

"This is a terrible conversation." She changed the subject. "Did you eat a good breakfast this morning?"

"I had toast and milk."

"I don't believe you. This package of bread hasn't been opened. I told you to make ham and eggs for yourself this morning, but you won't listen to anybody. Before you know it, you'll be suffering from malnutrition."

The woman never stopped talking, thought Tachibana with a wry smile. Fusae Nakayama was the only daughter of an antique dealer across from the Red Gate of Tokyo University, and their families had known each other for a couple of generations. She was five years younger than his wife, Nobuko, but they had seemed to hit it off well, and what with one excuse or another—delivering a gift, learning Western cooking, and so on—she had managed to visit quite frequently.

When Nobuko's illness took a rapid turn for the worse, followed by her sudden death, Fusae had cried so hard in front of everybody that even Tachibana was embarrassed. Then, almost before the seventh day of mourning was over, she had developed a peculiar enthusiasm for taking care of him—cleaning his apartment, doing his laundry, even preparing three good meals a day for him. Leaving aside the fact that she had told him how she had adored him as a young girl but thought of him as far above her, and forgetting the coquettish glances she sometimes cast at him, Tachibana had found her well-intentioned and extremely useful.

"You said you were going out this afternoon, so I'll make you an early lunch, and you'd better eat all of it," she said, cheerfully beginning to prepare the meal.

＊　＊　＊

"Well, what did you think of the professor?" asked Kinoshita, as they were waiting for a bus on the boulevard.

"I don't know. He didn't seem to be lying, and yet, I got the feeling I couldn't trust him completely. The hardest people for me to get a handle on are ones of his age, especially scholars like him."

"Still, it's a fact that Takeda was having him investigated. Isn't it strange that he didn't have any idea why?"

"Yes, that it is. But I couldn't pick up anything from his attitude. I might just as well have not been looking at him. People of his age who lived through the war went through a lot, and one thing they all learned was how to be inscrutable. It isn't easy to get the truth out of them if they don't want you to know it."

Takemura and Kinoshita next went to the private detective agency in Aoyama. "Yes, Mr. Takeda gave us a lot of business over many years," eulogized an administrator named Sawada who received them. "And if I remember correctly, just before he died, on the evening of July 3rd, that is, he called me at home with an urgent request that we investigate this Tomohiro Tachibana as quickly as possible."

Normally the detective agency maintained strict secrecy for its clients, even from the police, but as this client had been murdered and the police needed all the information they could get to find the murderer, Sawada was quite willing to tell them everything he knew. He said he had gotten the feeling on the telephone that something very unexpected had come up, and Takeda was considerably upset. He had requested that the agency check out Tachibana's identity and send him a report immediately, after which they were to send a follow-up report on his daily activities and the background of his trip to Togakushi.

"So we sent the first report, but then while we were working on the second one, this terrible thing happened," concluded Sawada, with a mournful look that might have expressed either his grief over the death of Takeda himself, or his lament over the loss of an important client.

"Then may I assume that after you sent the first report, you put a watch on Tachibana?" asked Takemura.

"Yes. We began watching him on July 5th. We found out later, of course, that at that time, Mr. Takeda was already dead. I believe it was on the noon news of July 7th that we heard about it. Naturally, we were astonished."

"So you had a watch on Tachibana from July 5th until you heard the news, right?"

"That's right. But didn't you say that Mr. Takeda's death took place before dawn on July 4th? So that means we can't establish an alibi for Tachibana."

"Yes, we'll certainly keep that in mind," said Takemura quickly. Putting on a smile, he thanked Sawada and stood up to go.

Kinoshita hardly managed to wait until they got outside. "What Sawada just told us about watching Tachibana from the 5th to the 7th does mean that Tachibana has an alibi at least for the time that the body was left on Poison Plain, right?"

"Looks like it, but even if they did have a watch on him, it was only during the daytime, wouldn't you think? They wouldn't know, probably, if he did anything after he got home at night. Besides, we aren't sure there was only one person involved, you know, so it wouldn't mean anything, even if he does have an alibi for the time the body was left."

"I guess not. Now that you mention it, the body was left on Poison Plain at night, wasn't it? That makes Professor Tachibana look awfully suspicious, doesn't it?"

"I'm not at all sure how he looks. I'm afraid my intuition seems to be letting me down," said Takemura with a frown.

3 Tachibana finally realized that the girl sitting beside him was behaving strangely. He had been aware for some time that she was continually putting a handkerchief to her face, but had assumed the action to be merely a habit. When he looked away from the stage at her, however, he noticed for the first time that she was crying. The handkerchief was not merely for perspiration. With closer scrutiny, he saw she was trembling all over, apparently trying to keep from sobbing out loud, and that made him wonder.

It wasn't that nobody ever cried during a Noh play, for many Noh plots contain strong elements of tragedy which can move an absorbed spectator to tears, just like an ordinary play or movie. In Noh, however, the spectator had to have quite a profound knowledge before being capable of that much empathy. The flowery language of Noh chants is entirely that of ancient poems and stories, and the Noh actor delivers his lines with a unique intonation in a voice which, furthermore, comes from behind his mask, making it an effort merely to distinguish the words. To understand enough to be moved by them, the spectator had to be quite well acquainted with Noh.

The girl beside Tachibana did not look very familiar. She was only an auditor at his seminar, and he guessed she must have entered the university that spring. She looked very young. It was rare to see such a young girl watching a Noh play at all, let alone understanding it so well as to be moved to tears. That in itself would put her among the most knowledgeable of Noh spectators.

There was just one small point that bothered Tachibana: the play they were watching was "Maple-Viewing," which belonged to the so-called fifth category of Noh drama.

In a Noh play, the leading actor is called the "doer." The doer's role may be one of five—a god, a military commander, a woman, a madman, or a demon. The play is classified according to the doer's role. In the first category he plays a god, in the second a man, the third a woman, the fourth a madman, and the fifth a demon. Plays of the first category are all stories of good omen, with happy endings which could make no one cry. Plays of the second through fourth categories, with their battlefield scenes and love stories, are filled with tragedy and romance, and a fine performance could well move a knowledgeable spectator to tears.

But plays of the fifth category feature demons. In the story of "Maple-Viewing," the military commander, Taira no Koremochi, comes to the Togakushi Mountains in autumn to hunt deer. There he meets a group of beautiful women holding a banquet in celebration of the autumn colors. They serve him saké and dance for him. He is overcome by drowsiness. Making sure he is asleep, they exit with the threatening words, "May you never awake from your dreams!"

Koremochi has a dream in which he receives a divine oracle which reveals that the women are actually demons. He unsheathes the supernatural sword beside his pillow and lies waiting. A demon soon appears. More than two meters tall, it tries to fly off with Koremochi by the head, but he runs it through and slays it.

The story is that of a hero against the supernatural, a story which might make a child cry, but hardly one to bring tears to the eyes of an adult. And yet, the girl beside Tachibana was crying with mournful abandon. He did not know quite what to make of her, but he nevertheless felt a surge of interest in the owner of such sensitivity and found it refreshing that such a young girl should be capable of so much feeling for the extremely stylized Noh drama.

* * *

The class leader of Tachibana's seminar, a boy named Minegishi, had suggested that they organize a Noh appreciation circle for the summer vacation. Quite a few students had thought it a good idea, and in the end, about twenty of them had agreed to participate. They would sit in the lowest priced seats, but they would attend professional performances of Noh plays from all five categories, and afterward discuss them over dinner with their professor.

Hearing that some of the students would even delay their returns home in order to participate, Tachibana had most willingly agreed. He was a little wary about the talk of collecting money for drinks with the meal, but decided finally that alcohol would serve to enhance the mood.

* * *

Tachibana was now seated in the last row. All of the twenty or so seats were more or less similar, but in order to give

his students a slightly better view, he had brushed aside
their embarrassment and insisted on sitting in the back. He
assumed that the girl was sitting there in the corner
because she was merely an auditor in his seminar and had
been embarrassed to take a better seat. It never occurred to
him that she might intentionally have sat there to be next
to him.

The Noh appreciation circle was a tolerable success. As
planned, they did splurge on beer and soft drinks at dinner,
but even Tachibana was happily convinced that they got
their money's worth. His tongue moved more freely than
usual and he flattered himself that he had given a pretty
good talk. He drank more than usual and toward the end
of the meal began to feel gloriously drunk. At this rate, he
figured, he was going to get home in a good mood for the
first time in a long while.

Then, as the dinner was drawing to a close and he was
starting to feel drowsy, from out of the murmur of voices,
he heard someone suddenly speak up from a corner of the
room.

"Professor Tachibana, from your talk a few minutes ago,
I think you must have only a superficial knowledge of the
story behind the play we just saw."

Tachibana was startled, but not so much as his students.
A hush fell on the room, and all eyes focused on the owner
of the voice. It was the girl. Tachibana was sitting some
distance away from her, but from his position, he had a
clear frontal view of her.

She was beautiful. Not pretty, but beautiful, having a
classic oval face and striking black eyes that glittered in the
slightest light. And those eyes were fixed, almost accusingly, on him.

"It's very rude of me," he said, "but I have a terrible
memory. I'm afraid your name escapes me."

"She's a new student, Professor," said Minegishi. "Her name is Noya. Yuko Noya, isn't it?"

The girl nodded. Noya was quite a rare surname. It was the first time Tachibana had ever heard it.

"But Miss Noya, that's an awfully rude way to speak to your professor," Minegishi reproached her.

"No, no, I don't mind. If we had to worry so much about how we word things, we'd never have any discussion about our studies," said Tachibana magnanimously. "If Miss Noya has a different opinion, I'd certainly like to hear it. After all, I might learn something. Now, Miss Noya, let's hear what you have to say."

"You talked as though the demoness was just a monster without a heart, Professor, but I think that's a terribly one-sided way of looking at her," said Yuko Noya, in a clear voice devoid of timidity. "There's nothing in the plot about how the women came to be having that feast in the mountains, so the play doesn't give a single hint about the origin of the maple-viewing banquet or its historical background. That makes it nothing more than a tale of heroism on the part of Taira no Koremochi. It totally overlooks the grief and resentment strong enough to have turned Maple into a demoness, and emphasizes only the symbolism of the evil karma lurking like a demon in a woman's heart, while it conveys nothing of how it got there. That makes it an awfully unfair and terribly shallow story."

"I see," said Tachibana, his eyes wide. Her argument aside, he had not recently laid eyes on a young person who spoke such excellent Japanese. "Then you think that before the play begins, an explanation should be presented to the audience concerning how Maple became a demoness?"

"Yes, I do."

"Well, I certainly think that your deep consideration of the matter shows your fine attitude toward the appreciation of Noh. And as a matter of fact, there are quite a few other examples where the omission of a prelude colors the story that is acted out on stage. For instance, there's the one about the hollyhocks from the *Tale of Genji,* where events leading up to the scene on stage are totally omitted, and the play begins abruptly with the wraith haunting the hollyhocks. Nowadays, of course, everybody knows the *Tale of Genji,* but it's hard to believe that many people did when the play was first produced. Even so, the bold technique of assuming that the audience does have prior knowledge is one of the peculiar characteristics of Noh, and one way of looking at it is that the part not acted out forces the spectator to use his imagination.

"Now, what about this Maple-Viewing play we just saw? I would imagine that, unlike the Hollyhocks play, the writer either didn't know or didn't care about the events leading up to what he depicted on stage. In other words, he intended no relation between the monster and the earlier 'doer'—the sensual beauty before she turns into a demoness. He was only trying to express the marvelous contrast between the splendid background of the Togakushi Mountains covered with autumn maples and the horror of the monster, and I think it's all right for the spectator to take it at face value. So all things considered, I don't think the grief and tragic history of Maple as a woman is terribly relevant to the play. But of course, I can't say that I don't understand how you, as a woman, would feel sympathy for her and want to defend her."

"No, it isn't sympathy. It's because I think that to understand Noh—this art of omission—it's very important to know what's omitted. For instance, sir, you offered the play 'On the Hollyhocks' as an example, but I think the significance of the omission in that play is totally different from the one in 'Maple-Viewing.' The people of those days were far more devoted to their religion and regarded it as much more absolute than we do nowadays. They would have felt instinctively what a demoness was, and I don't think it would have made any difference at all to their feelings even if they had been told how she became one."

Tachibana was amazed. For a girl of nineteen or so to be offering such an excellent argument in such fine language in this day and age was nothing less than a miracle. And indeed, the other students were gazing at Yuko Noya after her fervent speech as if she herself were a demoness.

"I see. I see. That's very interesting. And I certainly do think that's another good way of looking at it," said Tachibana. "But Miss Noya, you certainly do know your subject, don't you? To tell you the truth, I'm not that familiar myself with the story leading up to the 'Maple-Viewing' play. But from the way you talk, you must have made quite a thorough study of it. I wonder if we could ask you to tell us all about it?"

"Yes," she replied in a voice like a bell, and sat up very straight. "Actually, the reason I'm so familiar with the play is that the story is taken from a legend around my home in Nagano Prefecture. On the Noh stage, Maple is depicted as a demoness, but in the northern part of Nagano, especially around Togakushi and Kinasa, she's recognized as a real, historical character, and there are quite a number of very peculiar place names around Togakushi and Kinasa, whose origin can't be explained unless it is assumed that she did really exist. As a matter of fact, even the name Kinasa itself, meaning 'Village Without a Demon,' serves as para-doxical proof of her existence."

It stirred Tachibana to hear that Yuko Noya was from Nagano, and he was shaken when she mentioned Togakushi, feeling a bittersweet sentiment and a vague, inexplicable foreboding.

"Maple's infant name was Kureha, and she is said to have been born in the Aizu Region of northeastern Japan," Yuko continued. "As a girl, she was a beauty of some repute, and it was decided that she should go to the capital. There, she found favor with Tsunemoto, of the clan of Genji. That was when she changed her name from Kureha to Maple.

"Now, most prevalent theories take Maple as an inherently wicked woman. Some even make her a child sent in answer to a prayer to Marishiten, the Buddhist god of war. But looking at it with common sense and from a scientific point of view, those things just don't happen. I think her wickedness developed only when she decided that she wanted Tsunemoto's love all for herself. If I had been a country girl who went to the capital and received the favors of a man of power like Tsunemoto, I'm sure I would have been in such rapture that I would have become every bit as wicked as she did."

"Now, hold on there," laughed Tachibana, raising both hands. "I understand that you want to defend Maple, but don't be so subjective about it! Just tell us the story."

"I'm sorry." Yuko closed her mouth and her face reddened. For the first time, she displayed the naiveté and innocence of a young girl, which made Tachibana intensely happy. If she had turned out to be totally the prim young lady that her manner of speech indicated, he would most likely have found her unbearably stuffy.

She continued. "Maple's desire to possess Tsunemoto became stronger and stronger, until finally she thought of killing his lawful wife. Some views have it that she tried to use poison, others say it was witchcraft. Uh, my objective guess is that she must have learned something about poisonous herbs, and the hallucinatory powers of hemp.

"But her scheme was discovered before she could carry

it out, and she was exiled to the mountains of Togakushi, a poor area on barren land, known for the production of hemp. Lamenting her misfortune, she built a house for herself Kyoto style, to remind her of the capital, and she gave the names of places in Kyoto to the surrounding settlements—Higashikyo, Nishikyo, Ichijo, Nijo, even the river she named after one in Kyoto. The names are still used today. In Nishikyo there's the Kasuga Shrine, and the place where Maple lived is called Imperial Palace Remains.

"The villagers and the rough men of the surrounding mountains were charmed by her rare beauty, and that, along with her powers of witchcraft, turned her very quickly into a charismatic leader. The people cooperated to build her the 'imperial palace' of her dreams along with the surrounding town she desired, and they pledged their loyalty to her. Before long, the powerful clans of the region and even the warriors of the Zenko Temple became her followers, so it is said, which shows that she must have had quite considerable influence.

"But to support itself, this large band repeatedly raided and plundered the neighboring villages. Word of the raids reached the capital in Kyoto, and a military force under the command of Taira no Koremochi was dispatched to Togakushi. But Maple's band, protected by the natural stronghold of the Togakushi Mountains, built weirs and forts all over, and defeated the forces come to subjugate them. The memory of those weirs and forts is preserved today in some of the place names.

"Stymied by the stubborn resistance of Maple's band, Koremochi prayed to the Kitamuki Kuan-yin goddess in Ueda and was granted an oracle." Here Yuko paused, looking very sad. "The rest of the story sounds made up, and I don't like it very much, but anyway, with the gods behind him this time, Taira no Koremochi plans a general attack over a new route. The places where he crossed the Susobana River and where he set up camp are named for those events. Also, as the gods have instructed him to do, in order to determine where to begin his attack on the cave in which Maple has entrenched herself, Koremochi aims his bow at the sky and lets fly an arrow. The arrow flies west and lands with its point stuck in the ground. The place where it landed is called Arrowstand, and today there's a Hachiman Shrine on the site.

"Before beginning his final attack, Koremochi sneaks into Maple's camp alone. Discovered, he is naturally suspected of being an enemy soldier, and is brought before her. She knows at a glance that he is the enemy, but overcome by her longing for the capital from which he has come, she gives him a banquet. There are conflicting theories concerning whether it was Maple who offered Koremochi poisoned saké at the banquet, or whether it was the reverse, but whichever way it happened, the place is now called Poison Plain.

"Having succeeded in getting close to Maple, Koremochi finds his chance to draw his supernatural sword, with which he seriously wounds her. At the same time, his entire force charges. Unable to bear the mortification and hatred of it all, Maple finally turns into a demoness and tries to fight Koremochi off, but her wound is so serious that she is unable to use her witchcraft, and in the end, she is slain by Koremochi's supernatural sword.

"And that is the end of the Demoness Legend. After that, the name of the neighboring village was changed to Kinasa, or Demon-Free. In his old age, Taira no Koremochi built a villa in Ueda, where he spent his last years. The place is named after his villa, and his grave there is called General's Mound."

Yuko Noya had finished her long story. There was

silence for a moment, and then all at once, applause. Tachibana joined in, gazing in fascination at Yuko's shy, flushed smile. For some reason, over Yuko's beautiful face, there seemed to be superimposed the face of Taki Tendoh, so long asleep in his memory.

＊　＊　＊

In front of the restaurant, Minegishi hailed a taxi for Tachibana. Tachibana thanked him, and was just getting in when, from among the students seeing him off, Yuko Noya rushed up to him. She put her hand on his back, pretending to be helping him into the taxi, and whispered quickly into his ear, "Professor, you were the son of a viscount, weren't you?"

Tachibana turned in astonishment. She was looking at him with an enigmatic smile. "How did you know that?" he asked, but she merrily signaled to the driver to go ahead, and moved away from the car.

The driver pulled the door shut and started. Tachibana looked back to see Yuko waving to him from among the crowd of students.

Arrowstand

遺屍に立つ矢

The questioning of residents of the villa development on the Koshimizu Plateau was nearly concluded. "Three of the villas were still vacant, most likely because it's pretty early in the season," reported Detective Sergeant Yoshii, "but we've made a list of all the owners."

According to Yoshii's list, there were altogether twenty-six villas in the development. Most of those owned by companies were constantly attended by live-in managers. The name of the manager of the Fukumoto Machinery villa was listed as Mitsuo Murata. Takemura remembered Junko Murata, the woman who liked to talk the way his wife Yoko did.

"So far, we've asked everybody in the villas whether they had anything to do with Kisuke Takeda or whether they had a visit from him that night, but we haven't picked up anything yet that might help us," said Yoshii with a look of chagrin. A man of forty-two with a strong sense of duty, he was painfully irritated that he hadn't come up with anything helpful. "But we did pay special attention to the vicinity where you said a man who could be assumed to be Kisuke Takeda had been seen walking. One of the three villas whose owners we haven't been able yet to get in touch with is in that vicinity, and we did hear from the owner of the villa next to it—'next to it' being about a hundred meters away—that he had seen a light on there the night of the 3rd and heard a car going out and in."

"Oh? What time was that?"

"Well, he wasn't really sure, but he thinks he must have heard the car sometime between ten and eleven."

"You say he heard it going out, and then in?"

"That's right."

"In other words, he heard it twice, you mean? Both going out, and then coming in?"

"I think so . . . probably . . ."

"Come on! You know 'probably' isn't good enough. You said 'out and in.' That means first out and later in. I want to know how long it was between the going out and the coming in."

It was rare for Takemura to bawl out one of his men like that, but he was annoyed that Yoshii should have casually overlooked something that to him was only common sense.

"All right," said Yoshii, "we'll go back and check."

"I'd appreciate that. Also, which one on the list is the owner of that villa?"

"His name is Ishihara. He lives in Nagoya City, Chikusa Ward."

"Okay, split up your men and send somebody to Nagoya."

Two men each were immediately sent to Nagoya and Togakushi.

No further information had been picked up from the questioning of residents of the area around Poison Plain, where the body had been found. Nothing whatsoever about any suspicious person or automobile. No matter what time of night the body had been brought there, whoever did it must have known that the chances of not being seen were very slim, so whatever his purpose might have been, he knew he would be taking a big risk to accomplish it. Unless, of course, he had reason to believe it would be perfectly safe.

As Takemura listened to the reports of his men, he was looking hard at a 1:25,000 map spread out on the table. There was only one road to Poison Plain, and that was from the village of Imai. "Just looking at the place," said Takemura, "anybody wanting to bring a body there in the middle of the night would have had to know the area awfully well. Not only that, but he must have been sure of not being seen along the way. I don't like this."

"Maybe it was done by somebody local," said Kinoshita, quick to pick up Takemura's thoughts.

"That's a good possibility."

Obviously, if the murderer were somebody local, then the motive might well have been trouble over the building of the Togakushi Plateau Golf Course. Organized opposition to the course, though still weak, was said to be getting stronger. In addition, there were most likely quite a few people who might approve of the course itself but were angered by the strong-arm tactics employed by Takeda in other ventures. The police were, in fact, getting that impression from a lot of the residents. Some even declared coldly that Takeda had gotten the divine retribution he had coming to him.

"Still," said Takemura, "who would have opposed a golf course enough to kill somebody over it? Besides, that doesn't tell us why the body was left on Poison Plain. No, I don't think the motive for this murder could have been anything so obvious. It must be something much deeper. Otherwise, how do we explain why the body was left just where it was?"

That had been Takemura's feeling from the beginning, and the longer he worked on the case, the more convinced of it he had become. The poisoned body had been left on Poison Plain, and if they wrote that off as mere coincidence, then how would they explain the murderer's need to take the risk of getting it there? No, Takemura could only assume that the murderer must have been making some sort of display. But if so, then who was the display intended for, and why? If Takeda's killing and the placing of his body on Poison Plain was some kind of warning, then the murderer was likely not finished.

"I think perhaps we can expect another murder before long," said Takemura, with a gloomy look.

His prediction was to come true with unexpected speed.

✳ ✳ ✳

On his return to the villa development on the Koshimizu Plateau, Detective Yoshii had made his questioning more precise.

"The name of the family I spoke to is Segi, and the villa is privately owned," he reported to Takemura. "The son had gotten home from college at the beginning of this month, and on Saturday the 3rd, the whole family came up from Tokyo. The Ishihara villa is about a hundred meters away from theirs as the crow flies, and there's a rather thick stand of trees between them, so they don't have a good view of it. But at night, they can see its lights, and they remember somebody in their family commenting that night that their neighbors were there too. It was the college son who heard the car. He says he heard the engine start and the car drive off shortly after he went into the toilet, and he heard it come back and stop, and the door close just as he was leaving the toilet."

"What?" exclaimed Takemura. "You mean it went out and came right back?"

"Well, he says he probably spent five or six minutes in the toilet."

"Still, five or six minutes at most. Where could it have gone in such a short time?" Takemura considered the question for a moment, then asked, "Could it have been two different cars?"

"That's what I wondered myself, so I asked the boy just that question, but he says it had to be either the same car, or at least the same model. It seems he's a car buff, and he says he can tell the make and model of any car by the sound of its engine. It's a lot quieter out there than it is in the city, and he could very well be right."

"Hmm, I see. So, I guess they didn't notice any other activities in the villa next door—the Ishihara villa, I mean?"

"No, I'm afraid not. Except that they said they didn't see any lights on there the next evening, so I guess the people must have left during the day."

"So, what's your feeling about it, Sarge? Do you think Takeda might have visited the Ishihara villa that night?"

"Well, I'd say it's a strong possibility. From your conversation with the Murata woman, I don't think we could be wrong that Takeda went somewhere near the Ishihara villa after he left the hotel. We've been awfully thorough in our questioning in that neighborhood, and we've found no reason to believe that he might have visited any other villa. Of course, it's always possible that someone was lying, so maybe we'd better double-check, but I didn't get that feeling from anyone. Unless someone did lie, that would leave only the Ishihara villa, and its location is right. Besides, if Takeda had been headed for any place beyond the Ishihara villa, it would have been shorter for him to use the paved road that connects the Koshimizu Plateau Hotel and the Middle Shrine, so he would have had no reason to be walking on that lousy gravel road. So at this point, I think we have to assume that he was headed for the Ishihara villa."

"Okay, sounds great. We'll go all the way on your theory, Sarge," said Takemura, patting Yoshii appreciatively on the shoulder. "Now all we have to do is wait for your men to bring something back for us from Nagoya."

In that, however, they were disappointed. Yoshii's men just missed Mr. and Mrs. Ishihara. The only person at home was the elderly housekeeper, and she was not able to tell them much at all. "Mr. Ishihara only had to work until noon today, and he and Mrs. Ishihara just left a few minutes ago by car for their villa."

The detectives looked at each other. "You mean, their villa in Togakushi?"

"Yes."

It was a little past three. If the Ishiharas had left around three and taken the Chuo Expressway, it would take about two and a half hours to the Ihoku interchange. From there through Matsumoto and Nagano Cities to Togakushi over ordinary roads would take them quite a while, so the earliest they could be expected to arrive would be between eight and nine that night.

When he received that report from the men in Nagoya, Takemura decided to go to Togakushi himself. For some reason, he felt a foreboding that something was going to go wrong, and he had never known anything good to come of being given the slip by someone he wanted to see.

"Come on Kinoshita, let's go!" called Takemura.

Kinoshita looked glum. "Are we staking them out?"

"No, I just want to be there a little early, waiting for them."

"I guess we'll be back in the middle of the night, will we?"

"I imagine so. Why? Did you have something to do?"

"No, it's all right." Kinoshita hurried over to make a phone call in a corner of the room. By the way he kept bobbing his head, it looked like he was breaking a date.

Takemura and Kinoshita in one car, along with Yoshii and another detective in the second, headed for Togakushi.

"You did have something planned, didn't you? Did you go and break a date?" said Takemura, after they had traveled some distance. "You could have gotten somebody to fill in for you, you know."

"No, it's okay," said Kinoshita, with a look that meant it was too late to do anything about it now, anyway.

"You did break some kind of date, didn't you?"

"Yes, sort of."

"On the phone, you looked like you were begging for-giveness with tears in your eyes."

"I was not! I was only being polite."

"Well, I'm glad of that, but you know, I rely on you so much that I'm afraid I sometimes make unreasonable demands on you."

"Thank you, but I don't mind."

"If I've messed up your marriage plans, I'll give you my own wife, Yoko."

"I'd take her in a minute, Inspector. I've got a real crush on your wife!"

"Idiot! What kind of joke is that? Don't talk silly!" said Takemura, embarrassed.

"Aren't you the one who was talking silly, Inspector?"

said Kinoshita, quite offended. The conversation was taking an unpleasant turn.

"Hey, let's stop at the Middle Shrine for some buckwheat noodles," said Takemura. "My treat."

Kinoshita looked away, ready to laugh.

The police began their watch at 7 P.M. Takemura and Kinoshita waited in their car in the Segi villa driveway next door, watching for the Ishiharas to arrive. Yoshii and his partner waited in their car on the road beyond the Ishihara villa, ready, if necessary, to block any retreat.

All of the Koshimizu Plateau was enveloped in darkness by around 7:30, and the Ishihara villa remained completely dark. They all waited anxiously, checking with each other occasionally by walkie-talkie whenever they happened to think of it. The cool air felt good, but they had to keep their mouths shut to keep out the mosquitos. There was no question that it would have been more comfortable to close the windows and turn on the cooler, but they couldn't leave the motor running the way they could have done in the city.

"We should've bought some mosquito repellent," said Kinoshita, exasperated.

"You're asking too much," said Takemura. "Just be glad we've got the car, at least." He was about to add something about how it was when he was young, but he stopped himself. He was only thirty-three. It must have been the title of Inspector that was making him feel old. "That'll never do," he admonished himself aloud inadvertently.

"Okay, okay, I can take it," said Kinoshita, thinking Takemura was talking to him. His feelings were apparently hurt again.

Strange, thought Takemura, they weren't getting along

too well tonight. He hoped it wasn't a sign that something bad was going to happen.

The time passed quickly. Kinoshita had fallen asleep with his chin on his arm resting on the window. Takemura was annoyed, but thought it a shame to wake him, so concentrated instead on not falling asleep himself.

It was after ten, and still the Ishiharas had not appeared. Four cars had come by, but all of them had passed without stopping. Three of them had turned into the Fukumoto Machinery Company's villa. About now, thought Takemura, that cheerful Junko Murata would be all wound up entertaining guests. Come to think of it, it was she who had said that the poisoned body left that way on Poison Plain had to be the curse of the Demoness. If so, they were in for considerable trouble with their investigation. Such were the trivial thoughts passing one after another through Takemura's head.

"Inspector, wake up!" The voice of Kinoshita broke into them.

"Idiot! I wasn't sleeping!"

"But, your eyes were closed."

"I was only thinking. You're the one who was sleeping!"

"I was not!"

"Never mind. Has something happened?"

"No."

"Then what did you have to call me so loud for? What time is it?"

"Almost eleven."

"That's funny." Takemura looked out through the darkness, but there were still no lights on in the Ishihara villa. Even if they had stopped for supper somewhere along the way, they should have been here by now. He called the other car, but Yoshii and his partner had seen nothing either. Takemura became more and more uneasy by the minute.

"Do you think they could have suspected we were waiting?" asked Kinoshita.

"I shouldn't think so," said Takemura. "But they may have flown the coop anyway."

"Which would make Ishihara our man, then?"

"I guess so."

Shortly thereafter, Takemura called off the stakeout. The singing that had been coming from somewhere until a short while earlier was no longer to be heard, and the only sound now audible on the plateau was the buzz of mosquitos. The silence was broken by the noise of Kinoshita starting the engine.

"Hey, keep that down, will you?" snapped Takemura.

"How am I supposed to do that?" replied Kinoshita.

Superior and subordinate fell into an ill-humored, stony silence.

2 Takemura awoke with a start. He had been dreaming, but he couldn't remember about what. He knew from experience that when he awoke like that, he could hardly ever get back to sleep.

The dawn light was peeking through the window shutters. Beside him, Yoko was breathing regularly in her sleep, smiling slightly, as if having a good dream. Takemura remembered Kinoshita's face as he confessed to a crush on her. Well damned if Kinoshita could have her! He wanted her himself! Leaning over, he slipped a hand beneath her blanket. Just then, the telephone rang.

Yoko opened her eyes and looked at him blankly. What

could he do but take hold of her arm with the hand he had slipped under her blanket, shake it and say, "Hey, the phone's ringing!"

"I'll get it," she said, jumping up on a relex and rushing into the living room, where, finally awake, she turned and gave him a dirty look that said, "If you were awake, why didn't you get it?" before picking up the receiver.

"It's Inspector Katahira, from headquarters," she called.

Takemura looked at the clock. It wasn't even six! That meant bad news.

He got up and went to take the phone. "Takemura speaking."

"Good morning. This is Katahira. I've just gotten this report, and I'm afraid I don't have any details yet, but it seems that a car has been discovered with the body of a man and a woman in it at a place called West Arrow in Togakushi."

"What? Who are they?" asked Takemura, fearing he already knew.

"We haven't identified them yet, but the car had Nagoya plates, so I'm afraid this may have something to do with the Ishiharas you're looking for, Inspector, which is why I'm letting you know right away."

"Thanks. I'll be there shortly."

"Uh, one more thing, and this bothers me. There was an arrow stuck in each body."

"An arrow? Wait a minute! Didn't you say the place was called West Arrow or something?"

"Yes. That's what bothers me."

Takemura went cold.

* * *

The village of West Arrow was located just across the

Susobana River to the north of National Highway 406 on its way to Kinasa, on the same road that went through Imai to Poison Plain.

Getting out of the car, Takemura immediately felt something odd about the scene, and not only because of the police swarming all around. On either side of the narrow blacktop farm road was a small hillock. Barely twenty meters high, they were hardly worthy of the name, but in the midst of the surrounding bright pastoral scenery, they looked strangely dark. The one to the west of the road was covered with cedar, through which some sort of shrine was visible. The one to the east was somewhat smaller, with the shape of a triangular pyramid that made it look almost man-made. The trees on it were not very thick, and Takemura could see through them to the top, where a five-story pagoda stood. Of the two hillocks, this one was the more gloomy and mysterious.

The car with the bodies was parked off the road, heading to the west hillock, at the bottom of a crumbling stone staircase which led steeply up into the trees.

"That shrine up there seems to have two names," said Tsuneda, the chief of detectives at Nagano Central. "They call it either Arrowhead Shrine or Arrowstand Shrine." Tsuneda had gotten there a little ahead of Takemura and had already picked up some information. He looked quite unhappy about one brutal murder occurring right after another.

"Arrowstand, you say?" Takemura's foreboding became even stronger. First West Arrow, and now Arrowstand.

"Pretty nasty coincidence, isn't it?" said Tsuneda, the names evidently bothering him too.

"Then are these the Ishiharas?" asked Takemura.

"I think they must be. We couldn't find a driver's license, so I can't say for sure, but the plates are registered to

Ishihara. We've contacted Nagoya, and we should have someone here who can make a positive identification first thing this afternoon."

Looking into the car through a small gap left by CID, Takemura saw that the bodies had apparently just been thrown into the back seat, where they had sprawled partly on the floor. They were dressed, but out of each of their backs protruded a white-feathered arrow.

"I was told those are ceremonial arrows used at the Togakushi Shrines," said Tsuneda. "For some kind of exorcism, I guess. Somebody must have sharpened the tips and stuck them into the bodies. No sign of bleeding though, so it must have been done some time after they died."

"What was the cause of death?"

"Same as Takeda, the doctor says."

"Poisoning? Looks like the same murderer, then, doesn't it?"

"Looks like it."

"Who found the bodies?"

"An old woman. I don't know how much we can get from her, but I suppose you'd better talk to her anyway."

The old woman, nearly seventy-eight, was named Iku Katoh. She was in the habit of getting up every morning before the other members of her household and going out to sweep the area in front of the shrine as a daily chore. She had gotten up around five this morning as usual, just as the dawn was breaking, and gone out with her broom to the worshippers' entrance of the shrine, practically next door to her house. This time, however, she had found the car enshrined there, right at the bottom of the stone staircase. Annoyed because it was in her way, she had taken a peek inside and seen the bodies.

She tried her best to tell Takemura all about it, but her

language was so thick with dialect that she was quite difficult to understand, and it took him some time even to get as much as he did from her.

The car must have been parked there during the night. Several people questioned said they had heard it. The consensus seemed to be that it was around two in the morning. Although Iku Katoh's bedroom was closest to the spot, she said she had been sleeping and hadn't heard anything. Even had she been awake, she was hard of hearing and most likely wouldn't have heard it anyway.

Takemura took great pains to hear everything she had to say. After he finished the more relevant questioning, he asked her about the strange triangular hillock on the east side of the road.

"Hill? 'Tain't no hill. 'Tis a mound. Demon's Mound, they calls it hereabouts."

"Demon's Mound?"

"Ay, that's what they calls it. But that ain't what it is. Nope. It oughta be called Miss Maple's Mound. That there's Miss Maple's grave, it is."

"Miss Maple? You mean the Demoness Maple?" Takemura was surprised to run into the Demoness Legend again, but more interested in the fact that the old woman had attached a polite "Miss" to Maple's name. From further inquiries, he learned that this place, West Arrow, had played an especially important part in the Demoness Legend, the story being that before his final attack, Taira no Koremochi had, after praying to the gods for assistance, shot an arrow from the top of Mount Shimoso on the south side of the Susobana River, trying to determine the best route to follow in attacking Mount Arakura, where Maple's band had entrenched itself. He aimed his arrow toward the sky, and it landed on a hillock on the opposite side of the Susobana, with its point stuck in a rock. At the place where it landed, a shrine was built to Arrowhead Hachiman, the god of war, and on Mount Shimoso, a shrine was built to Arrowshot Hachiman. The names still exist, giving some credence to the legend.

The cause of death was determined to be poison, of the same kind that had killed Takeda. The arrows had been stuck into the bodies at least two hours after death. They had been stuck into people already dead for hours! Feeling the bile come up into his mouth, Takemura knew he was dealing with something abnormal. The act of murder would itself have to be called abnormal, but at least in impulsive cases of robbery-murder or grudge-murder, when the victim is dead, the job is finished. With the death, the murderer is either satisfied, or else comes to his senses, but in either case, he does not try to further desecrate the corpse. He may of course try to cover the traces of his crime by setting a fire or otherwise disposing of the body, but such actions testify to his normality rather than abnormality.

For the bodies to have been thus violated, and that some time after the murders, would mean not only that the motive had been a grudge, but an extraordinarily deep one, and it would mean most of all that the murderer was suffering from some extreme psychosis.

In addition, the bodies had been left at this place called Arrowstand with arrows standing in them. That made it even more obvious than it had been with the poisoned body left on Poison Plain that the murderer had some special intention. It also left no doubt that the two cases were related.

* * *

In the afternoon, a number of people connected with the Ishiharas arrived from Nagoya: their elderly housekeeper,

Shizu Kasai; their married only daughter, Hisako, and her husband Koichi Hirai; a director of Ishihara's Chubu Advertising Agency named Iwata; and the agency's general affairs manager, a man named Sueyasu. They arrived in separate parties. The first to arrive, alone, was Shizu Kasai. Next came Mr. and Mrs. Hirai, and finally the two men from the company. It was understandable enough that the men from the company should have come separately, but less so that Shizu Kasai should have come by herself, especially since Mr. and Mrs. Hirai had come by car and could easily have saved her money and trouble by giving her a lift.

Even stranger was the fact that when Shizu and Hisako came face to face, they both turned away without so much as a word of greeting. Such behavior at a time like this could only mean some extreme discord between them.

When Shizu Kasai was shown the bodies, and Takemura asked if there was any mistake, she answered tearfully that there was not.

Hisako Hirai, however, replied, "Yes, this is my father, but that woman is not my mother."

"What do you mean?" asked Takemura, surprised, with a look at Hisako's husband. Koichi, however, looked at the floor and said nothing, apparently afraid of his wife. Shizu was called in once more, and she confirmed that the woman was indeed Mrs. Ishihara.

In the midst of the confusion, Iwata and Sueyasu arrived, and both confirmed that the bodies were indeed those of their boss and his wife. They told Takemura that Hisako was unwilling to recognize Ishihara's wife, Kayo, as her mother. Kayo was Ryuji Ishihara's second wife, in other words, Hisako's stepmother, but there had been very bad feeling between the two women.

Considering their relative ages—Ishihara was fifty-nine,

Kayo thirty-eight, and Hisako thirty-three—the enmity that Hisako bore toward her stepmother was not incomprehensible. She would not likely have enjoyed calling someone only five years older than herself "mother," and it was also easy to imagine that she might be afraid Kayo would wheedle the family fortune out of her father.

Shizu Kasai, who was nearly seventy, was a maid whom Kayo had brought with her when she married Ishihara. Although the fortunes of Kayo's own family had declined since the end of the war, it had once been a distinguished family of the Suwa region of Nagano Prefecture. Shizu was reduced to weeping and wailing about where the gods could have been to let such a thing happen to her mistress, but this did not deter Hisako from coldheartedly regarding the miserable old woman as an enemy.

"This ends your connection with our family, so you can just take that woman's bones and go!" railed Hisako at Shizu, right in the middle of the police station.

Even Hisako's husband was unable to let that pass. He admonished his wife that enough was enough, but she was on the verge of total, uncontrollable hysteria. There was nothing for Takemura to do but forget the couple and question instead the two men from Ishihara's company, who were no relation to the family.

The Chubu Advertising Agency was based in Nagoya and did business mainly with clients in that area. Established in 1960, it was a leading local agency, with thirty-odd employees. Both Iwata and Sueyasu insisted they could think of no possible reason whatsoever for the murders, and since these two had been Ishihara's right-hand men, if they had no idea, it was hardly conceivable that any other employee would. The questioning did, however, turn up a connection between Ishihara and Kisuke Takeda.

"Why yes," said Iwata, "as a matter of fact, Mr. Takeda was one of our stockholders. We also did some business through his firm. I've heard that Mr. Takeda and Mr. Ishihara were old friends."

"I suppose you knew that Mr. Ishihara owned a villa in Togakushi?" said Takemura.

"Yes, of course."

"Well actually, we have reason to believe that Kisuke Takeda paid a visit there the night he was killed. Can you tell me whether Mr. Ishihara was at his villa that night?"

"The night Mr. Takeda was killed? That was the 7th, right?"

"No. The 7th is when his body was found. He was killed sometime during the night of Saturday the 3rd."

"Oh. Well, if it was the 3rd, I can tell you for sure that the boss was not at his villa. On Sunday the 4th, we had to entertain clients at a golf tournament in Takarazuka, so all the important employees of our company stayed overnight there the night before, including the boss, of course. I saw him with my own eyes playing mahjong with guests until late that night." Iwata looked at Sueyasu for confirmation, and Sueyasu confirmed.

"Well then, what about Mrs. Ishihara, or Mr. Ishihara's daughter and her husband? Could any of them have been there?"

"Well, er, yes. That's a possibility, I suppose." The two men exchanged uneasy glances. Takemura had apparently touched on some sensitive spot.

"Did anyone in the Ishihara family, including Mr. Ishihara himself, have any reason for hating Mr. Takeda?" asked Takemura.

Both men clammed up.

"Now look, I'll see to it that no trouble comes to either of you for any of this. This isn't just idle gossip I'm asking you for. All right, I'll make it easier for you. I'll tick them off one by one." Takemura bent one finger. "First, what about Mr. Ishihara?"

They shook their heads grudgingly, like naughty children.

"Then what about his wife, Kayo?"

They shook their heads again.

"Hisako?"

They nodded at each other, in agreement that there was no help for it. Iwata spoke. "It is possible that she might have disliked Mr. Takeda to some extent. It was he who got her father and Kayo together."

"Oh really? Okay, then what about Hisako's husband, Koichi Hirai?"

"No, I think he rather sympathized with Kayo. He thought his wife was much too hard on her. Hisako hated Kayo so much that it even bothered us."

"So he would have had no reason for any bad feelings toward Mr. Takeda?"

"I don't think he even knew very much about Mr. Takeda at all."

"Well, thank you very much. I guess that's about it for now."

Takemura dropped his questioning of the two men for the time being. He had neglected to press them hard enough, however, about one person's relationship with Takeda, and this oversight was to delay his solution of the case.

Afterwards, he spoke individually with Shizu Kasai and Koichi Hirai again.

Shizu Kasai was so distracted as to be almost incapable of answering his questions. She seemed almost physically ill. He always found it most difficult to question such a person.

"Now, I'm going to make my questions easy, and I want you to take your time answering them," he said. "On Saturday, July 3rd—oh yes, that was the day Mr. Ishihara stayed overnight in Takarazuka for a golf tournament—on that day, did Mrs. Ishihara—your mistress, Kayo—go to the villa in Togakushi?"

"No, she didn't," answered Shizu, without changing her expression or looking at Takemura.

"Then she was in Nagoya all the time, at home?"

"Yes, she was."

"What was she doing?"

"I don't know."

"But, you must know something about what she was doing. For instance, was she watching television, or . . ."

"Yes, that's it. She was watching television."

Takemura could see he would get nowhere with her. He gave up and called in Hirai.

Koichi Hirai, as an employee of one of Ishihara's client companies, had been in Takarazuka at the golf tournament.

"Was your wife with you?" asked Takemura.

"No, she wasn't," answered Hirai.

"Then did she stay home to take care of the house?"

"Yes, you could say that."

"Do you know if she was home all the time?"

"What do you mean?"

"I mean, Mr. Ishihara owned a villa in Togakushi, didn't he? Do you think she might have gone there by herself?"

"Are you kidding?" laughed Hirai. "My wife doesn't have the courage to go to a lonesome place like that by herself. She may act fierce, but when it comes right down to it, she's still a woman."

Hirai's timid manner of shortly before had undergone a

complete change. He was now spirited with a vengeance. Takemura couldn't tell whether it was mere bravado in the absence of his wife, or whether he had simply remained silent earlier out of respect for her feelings.

"Besides," added Hirai, "she had the boy to take care of. We have a son going on four."

"Oh, then she wouldn't have been all by herself, right?"

"Yes, that's right. But may I ask what you're getting at?"

"Nothing in particular. By the way, does your wife drive?"

"Oh yes. As a matter of fact, she drove us here today."

"What about Kayo?"

"You mean, did she drive? Yes, of course. But my father-in-law didn't."

"Okay. I've got one more question. Where were you and your wife last night?"

"Where were we? What do you mean by that? Do you suspect us?"

"No, I don't. This is merely for reference."

"Good. I was out playing mahjong with friends. I must have gotten home around 11:30. My wife was at home all evening. Of course, if you asked me, I wouldn't be able to prove that, but then, there's no end to the things one can't prove. Besides, Inspector," said Hirai, with an expression of undisguised displeasure, "and this is a private matter that I'd rather not talk about, except that you'd probably get it out of me anyway—as far as that villa goes, the fact is that my wife and I have never once been there. My mother-in-law, Kayo, had practically appropriated the place for herself. I don't imagine even my father-in-law had ever been there."

"What? Not even Mr. Ishihara?"

"That's right. He didn't like Togakushi, and he had

never wanted that villa. Anyway, that should tell you you'd be wasting your time suspecting us." Hirai looked like he would resent any further questions.

✳ ✳ ✳

That day at noon, the sign "Togakushi Serial-Murder Investigation Headquarters" was put up at Nagano Central. This recognition of the murders as connected—by authorities who had been reluctant even to declare the death of Kisuke Takeda a case of murder at all—was owing to the argument of Inspector Takemura.

"We've got to be on guard against another murder," said Takemura, pressing his superior, Miyazaki.

"You're not just trying to frighten me, are you?" said Miyazaki.

"Hardly. I had a hunch after the first one that there would be more, and after this, I'm absolutely sure. Any way you look at it, our murderer is sending somebody a warning."

"A warning?"

"Well look. First he leaves a poisoned body on Poison Plain, then he sticks arrows in a couple of bodies at Arrowstand. Anyone who would run risks like that has got to be abnormal, of course, but he must also have some very strong motive. We can only assume that he wants somebody else to know that he intends to kill him. In killing Takeda, he must have been sending a message to let someone know why, and he did the same thing with the Ishiharas at Arrowstand. We've got to believe he was sending a message to his next victim. So it will hardly be surprising if there is one."

"So you really think we've got to take these weird killings as notice that another is in the making?"

"That's exactly what I think. If we don't treat these two

cases as connected, we don't stand much chance of solving either, or even of preventing another murder."

"Then you mean that Takeda and the Ishiharas must have had something in common that gave the murderer a motive for killing all three of them?"

"Yes, that's what I mean."

Takemura was sure of that much, but he had not the slightest idea what that common factor might be. The only relations turned up so far between the two men seemed perfectly businesslike: Takeda had supplied capital for the establishment of Ishihara's company, and Ishihara had gotten some of his clients through Takeda's enterprises and connections. That had been twenty-odd years ago. It could be assumed that the two men had known each other since some time before that, but Takemura could find nobody who went back that far with them. Even Ishihara's daughter Hisako, Takemura learned, had only become aware of Takeda's existence two years ago, when her father had married Kayo through Takeda's introduction. And even that could have arisen out of everyday business dealings— and those not especially secret.

It did not seem likely either that Takeda and Ishihara could have had a common business enemy. According to both Iwata and Sueyasu, any favors that Takeda ever did for Ishihara's advertising agency were insignificant, and aside from Takeda's assistance in the establishment of the company itself, they had never cooperated in any joint venture. In other words, there had never been any dealings between them of a sort that could have earned them a common enemy.

That was confirmed by Takeda's secretary, Izawa, who said that since he had joined the firm, there had been no contacts between Takeda and either Ishihara's agency or Ishihara himself that had not been straightforward business. Even the marriage arrangements for Ishihara and Kayo had been entrusted to Izawa and completed without Takeda's attention.

"All Mr. Takeda did was ask me if I could handle it. Apparently he hadn't even considered using an intermediary," said Izawa. "If I had told him I didn't have time, I think that would have been the end of it. I had the feeling that neither he nor Mr. Ishihara wanted to have too much to do with each other."

His boss dead, Izawa was speaking frankly, and it all seemed perfectly credible. But he was painting a picture of quite a distant connection between Takeda and Ishihara, so it seemed at this point that there was nothing whatsoever to suggest any possible reason why the same person would want both men dead.

Having declared the two cases related, and even that another murder could be expected, Takemura was really out on a limb, but he still trusted his intuition. The cases were similar in that both presented a lot of riddles, at least. For instance, the police had been able to pick up nothing at all about the Ishiharas' whereabouts or actions between the time they left Nagoya and the time their bodies were found at Arrowstand in Togakushi, just as detectives had not managed to trace Takeda's whereabouts and doings between the Koshimizu Plateau Hotel and Poison Plain. The deaths of the Ishiharas were estimated to have occurred sometime between 8 P.M. and 11 P.M. the night before their bodies were discovered, so they must have been poisoned while Takemura and his men were fighting off mosquitos at their stakeout of the Ishihara villa. Where could the Ishiharas have gone after they left Nagoya? Had they been lying when they told Shizu they were going to their villa in Togakushi?

3 Yuko Noya had shaken Tomohiro Tachibana to the core. He couldn't imagine how she could have known about his past. That the heads of the Tachibana family had in the old days held the title of viscount could not have been known to anyone outside an extremely limited number of people. He himself had never told anyone. The fact was that he hated the very word "viscount," because even the mention of it was sufficient to bring back to him the memory of the tragedy with Taki in Togakushi.

Yuko's satanic whisper about his being the son of a viscount still rang in his ears. He could see her classic oval face and her large eyes. And then the face would fade as in a movie scene, changing to the face that try as he might he could never forget, Taki's face. Taki had been just Yuko's age when he lost her—his life's treasure. Was he simply trying to find her again in Yuko? No, he thought, there was more to it than that.

Yuko, with her eyes glittering as she talked, had looked to Tachibana just like Taki used to look when she was in a trance, speaking of the wonders of heaven and earth as she foretold the future. And it gave him an even more eerie feeling that Yuko should have been telling the Demoness Legend of Togakushi.

He telephoned the office of the dean of students. The college was on vacation, but the dean, a good friend of his, was still at work. "I'm awfully sorry to trouble you," apologized Tachibana, "but I wonder if you could get me the home address of a girl named Yuko Noya, who just entered this year. She requested an early report, and I gave it to her. Now I find there's a correction I need to make, but she's apparently already gone home for the holidays, and I'm afraid I can't get in touch with her." He was going to feel guilty about this, thought Tachibana, the lecherous old man.

"Sure," said the dean lightly.

It seemed an absurdly long time—someone must be having a lot of trouble finding the information—before the dean called him back to tell him that Yuko was from Yashiro, Koshoku City, Nagano Prefecture.

Having unconsciously expected to hear that she was from Togakushi, he felt a pang of disappointment. "Yashiro, you say? Pretty far away, isn't she? Oh well, no help for it, I guess. Let's see, I believe her Tokyo address was in Takehaya, wasn't it?"

"No, it's in Sengoku, Bunkyo Ward."

"It is? I must have written it down wrong, then. No wonder I couldn't get in touch with her. Would you mind letting me have that address?" Now he was adding fraud to his lechery, thought Tachibana with a wry smile.

The unsuspecting dean immediately gave him the address and even the telephone number. Tachibana thanked him, hung up, and dialed her number right away.

"Hello, this is Yuko Noya," she answered.

Not expecting her to answer the phone herself, he was caught off guard. He had guessed from the name of her apartment house that it was the type of place where the manager would answer the phone and summon the tenant the call was for. He had been so sure of that, that for an instant, he was speechless.

Finally he managed to say, "Oh, uh, Miss Noya? Tachibana here."

"Oh! Professor? What a surprise! Thank you so much for the other day, and I'm very sorry I said so many rude things. I've been thinking of paying you a visit to apologize," she said without a pause, ending breathlessly.

"Oh no, you don't have to worry about that. But there is something I would like to ask you."

"Yes, I know. About my saying your father was a viscount, isn't it? I'm so sorry about that. It came out sounding like I was making fun of you. That's really been bothering me. But I'm so happy to be able to talk to you about it."

"But I don't understand how you could have known a thing like that."

"That's a very long story. If I won't be causing you too much trouble, could I come visit you now and tell you all about it?"

"You mean right now? Today?"

"Yes, I'm afraid I'm leaving for home tomorrow."

He told her to come, then just sat there at the phone in blank amazement at the whole new situation that faced him. She had said she could be there in thirty minutes. He looked at his watch. It was nearly eleven-thirty. Fusae Nakayama was there cleaning house and preparing to make lunch. The usually calm Tachibana fidgeted around the room and kept going to check the already perfectly tidy entryway.

Finally the doorbell rang, and he heard Fusae's footsteps as she went from the kitchen to answer it. There was the sound of the door, and the voice of a female visitor saying a few words. After a pause, Fusae looked into the room he was in without knocking. "You have a visitor," she whispered. "A girl who says her name is Noya or something." Fusae looked sulky. It dawned on him that this was probably the first time he had had a female visitor since she had started coming to do his housekeeping.

"Oh, must be one of my students. I wonder what

she wants," said Tachibana apologetically, feigning ignorance. Then he brushed past Fusae and hurried to the entryway.

"I'm sorry to drop in on you so suddenly," said Yuko, sizing up the situation with a look at Tachibana's face and greeting him as though the telephone call had never taken place.

She was neatly dressed in a white linen blouse and a light wool maroon skirt, but her glossy black hair was dancing around her fair-complexioned face as she looked straight at him with a slightly mischievous smile. With a dizzying shock, the image yanked him back forty years. She looked just like Taki, he thought, but quickly forced the thought out of his mind.

"Uh, am I intruding on something?" said Yuko uneasily.

"Hmh? Oh, no, no, not at all," said Tachibana, dazzled by her eyes, barely managing a smile. "Well, come on in," he said.

He turned and went into the parlor without looking back at her. To Fusae, who was watching the proceedings from inside the study door, he said, "Could you bring us some tea?" He could not calm himself, and even before Yuko was seated, he had lit a cigarette and was puffing out clouds of smoke.

Yuko entered nervously, sat down on the edge of the sofa, small and quiet, and glanced curiously around the room. Tachibana watched her, considering the shock he had just received. He must have considered it for much longer than he thought.

"Professor, the ashes!" said Yuko suddenly.

Bewildered, he did not react fast enough. All of the long ash fell into his lap. His exclamation did not become his position, as he pounded his lap on a reflex, sending a powder of disintegrating ash flying everywhere. As he tried to wave it away from his face, Yuko sat primly, handkerchief pressed to her lips, trying not to giggle.

With a quick knock, Fusae re-entered. Yuko jumped up from the sofa, stepped a little away from it, and made a respectful bow. "Oh, you must be Mrs. Tachibana! I'm afraid I was rude when I came in. My name is Yuko Noya."

Fusae's sulky look dissolved immediately into a toothy smile. "Me? Oh dear me, no! I'm not Mrs. Tachibana!" she said, with an unusually ladylike air. The mistake had put her in a very good mood.

"This lady is a neighbor of mine, Fusae Nakayama," said Tachibana. "She has been kind enough to take care of me."

"Oh, I'm sorry! I've done it again! But you look so well together," said Yuko.

"I'm honored that you should say so," said Fusae, giggling as she put the tea on the table.

Tachibana was not terribly happy about the error, but he was pleased enough for Yuko that she had managed to charm the somewhat bothersome Fusae.

After Fusae went out, Tachibana, teacup in hand, said softly, "My wife died this spring."

"Yes, I know."

"You do?" Tachibana almost spilled his tea. "What do you mean?"

"I checked into a few things about you, Professor."

"But you just . . ."

"That was because she didn't look very pleased to see me," Yuko said with a shrug, briefly showing her pink tongue.

"You mean you did that just to make her pleased with you?" said Tachibana in amazement, wondering about her. He didn't know whether to take the act as clever or disagreeable, but whichever it was, there was no denying that it had worked.

"That's not a very nice habit you have, playing with people like that," he said, but he couldn't help smiling.

"Are you talking about my saying that you were the son of a viscount, too?"

"No, that was different."

Looking straight at Tachibana, her lips pursed, she said, "I wanted so very much to meet you, Professor, that I've been doing everything I could to get you to notice me. That's why I took the seat next to yours when the class went to see Noh."

"Well, I must say I'm greatly honored, but why in the world would you want to meet an old fogey like me?"

"Because I've known about you ever since I was a little girl. That's why I chose the university you were teaching at."

"Really? You amaze me even more. But how did you know about me?"

"I saw your name in a book in my house."

"You did? My name? Hm, let's see. If it was when you were a little girl, that must have been maybe ten years ago. About the time I published *A New Interpretation of Past and Present Tales*, I think."

"No, I don't mean that kind of book. It was a concise dictionary."

"A what?"

"An English dictionary. And the name Tomohiro Tachibana had been written in it with a pen."

Tachibana sat speechless.

"I think I was only in the second or third grade in elementary school, but every time I saw your name, I wondered who you were. Finally I asked my mother, and she told me you were the son of a viscount. I didn't really know what a viscount was, but my mother told me that a viscount was an even greater man than the great baron who she said grew the potatoes that were called 'baron' potatoes. So I figured you must be a very great man. Then when I entered junior high school and my Japanese teacher said we were going to use a supplementary reader written by Professor Tachibana, I was really surprised. Then . . ."

"Hold on a minute," said Tachibana, checking Yuko's glib tongue. "How did that concise dictionary happen to be in your house?"

"I don't know. Actually, only a little while after I asked my mother about it, it just disappeared, and a new one appeared in its place on the bookshelf. It was a pretty old dictionary, so I figured maybe that was why my mother had bought a new one to replace it, but when I asked her, she said grandpa had told her to do it. I was happy about the new dictionary, of course, but I missed the old one, too. When I asked what had happened to it, though, nobody would tell me, and I remember feeling kind of lonely for it."

Tachibana felt a pain in his chest, as of something clutching at his heart. He had a dim memory of a concise dictionary he had given away to someone, but he wondered how it had gotten to Yuko's house. Of course, that had been a period when nobody had any property at all, let alone books, so the dictionary could have made the rounds of secondhand bookstores, finally coming into the hands of Yuko's mother, or her grandfather when he was younger. But if that had been so, how would Yuko's mother have known about the Tachibana family being viscounts? Unless, perhaps, he had pretentiously written "viscount" beside his name in the dictionary. Having been brought up among people who addressed him obsequiously as "young master" and such, he would have been capable of such folly.

"Your home is in Yashiro, isn't it?" he asked.

"Yes, that's right. But how did you know, Professor?"

"Hmh? Oh, er, I checked on a few things about you, too."

"Did you really? Oh, that makes me so happy!"

"By the way, how long has your family been living there?"

"Since my great-grandfather's time."

"And where is your mother from?"

"Oh, it was my father who was adopted into the family to marry my mother."

"I see." Tachibana was disappointed. "You were so familiar with the Togakushi legend that I had assumed you were from Togakushi."

"My mother used to tell me stories about the Demoness, then when I entered high school, I began doing a little research of my own. My mother said that grandfather and great-grandmother used to tell her the stories. I heard that my grandfather's parents once lived in Togakushi for a while."

"Oh, where?"

"A place called Hoko Shrine."

"Hoko Shrine?" Tachibana slumped deep into the arm-chair with a suffocating feeling. Could it be? Was it really possible? "Was your great-grandfather by any chance named Keijiro?"

"Yes, he was. Keijiro. Did you know him?"

"Mhm." His chest tight, Tachibana remembered the old couple telling him of a son in the army. "So that's it. But I didn't know the family name, Noya. So, it was Keijiro's . . ."

Again he looked hard at Yuko. Innocently, she returned his gaze. There was a resemblance, he thought, tense again. Not to Keijiro or his wife, of course. No, she looked like Taki, though he couldn't put his finger on just where the resemblance lay.

"Your grandfather's wife," said Tachibana, "what was her name?"

"I don't know."

"You don't know?"

"No. Neither my grandfather nor my parents ever seemed to want to talk about her. They would only say that she was dead. They never told me her name or where she came from."

"Hmm, that's strange, isn't it?" said Tachibana, guessing that Yuko's grandmother must have been Taki. It would hardly have been surprising if Keijiro's son had married Taki when he came back from the war. That would mean that Yuko's mother was their daughter. The idea of transmigration of souls was not inconceivable to him. What if Taki's soul had found its way into Yuko's body, and fate had brought her before him again?

Unable to get enough of looking at her, he suddenly realized that her white blouse and maroon skirt reminded him of a shrine maiden's dancing costume. That must have been what had given him such a shock when he first saw her in the entryway.

"Do you like to wear clothes like that?" he asked her.

"Yes, I do. Actually, I'd rather wear a skirt that was a little brighter red, but my friend says it would look too gaudy."

Taki had always looked good in her shrine maiden's costume and always been eager to put it on. When she reached puberty and had to stop dancing at the shrine, she had cried constantly. She had lived to put on that costume and dance. She once told Tachibana that while she was living with his family, she would often put it on in the privacy of her room. And while he was living with her family, she had worn it nearly all the time.

While wearing it, however, she had sometimes been seized by spells of seemingly supernatural possession. In the middle of some ordinary act, she would suddenly fall silent and still, her eyes fixed on a particular spot. Then she would begin to dance, the sleeves of her Shinto robe fluttering as she chanted something that sounded like a prophecy. After a short time she would come to herself again with a shy smile and go back to whatever she had just been doing.

The first time Tachibana had seen such a spell, he thought she was just having some fun with him, but time and again, her prophecies had seemed to come true—at least in so far as their vague language could be construed as a prediction of some occurrence. For instance, once she chanted something about the "trees flowing," and the next day torrential rains caused a landslide that resulted in several deaths. To be sure, the trees had flowed, but disparaging comments were heard to the effect that she should have chanted about the "mountain collapsing."

Nevertheless, the majority of the villagers believed in her prophecies, and even Tachibana had not taken her spells as evidence of insanity. He thought of them vaguely as some kind of possession. Student of literature that he was, he had not felt competent to comment scientifically on the existence of foreknowledge, but he believed at least that she was gifted with some extraordinary powers.

Taki's parents had been very worried about what would become of her, their only daughter, and what worried them most seemed to be just those extraordinary powers. Whenever she had one of her spells, they would voice their worries to the "young master" of the Tachibana family, who must have been their one great hope. At such times, he would assure them that they need not worry, because he was going to see to Taki's happiness. He was trying to tell them that he intended to marry her. He was never sure whether they had understood that or not, but his words had seemed to reassure them.

Tachibana had deeply loved Taki. From the first time he saw her in his first year of junior high school, he had felt a conviction that she was his destiny, and the longer he knew her, the stronger that conviction had become. Taki had seemed even more sure of that destiny than he. She had felt perfectly secure as long as he was right there, but when he was not, she would sometimes come looking for him with great fear in her eyes, and finding him, would cling to his arm so hard that it hurt.

Looking back, Tachibana suspected she must have had a premonition of tragedy, both their own personal tragedy and their country's plunge toward destruction in the war, for her spells ceased to be accompanied by joyous dancing and became expressions of dark fear. Time and again he saw her wearing a look of despair. Finally, the spells ceased altogether, leaving him with no key to what she saw. He had not grasped the meaning of her fears until they were realized. Even when her parents died, she had not grieved so much as he might have expected. Not until later had he realized this was not from any lack of feeling, but rather because she had seen an even greater tragedy looming beyond.

"Professor?" Yuko's voice, slightly tinged with reproach, brought him back to the present. He knew he had not been dozing, but he did have a sensation that he had forgotten where he was, if only for a short time. He had not even noticed that she had stood up.

"Uh, I guess I'd better be going," she said, bowing sadly.

"No, please don't go yet," said Tachibana hastily. "I'd like to hear more. Won't you please stay awhile?"

"I don't mind, but you . . ."

"No, no, I was just thinking about something. Anyway, please, sit down."

Reassured, she sat down again. At the moment, she looked like any other naive freshman, but remembering how she had just handled Fusae Nakayama, Tachibana knew he had better be careful.

"May I ask your mother's name?" he said.

"It's Katsura. The name was taken from the first character of my great-grandfather's name."

"Katsura? That's a nice name." But there was nothing in it to connect it with Taki. "What does your father do?"

"He runs a laundry and dry-cleaning chain."

This was getting really far away from what he had expected. "What do you do during your summer vacations?"

"I go back to the country and work. In summer there's piles of laundry from the villas and tourist homes and so on, and the company is always shorthanded. I get my own route this summer. I got my driver's license during the spring vacation just so I could do it. They promised me I could have Togakushi, the Iizuna Plateau, and Kinasa. That's where the study circle is."

"What study circle?"

"The one that studies the folk tales and legends of Togakushi. I've been a member since high school."

"Oh, I see. You must be anxious to get back there, then."

"Oh yes, I'm really looking forward to it. Are you going anywhere for the summer, Professor?"

"No, I guess I'm just going to laze around my study all summer."

"Then why don't you come visit Togakushi? I'll show you around in my car."

"Togakushi?"

"It's a great place, really."

"Oh, yes, I imagine it is. . . . Togakushi . . ." Something made him stop before telling her that he had just been there.

The Curse of the Demoness

 The investigation was stuck. The police had not been able to find a shred of information suggesting a common motive for the two cases involving three murder victims.

Section Two was continuing its search for a political or financial motive, on the assumption that the murders could have arisen out of some big conflict of interests with a gigantic organization. Kisuke Takeda had at one time been involved in a battle with a group with powerful capital interests led by an important politician from Niigata, for acquisition of property rights to land along the dry bed of the Shinano River. Takeda had yielded, at least on the surface, but rumor had it that he had come out of the deal quite a bit richer.

"It looks like Section Two is working on a pretty good bet for the motive, don't you think?" said Miyazaki, apt to become fainthearted in such situations. When his own section was stymied, the grass always looked greener to him elsewhere.

"Why don't we just let them work on it?" said Takemura. "If they solve the case, it will take a big load off of us. That would be a godsend."

"Godsend! It would be a disgrace! Don't forget, this business started with the governor himself. The honor of Section One is hanging on it!"

"Yes, I know."

"Then, just this once, why don't you try looking for information along the same lines? You know, cooperation is the whole basis of the police organization."

"You don't need to tell me that, but I'd be wasting my time."

"I don't think so."

"Well I would. I've been trying to tell you that this case has got nothing to do with politics or finance or business deals. It smacks of some deep personal grudge. And anyway, if you want to treat it as political or financial, then I'd appreciate it if you'd take me off of it, because I'm not suited for that sort of thing."

"Now, now, no need to talk like that! I never said you were wrong. I'm just trying to play it safe. But if you feel that strongly about it, I won't force anything on you," said Miyazaki, beating a hasty retreat. As Takemura was leaving, though, he added, "But why don't you just drop in and see what Section Two is doing?"

"Okay," said Takemura, forcing a smile.

Superintendent Fukami, the head of Section Two, was of the so-called elite career class. Two years younger than Takemura, he already outranked him, and would probably receive another promotion after the next test.

Sections One and Two were both in the same department, but their functions differed greatly. Drawing an analogy to a business enterprise, one could say that Section One consisted of blue-collar workers, and Section Two of white. Or, another way to regard their relationship would be as that of sales department to general affairs department.

It is the doings of Section One that make the stuff of TV police dramas, to whose viewers those showy and powerful detectives—the center of action—are the stars of the force. To members of Section Two, though, those same detectives are mere physical laborers, and their own elaborate work is much higher class. They would not, of course, come right out and say it, but they think of their Section One counterparts as mere thief-catchers.

Doing as Miyazaki asked, Takemura dropped in at Section Two. But the inspector in charge of the case was nowhere around, and Fukami himself quickly caught sight of him instead.

"Ye-e-es?" Fukami had a habit of putting a peculiar, provoking, upward intonation on the word.

"Er, I was wondering if there've been any new developments?" said Takemura.

"New developments?" Fukami looked away. "No, I don't think so. But then, that case is not really quite in our line here. We prefer to leave murders to you."

"But I'm afraid we're mere novices when it comes to political and financial circles, so if you won't teach us a few things . . ." Takemura was trying to be diplomatic. The man might prove unexpectedly useful.

Fukami laughed. "Oh, I don't believe you're novices, but if there's something in particular you want to know, go ahead and ask."

Sure enough, the approach had worked. Though Fukami might be steeped in scholarly learning, in affairs of the world, it was he who was the novice.

"Could there be anyone who might have been an enemy of both Takeda and Ishihara?" asked Takemura, putting out a feeler.

"Probably so, since they were connected both in their work and in their financing. There must have been some deals where Ishihara acted as a front for Takeda, which means that if we could just learn how the deals worked, and find out what enemies Ishihara might have made in the course of them, we could make an awfully good guess that the same people must have been enemies of Takeda as well. Of course, whether or not there would have been enmity enough for murder would be another question."

"Do you think there could have been?"

"I can't imagine how, but I wouldn't want to rule out the possibility completely."

"Then you mean at least that no such person or organization has shown up so far in your investigation?"

"Well, er, at this point we, uh . . ."

"To go as far as murder, it would have to be a deal or a negotiation on quite a large scale, or at least something that the participants would have believed to have that kind of potential. Anything like that?"

"Yes, it would have to be that, certainly."

"Then you haven't come up with anything like that, right? In other words, we can assume that these murders did not arise out of any kind of business deal, can't we?"

"What?" Fukami glared at Takemura from behind his glasses.

"If your excellent staff here in Section Two has been working on it all this time and hasn't come up with anything by now, then I think we can be sure that nothing on a big enough scale exists."

"That will do, Takemura!" The young section head took a quick glance around the room. Takemura had not been trying to keep his voice down, but there was nobody right near them, and the rest of the room was abuzz with people on the phone and such, so there was really no danger of being overheard.

"Let's go into the next room," said Fukami, getting up and leading Takemura into the adjoining reception room. "That wasn't very smart. I can't have you saying things that would damage morale."

"I'm terribly sorry. I'm afraid I didn't realize what I was doing."

Fukami snorted, then grinned. "But you have hit the nail right on the head. To tell you the truth, I've got the same feeling. It doesn't look as though these murders are a job for Section Two."

Takemura was astounded—and deeply impressed. It was not in the book of elite officialdom to change direction so easily just because it was a waste of time to continue in the same direction. But here was someone different. He had seen what he ought to see, and he knew how the organization was supposed to work.

"Which is why we're going to get ourselves out of the investigation," continued Fukami. "But until we get through the necessary procedures, I'd appreciate it if you'd keep this conversation off the record."

"Yes, of course. I'm embarrassed to have been so terribly presumptuous."

"Forget it. I see you really are the great detective they say you are. It's a shame your talents are wasted in Section One," said Fukami with a grin. Takemura decided he was going to like this greenhorn superintendent.

* * *

At any rate, Fukami's seal of approval had given Takemura more confidence in his own thinking, and that was an unexpected harvest. Now he could ignore any static and devote himself entirely to the investigation as he thought it should be conducted.

He went through the whole case again in his mind. On the evening of July 3rd, a little after six, Kisuke Takeda had excused himself from the dinner party at the Koshimizu Plateau Hotel and retired to his room. A little before seven, he left the hotel and walked to the villa development, where the last person to see him was Junko Murata.

Questioning of neighbors suggested that his destination must have been the Ishihara villa, and the subsequent search of the villa after the Ishihara murders did indeed turn up his fingerprints and a few strands of his hair, though it could not be established that they had been left on the day of his disappearance. Ishihara family members and connections stated that none of them had been at the villa that night, so if he was there, it was without their leave. Since a light had been seen there from the neighboring Segi villa, the probability was quite high that he had been there—either alone or with others.

Next there was the question of the car heard going out and then coming back in. Since Takeda had walked to the villa, someone else must have gone there by car. Who? And where would the car have been going at ten or eleven at night?

Takemura made the important assumption that Takeda was still alive at that point. If that were the case, it could mean that he had been taken someplace else in the car and killed there. Where? And was his body kept there until deposited on Poison Plain, or moved elsewhere again? If so, how and where?

Having gotten that far, however, Takemura found that what still bothered him most was the weird act of leaving the poisoned body on Poison Plain.

Takemura had gone through Kisuke Takeda's actions on July 3rd many times by now, following his habitual method of trying to put himself in the other man's place. Any human action could be assumed to have some goal and some kind of logic. Even if it seemed contradictory, it had to have some particular drift. If the drift changed or stagnated unnaturally, it could be assumed that the action had encountered some obstacle. Thus, if one could only follow the course of the drift, one could discover the person's aim.

In Takeda's actions on that day, there were several points that seemed unnatural. First, he had excused himself from the dinner party. Second, he had gotten rid of his secretary, Izawa. Third, he had gone off without a car. Obviously, he had been trying to do something without anyone's knowledge. What could it have been that was so secret he wanted to keep it even from his trusted personal secretary, Izawa?

Suddenly, Takemura had it. It took only an instant for the thought to pass from hypothesis to conviction.

"Hey, Kinoshita, we're going out!" he called.

"Right. Where to?" said Kinoshita, who was at the window absentmindedly pulling hairs out of his nose.

"Nagoya. By train," said Takemura on his way out of the door. Kinoshita grabbed his jacket and raced after him.

2 Shizu Kasai received the two detectives apprehensively. Though she was an old woman of inscrutable expression and unfathomable thoughts, they definitely got the prickly feeling that they were not welcome.

"May we come in?" said Takemura.

"Please."

With that brief exchange they were admitted, shown to the parlor and served cold barley tea without another word from Shizu. Either she was very unsociable, or else she was trying to avoid saying anything she didn't have to for fear of making some kind of blunder. Probably both, thought Takemura.

"I imagine you must be lonely, all by yourself in such a big house," said Takemura.

"No." Shizu had apparently taken the comment as a mere attempt at polite conversation.

Takemura smiled ruefully. Detectives are apt to be thought of as brazen, hardheaded people, but he, at least, was rather the reverse. He was considerate almost to a fault of the feelings of the person he was dealing with. When he thought of the position in which this old woman had been placed, he could quite well understand her behavior.

"You're in for some considerable troubles, I would imagine," said Takemura. "It will be hard for you, I'm sure, but you've got to stand up for your rights and secure your own happiness now. If there's any way that we can advise or assist you, please let us know."

Shizu had not expected to hear anything like that. She melted, revealing a lonely old woman trembling with sorrow and anxiety. "Can you really help me?" she asked.

"Of course we can. Just tell us the trouble."

"I'm going to be thrown out of this house."

That was what Takemura had thought. "So Mr. Ishihara's daughter, Hisako, is treating you badly, then?"

"Yes, yes, she is." Once the dam was broken, there was no stopping her. The young Kinoshita looked displeased, but Takemura listened to her patiently. When she had said all she had to say, she mumbled distractedly, "But now that my mistress Kayo, is gone, I can't just stay in this house forever."

"Don't you have any relatives?" asked Takemura.

"No, no blood relatives at all. The only thing I could do is return to my mistress's family home in Suwa, but I'd only be a nuisance to them."

"Nonsense. Besides, the Ishihara family should settle some reasonable amount on you, too, in acknowledgment of your service to Kayo. They can't just treat you as someone who's in the way. If you don't want to return to Kayo's family home, you should be able to live by yourself."

Takemura cheered Shizu up with a promise that he would help her with the procedure and tell her the proper office to go to for whatever she wished to do. She was so happy she almost cried.

After thanking him over and over again, she paused, and then said, "Uh, Inspector, I'm afraid I have an apology to make."

"I know," said Takemura cheerfully. "You lied to me about Kayo, didn't you?"

"How did you know that?" She stared at him in amazement. He smiled back at her. Kinoshita leaned forward, staring at him too, wondering what Shizu had lied about.

"Well, I'm not sure exactly how I knew. I guess after being a detective for so long, a person just sort of knows these things. Some kind of intuition, I suppose."

"Really? Then I guess it was useless to try to hide it after all."

"Oh no, I wouldn't say that. You were lying to protect your mistress's reputation, weren't you? But now there's no need to lie anymore. Far from it. If you don't tell me the truth now, we'll never catch whoever killed her and Mr. Ishihara."

"I'm very sorry I lied to you," said Shizu, bowing her head in shame. "I'll tell you the truth now. I lied when I said that my young lady—I mean, Mrs. Ishihara—had not gone to Togakushi on July 3rd. As soon as Mr. Ishihara left that day for Takarazuka, she started out for Togakushi by car. If he called, I was to say that she was indisposed, in the toilet or the bath, and would call him back later."

"I see. Then she was going alone to the villa in Togakushi to meet Kisuke Takeda?"

"Yes," answered Shizu, in a voice as soft as the buzz of a mosquito. Kinoshita looked on, mouth agape.

"Mr. Takeda had been having an affair with Kayo, hadn't he?"

"Yes. Well, no, not an affair. He led my young lady astray, is what he did. But his own wife is so dreadful that he had to force my young lady on Mr. Ishihara. Then before long, he set it up so they could have secret meetings at that villa in Togakushi, and . . ."

"A terrible person, wasn't he, this Mr. Takeda?"

"A horrible, horrible man, to seduce such a pure inno-cent lady."

"Didn't Kayo's parents speak to him about it?"

"They couldn't. They were at his mercy. They had been an important family of the Suwa area for more than ten generations, but had been cheated out of the family busi-ness by Mr. Takeda and forced to sell their land to him cheap. Finally, he even got his hands on their daughter. She was like a human sacrifice. But he couldn't marry her. At first, she hated him, but then—I don't know why—she began to look forward to his visits. An evil man, he was. A terrible, evil man. But even he had to keep up appearances, and besides, he was afraid of his wife, so to hide his evil, he forced my lady on Mr. Ishihara. Then he found ways to keep seeing her secretly. This spring, she told Mr. Ishihara she wanted to buy a villa in Togakushi. He told her he didn't like Togakushi, but she insisted and forced him into it. But I'll tell you, I'm sure it was Mr. Takeda who was behind it!"

To hear Shizu Kasai talk about him, Kisuke Takeda must have been the Devil himself. Takemura was careful to take what she said with a grain of salt, though. Even supposing that Kayo's family had been outwitted and taken in by Takeda, they could hardly have been so innocent themselves. Their story sounded like a typical example of the decline of a great family. Nor could Kayo herself have been so innocent that she could not have broken off, even after marriage, a relationship with a man old enough to be her father, and hardly a very attractive man at that.

"Then did Kayo get home on the morning of the 4th?" asked Takemura.

"Yes, but it was almost noon. It was a Sunday, and there was heavy rain in Nagano. She said traffic was all tied up, and she had spent a long time on the road."

That would mean that she had left Togakushi early in the morning.

"From then until the 7th, did she go out anywhere for long?"

"How long?"

"Say, five or ten hours."

"Oh no, not for that long."

"Then the next time she went to Togakushi was with her husband on July l0th?"

"Yes, that's right."

If so, then Kayo could not have been the one who left

Kisuke Takeda's body on Poison Plain, so if she did kill him, she must have had an accomplice.

"All right, now, this is a very important question, so I want you to listen calmly and then answer frankly," said Takemura, straightening up and looking the old woman right in the eye. "Do you think it's possible that Kayo could have killed Kisuke Takeda, or do you think it's absolutely impossible?"

Shizu paled, but Takemura's earnestness forced her to think about the question as hard as she could, before answering carefully, "No, she absolutely could never have done such a thing. As sad as it may be, Mr. Takeda had taken possession body and soul of my young lady. If anybody in this house had killed him, it would have been me or Mr. Ishihara."

"What?" Takemura was caught by surprise now. "You mean Mr. Ishihara knew about her affair?"

"Yes, I think he must have had a feeling. Then when he heard about the murder and read in the newspaper that it wasn't known where Mr. Takeda went after he left the hotel, he asked my lady if it hadn't been the villa he went to, for a meeting with her. I'd never seen him question her so hard before. He asked her if all the excuses she had been making to go to Togakushi had been just so she could see Mr. Takeda. There were tears and accusations for two days, but she just kept shaking her head. Finally, on the afternoon of the 10th, when he got home from work, he practically dragged her off to Togakushi."

"What were they going to do there?"

"I don't know. I guess he was going to try to find out for himself whether she was telling the truth or not."

"It sounds like Mr. Ishihara was very much in love with Kayo."

"Yes, he was. I felt sorry for him, because I knew her feelings were for Mr. Takeda."

Takemura seemed to have gotten just about everything he needed from Shizu Kasai. He had just one more question, about something that had been bothering him since he entered the room. "Do you mind if I ask you, those two things that look like bowls, standing side by side over there, what are they for?" He was referring to two enameled basins that looked like some sort of sacred offering, placed ostentatiously on a side table. Each was about four-fifths full of a slightly cloudy, light green liquid. "The liquid is the color of tea. Is that what it is?"

Takemura got up and went over to the basins for a closer look. Shizu followed him, looking troubled.

"Yes, that's tea."

"Oh, so it is tea. But what's it for? Some kind of charm?"

"Er, yes, something like that." She hesitated.

Takemura looked at her. "Won't you tell me about it?"

"It's the Curse of the Demoness."

"The Curse of the Demoness?" He felt cold all over. "What sort of curse is that?"

"It's supposed to be a secret spell used a long time ago by the Demoness Maple in the Togakushi Mountains."

"What's it supposed to do?"

No response.

"Is it supposed to put a death spell on somebody?"

She nodded.

"How do you cast it?

"You make the tea in the morning, then you pour it into the bowl while facing in the direction where the person you want to put the curse on is located. As you do it, you say, 'Die, die.'"

"I see."

"Then in the evening you take the bowl outside and do the same thing again as you pour the tea out on the ground."

What was he on to now, he wondered sadly. "You keep doing this every day?"

"Yes."

"Do two bowls mean the curse is on two people?"

"Yes."

"Then I guess one of them must be for Mrs. Takeda in Nagano. Who's the other for?"

Again, no response.

"Is it for Hisako Hirai?"

"Yes, now. But not when my mistress was alive."

Takemura realized who it must have been for. "Then it was for her husband, Mr. Ishihara?"

The old lady nodded.

"Then it was Kayo who was trying to cast the spell?" Had the woman been that horrible? Then Takemura thought of something even worse. "You just said it was different when Kayo was alive. Do you mean you're trying to carry out her wishes even now that she's dead?"

Shizu stood there as stiff as a board.

"So you are, then." Takemura shook his head sadly.

"Well, I ask you to stop. Wouldn't you say that Kayo's curse has already worked?"

"It has?"

"Well, look. In the direction she put the curse, Mr. Takeda, Mr. Ishihara, and even Kayo herself are all dead."

"Oh my!" Shizu began to tremble. That had never occurred to her.

"Don't you know the saying that curses, like chickens, come home to roost? Kayo shouldn't have been doing it, and for you who have got better judgement, it's even worse. Do you think you can get happiness for yourself by making someone else unhappy?"

Shizu flopped down on the floor. Arms dangling at her sides, she began to wail like a baby. Takemura put his arm around her shoulders and helped her to the sofa, then waited patiently for her to calm down.

Finally recovering enough to regain a sense of shame, she wiped her eyes with a tissue and said, "I'm sorry to let you see me so upset."

"No, no. A shock like that would upset anybody," said Takemura gently. "By the way, do you know where Kayo learned the curse?"

"She said it was at a place called the Hall of Heavenly Wisdom, in Togakushi."

"The Hall of Heavenly Wisdom?"

"Yes. There's a shrine maiden there who tells fortunes."

"Oh? I guess Kayo must really have believed in her!"

"She did. She had her fortune told there almost every time she went to the villa."

"Oh did she?" laughed Takemura. "Then I guess she must have used that as her excuse to her husband for going to Togakushi, right?"

"She did use to tell him that was why she was going. But I don't think it was only an excuse. I do think it was really half her reason for going. She had heard about the shrine maiden from somebody this spring on one of her visits to Togakushi. After having her fortune told once, she became a believer. Afterward, whenever she had any kind of problem, she would go right off to the Hall of Heavenly Wisdom to consult her fortuneteller."

"Then is it possible that that's where she and her husband were going in Togakushi on the 10th?"

"I don't know, because they couldn't have gotten there before night."

"Oh yes, that's right."

Still, had Ishihara doubted his wife's story, the Hall of Heavenly Wisdom would have been the place for him to check it out. Takemura came away thinking that he might have picked up something else quite valuable.

On the train going back, Kinoshita suddenly blurted out loud, "Inspector, that must mean that the car the boy heard from the toilet next door was Kayo's!"

All the passengers around them turned to look at the source of the peculiar outburst. Takemura flinched and ducked his head.

"Probably so," he said.

"What? You don't seem too surprised."

"Surprised? Oh yes, I'm surprised. I'm surprised at you and your ridiculous shout."

"But if that was Kayo's car, doesn't it mean that she must have killed Kisuke Takeda? With a car, it would have been easy to get the body to Poison Plain."

"But that car went out and came right back, didn't it?"

"Well, maybe she didn't take the body all the way to Poison Plain just then. She could have been just taking a run around the neighborhood looking for someplace nearby to put it."

"Yes, but the time of death was estimated to be a little later than that."

"The estimate could be off some."

"Boy, wouldn't Inspector Kojima, the examiner, love to hear that! But that aside, Shizu Kasai declared that Kayo could not have killed Takeda."

"So how far can you believe an old woman like that? But Inspector, may I ask how you would explain the car?"

"It was Kayo's, of course."

"Was she alone?"

"No, Takeda was probably with her, but alive."

"What?" Kinoshita looked puzzled. "But where in the world were they going?"

"Well, now," Takemura smiled, "maybe they were just taking a run around the neighborhood, as you suggested."

"Oh, I see. Then maybe she killed him after that, right?"

"If she did, what did she do with the body? If she had left it anywhere in the vicinity that evening, it would probably soon have been found, and she left for Nagoya the next morning. That would mean she had to have left the body in the villa."

"Maybe she had an accomplice."

"Okay, so you insist she must have done it? Then tell me, who killed her and her husband? The accomplice?"

"Yes! Yes, that's it! That solves it!"

"Well, I'm ready to offer you my congratulations. Who's the accomplice?"

"Pardon? Oh, a little further investigation should clear that up."

"That would be nice."

"You're not taking this seriously."

"Oh yes I am. Very seriously."

"That's hard to believe. Or, have you got another idea of your own?"

"Oh, I can't say that I don't, now that we know the car was Kayo's."

"So what do you think?"

"Well, I think I can make a pretty good guess as to where the car was going and for what."

"You can? Really? Where?"

"To the Koshimizu Plateau Hotel. Kayo was taking Takeda back there. It would have been awfully difficult for him to have to walk back on that road at night."

"What?" Appalled, Kinoshita looked at Takemura, almost with contempt in his eyes. "Are you putting me on?"

"No, I mean it. Judging from the length of time the car was gone, doesn't that seem like the best guess?"

"I suppose so. Then, instead of getting out, he went back to the villa with her? Is that it?"

"I had no idea you were so stubborn. No. We can be sure at least that he got out of the car in as inconspicuous a place as possible. The question is, what happened after that?"

"Oh, I see. Then, was he attacked somewhere between the car and the hotel?"

"Well, your ideas certainly do lack imagination, but I wouldn't say that's entirely impossible."

"Lack imagination? But what else could have happened?" said Kinoshita with a sour look.

"Well, now . . ." said Takemura, his voice trailing off.

3 In Togakushi, the height of summer was approaching. On the plateau, where the snow piles high during the long winter months, magnificent natural changes take place during the brief period between spring and autumn. Summer is truly a feast of all nature, in the midst of which the crowds of humanity that flock there are no more than extras playing a mob scene. The leading characters are the sky, mountains, trees, and birds.

Takemura had Kinoshita stop the car in front of a park and got out. They had barely started out for the Togakushi Plateau, but having climbed up from the bottom of the basin in which Nagano City was located, they were already bathed in exhilarating sunlight. A breeze with the fragrance of forest caressed their cheeks.

"Hey, how about some buckwheat noodles?" said Takemura.

"Buckwheat noodles again? You sure do like them, don't you, Inspector?" said Kinoshita with a smile, getting out and following him.

That was true, and Takemura thought it funny himself. Whenever he ate out, if he could find a buckwheat-noodle shop anywhere around, that was what he always had. It had become a sort of routine. When first married, he had tried, out of consideration for Yoko, to adjust his eating habits to hers. But not for long. She had not liked buckwheat noodles. If she ate noodles at all, they would be Chinese noodles, or at most, ordinary Japanese white ones. Before he knew it, however, she had undergone a complete change and begun to eat buckwheat noodles along with him, and now, at times she even suggested herself that they have them. Her husband's likes had become her own.

A woman was a creature who would do anything for the man she loved, reflected Takemura. There was no end to the heinous crimes committed throughout history by tormented women. A woman was capable of a terrible vindictiveness that a man was not. That was probably what had motivated Kayo Ishihara, who had given herself heart and soul, not to her husband, but to Kisuke Takeda. But in this case, the vindictive woman herself had been killed. If it must be assumed that the same person had killed Takeda, Ishihara, and Kayo, then what could the motive have been?

No one had been found so far with a motive for killing all three. Or more to the point, no common factor had been found which might provide such a motive. It was of course possible that either Ishihara or Kayo had been killed only to eliminate a witness. Such a hypothesis would greatly simplify the search for a motive, making it a search for some common factor between Takeda and either Ishihara or Kayo.

Even so, Takemura would still not readily be able to name a suspect. Takeda's wife, Sachie, came to mind. From the point of view of motive alone, she would of course make a perfect suspect for the murders of Takeda and Kayo. A proud woman from a distinguished bloodline, if she had discovered the infidelity of a husband who might now be master of the house but had once been a mere servant, she would hardly have taken it lightly. Possibly it had not even been the first time, and she just hadn't been able to endure it any longer. But this case was not one of simple, impulsive murder. It was in fact a very intricate crime, abounding in almost absurd behavior, and carried out with skill and ingenuity, leaving not a trace, which almost aroused Takemura's admiration. It was not a crime that had been committed on impulse by someone crazed with jealousy.

✳ ✳ ✳

The shop was too crowded for Takemura to enjoy the buckwheat noodles he had been so eager for, making him wish he had waited until they got to the Okubo Teahouse, or better yet, the Middle Shrine.

Shizu Kasai had told them that the Hall of Heavenly Wisdom was located between the Hoko Shrine and Middle Shrine villages. They did their best to spot it from the car, but must have missed it, because before they knew it, they had entered the Middle Shrine village.

"We'll just have to go back and look more carefully this time," said Takemura.

"I'm afraid you'll have to do most of the looking, Inspector," grumbled Kinoshita as he made a U-turn and headed slowly back.

In the low-lying area to the left of the road, there was an irrigation pond, and beyond it a stand of cedar stretching toward the Hoko Shrine village. "It should be somewhere around here," said Takemura. "You can let me out for a look."

Kinoshita pulled over and stopped. Takemura got out onto some grass and looked as far as he could into the trees, but couldn't make out anything. Kinoshita spotted a station wagon coming slowly up the hill, on the side of which was the name Hokushin Laundry. The driver was a girl.

"Hey, Miss!" he hailed the car rudely, at the top of his voice.

He could have been a policeman or a punk, but she stopped, with a contemptuous look. Her face was that of a young girl, with no make-up at all, but Kinoshita saw at a glance that she was very pretty. He abruptly changed his manner, partly because of the man sitting next to her, who looked of an age to be her father.

"Er, there's supposed to be a place around here called the Hall of Heavenly Wisdom. You wouldn't happen to know where it is, would you?"

"Oh, yes. Just a little way down the hill there's a narrow lane running off to the left. Just follow it to the end, about three hundred meters. There's a little sign beside this road where the lane goes off," said the girl.

"Oh, good. Well, thank . . ." Kinoshita stopped, his eyes having fallen on the man beside her. "Say, aren't you the gentleman we visited in Tokyo?"

"Why, you were one of the detectives, weren't you? Well, well, what a coincidence!"

Takemura hurried over to the car. "Why, Professor Tachibana!"

He looked totally different in the sporty clothes he was wearing, but the gentleman sitting next to the girl was indeed Tomohiro Tachibana.

"What? You here too, Inspector?" said Tachibana easily, almost glad to see them again. "Still on the job, I guess?"

"Yes, still investigating the same case. And you, Professor?" Takemura's eyes strayed to the girl.

Afraid of giving the wrong impression, Tachibana said with forced smile, "This young lady is a student of mine. She's working here for the summer and offered to show me around on her route. She has to make a lot of stops, but that's just fine with me. This has turned into a much more enjoyable summer vacation than I had expected."

"Well, I'm glad to hear that. Are you staying at the Koshimizu Plateau Hotel?"

"Yes, that's right."

"I may be wanting to talk to you again, so, see you there, perhaps."

They said goodbye, and the car started off a little jerkily on its way up the hill.

"There's something fishy about that guy hanging around here," said Kinoshita, watching with folded arms as the car disappeared. "Do you think the girl is safe with him?"

"What? You liked her, did you? I think I'll tell her," laughed Takemura.

About a hundred meters down the road, they found the lane. Looking carefully, they saw the small sign with the words "Hall of Heavenly Wisdom," hidden in some tall grass. The lane was of rough gravel, barely wide enough for a single car. It must once have been a lumber road or something. As Kinoshita was wondering what he was going to do if he met a car coming toward him, they came out on a clearing in which stood a crude, thatched-roof cottage. There were three cars parked in front of it and several people standing around under the eaves or in the shade of the trees. All of them were standing perfectly still, with the air of people waiting for someone. Takemura and

Kinoshita got out of the car and headed for the dark hole of an entrance under the low roof.

"Hey you, why don't you wait your turn?" said a thin man of about forty. He and a woman standing beside the entrance both gave them reproachful glares.

"Our turn?"

"Yeah, everybody else is waiting." He nodded toward two others in the shade of the trees, who were watching apprehensively, afraid that Takemura and Kinoshita were going to cut in.

"But we're . . ." Kinoshita imperiously reached for his badge. Takemura quickly stopped him.

"Sorry," said Takemura. "Thoughtless of us. We'll just wait too. But she sure does have a lot of customers. Is she really that good, this fortuneteller?"

"Oh yeah, she's real good. Your first time, then?"

"Yes, our first time. You're from Osaka, are you?"

"Why yes, Izumi-Otsu. But it looks like we're out of luck today. The last time we were here, too, there were about ten people ahead of us, and we waited nearly all day, but she stopped before she got to us."

"Just like that?"

"Yeah. When she gets tired of it, she doesn't care how many people are waiting. She just quits for the day. That's why people get so mad when somebody tries to break in. But I'm sorry I spoke to you that way just now."

"No, no, I can certainly understand how you felt. Our fault completely."

Takemura took Kinoshita by the arm and led him away to the edge of the clearing. "We'll just have to wait," he said. "If we make the fortuneteller cranky, we'll be causing a lot of trouble for those people."

Having calmed the disgruntled Kinoshita, Takemura stepped into the shade of a locust tree. There was a little brook just beyond the tree that made the place feel cool. As he squatted down with an uninhibited shout of relief, he spotted something very rare on the ground in front of him. This part of the ground, probably under water when the brook was high, was practically all sand. In it a doodlebug had dug a cone-shaped hole.

"Hey, come look at this!" he called to Kinoshita.

"What is it?"

"It's a doodlebug hole! The larva of a mayfly is in there."

"Gee! That's a doodlebug hole?" Never having seen one before, Kinoshita looked at it with great interest. As he was doing so, an ant crawling nearby chanced to fall in. The unfortunate ant tried its best to climb out, but the sand kept crumbling under it, and it ended up at the bottom of the hole. As soon as it got there, the sand lifted, and a strange, ugly little black creature appeared. An instant later, ant and creature both disappeared, faster than the eye could follow the action.

"What a horrible little bug!" said Kinoshita, glaring at the hole with a scowl. Then suddenly he raised his foot and destroyed it with the heel of his shoe.

"Hey, that was a rotten thing to do," said Takemura.

"What do you mean? It was only justice."

"What kind of justice do you call that? I call it 'might makes right.'"

"But isn't that how the police do things?"

"Oh?"

Takemura saw another side of Kinoshita's personality, which captured his interest. A long time on the police force sometimes gives a person the idea that he is somehow different from the ordinary person, and he acquires the Establishment feeling that might does make right. Takemura always cautioned himself never to forget, even when dealing with a suspect, that human pain was still human pain.

Some of his colleagues, of course, considered him a bleeding heart. They felt their job was to exercise the authority of the state to its limits, and any sympathy toward the target of an investigation was to them taboo. Takemura had no wish to criticize them. Perhaps the road one chose was a matter of personality. There was something to be said for both attitudes. He could see that Kinoshita was at the crossroads between the comfortable feeling that he was exercising the authority of the state and the sympathetic feeling for the pain of the weak.

✳ ✳ ✳

They had to wait a full hour and a half for their turn, and two more parties arrived as they waited. The woman in the party just before them must have received a prediction of ill fortune, because she went away with her handkerchief pressed to her eyes.

Entering the cottage, they found themselves on a dirt floor like that of an old farmhouse. It took quite a while for their eyes to adjust to the dim light inside. Takemura stumbled at the place where shoes were supposed to be removed, giving himself a nasty bump on the shins.

"Come in," said a woman's voice from the back. Taking off their shoes and stepping up onto a board floor, they crossed it to a dark, shiny, wooden door. Slowly opening the heavy door, they were met by a light blue cloud of smoke accompanied by an odor which made Takemura flinch.

Beyond the door was an even darker room, in which sat a hazy, dimly illuminated figure dressed in the easily recognizable costume of a shrine maiden. Behind her was a simple altar, but they couldn't make out what was on it. On the floor in front of her was a small incense burner. The fire flickering there, nearly as small as a pilot light, was apparently the source of the pale blue smoke which filled the room. The only illumination was provided by the incense burner and four candles standing in candlesticks in each corner of the room. Closing the door behind them, they felt helpless in the near darkness.

The shrine maiden did not say a word, so Takemura and Kinoshita sat down facing her without leave. She sat motionless and erect, but with head slightly lowered, so they could not tell her age.

"Dogs," she suddenly muttered.

They looked at each other, wondering whether she meant them.

Slowly, she raised her head, an enigmatic smile on her lipsticked lips, her long, narrow eyes glittering with malice in the light of the incense burner.

"I smell dogs," she said.

This time her meaning was unmistakable. Kinoshita's temper flared. "Dogs" was a contemptuous term for the police. But how had she guessed?

Takemura could not help marveling. "I'm Takemura, Nagano prefectural police, Investigative Section One, and this is Detective Kinoshita," he said, quickly deciding there was no point in trying to fool this woman. Having so decided, he could calmly gather his wits for the struggle.

"Hmh!" she sneered, but the malice in her eyes seemed to abate somewhat.

"We're sorry to barge in on you like this, but we'd like to ask you a few questions about a case we're working on."

She did not condescend to reply, but neither did she give any sign of refusal.

"I believe you know a woman named Kayo Ishihara?"

Her expression did not change. Takemura took a photograph out of his briefcase and held it in the light of the incense burner for her to look at.

"Yes, I know her," she replied in a peculiar, low tone of voice, without changing her expression or bothering to look at the picture. She must have recognized the name right off.

"I believe she came here quite often," said Takemura. "Do you remember when she was here last?"

"The beginning of this month."

"You mean July 3rd?"

"I think so."

"She didn't come again after that? Like around the 10th?"

"No."

"When she came on the 3rd, was she alone?"

"Yes."

"How did she seem to you that day?"

"What do you mean?"

"For instance, did she seem worried about anything?"

"Do you think I ever get anybody here who isn't worried about something?" chuckled the shrine maiden.

"But Kayo was trying to kill someone with a curse, wasn't she? Something called the Curse of the Demoness. Aren't you the one who taught it to her?"

"Those things don't work."

"Oh? They don't?" This really surprised him. "But Kayo believed in it. She was going through the ritual every morning and evening."

"So? It made her feel better, didn't it?"

There was some truth in that, thought Takemura, but it was tantamount to fraud.

"Look, this is useless," said the shrine maiden. "Go away!"

With that, she fell back into silence.

Outside again, Kinoshita said in disgust, "Nasty bitch, isn't she?"

"But she does a terrific job of seeing through people. That was really something, figuring us out like that."

"Maybe it was just a bluff."

"Oh, I think it must have been more than that. That Curse of the Demoness business was worthy of a psychologist, don't you think?"

When they got into the car and Kinoshita put his hands on the wheel, Takemura said, "Be careful now. Do you feel all right?"

"What? Yes, I feel great. Why?"

"Well, I'm glad, but didn't that smoke bother you?"

"Now that you mention it, it was awfully smoky in there, wasn't it? What do you suppose she was burning?"

"Pot, I imagine."

"What?" Kinoshita yanked the emergency brake. "But we can't let her get away with that! Are you sure?"

"It wasn't enough to be that bad. She'd get no more than a warning."

"But it's a violation of the Drug Control Act. We've got to report it to Section Four."

"Now, just hold on!"

"What? Why?"

"Because I was just pulling your leg," laughed Takemura. "She wasn't burning pot. Only the hemp that it comes from. And she was only burning the stalks. They were stacked up beside her."

"What do you want to do that to me for?"

Takemura did not believe it had been only the stalks, but he didn't want the kind of fuss Kinoshita would have made. He had not rid himself of the idea that the Ishiharas might have gone to see the shrine maiden that night, and he wanted to save a narcotics rap for a last resort.

Transmigration

輪廻転生

 Tachibana awoke to the song of mountain birds. Opening the curtains, he found that West Peak of the Togakushi Mountains—usually visible from his window—was completely hidden by fog.

He washed, dressed, and went down to the restaurant. Though he normally skipped breakfast at home, he was quite hungry this morning, and most of all, he was dying to enjoy a leisurely cup of hot coffee. Taking his time over a light breakfast of bacon, eggs, and toast, he saw groups of people here and there who had already eaten and were leaving, though it wasn't even eight.

He wondered what their hurry was. How peculiar that young people—who still had plenty of time—always liked to rush, while old folks like himself—who were running out of time—liked to take it easy. Strange world!

A number of rooms that he passed on the way back to his own had already been vacated, their doors left open. An old cleaning lady was pushing around a handcart with a big bag, into which she was putting dirty sheets and towels. Soon, Yuko Noya would be there with the station wagon to collect the laundry.

His phone began to ring just as he entered his room.

"Good morning! Have you had breakfast?" came Yuko's cheerful voice over the line. "I've brought my mother with me. Would you like to meet her?"

"Yes, of course."

Having arranged to meet them in the coffee shop on the first floor, Tachibana brushed his teeth and shaved in high spirits, hoping that Yuko Noya's mother, Katsura, would turn out to be Taki's daughter. Yuko's resemblance to Taki might be only his imagination, but if Katsura was Taki's daughter, perhaps she had inherited Taki's personality and rare beauty even more clearly than Yuko.

When he met her in the coffee shop and made so bold as to take a good look at her, however, he was forced to admit that she bore no particular resemblance to Taki. She was pretty, to be sure, but she lacked the elegant beauty Taki had been blessed with. Even allowing for her age, probably thirty-seven or thirty-eight, he could not believe that she had ever come close to possessing Taki's beauty. Still, whether she looked like Taki or not, she definitely reminded him of someone, though he couldn't think whom.

"Take your time. I have work to do," said Yuko cheerfully, dashing off after making a brief introduction.

Yuko gone, Tachibana and Katsura quickly became stiff and formal. He called the waiter over and asked her what she would have. She requested coffee, and he ordered a cup for each of them.

"You are being very kind to Yuko," she said, in a voice with a calming effect. Her singing voice would be alto, thought Tachibana, not unlike Taki's.

"No, no, it's she who is going to a lot of trouble over me.

I'm really enjoying myself more than I ever thought possible."

"But she's just gotten her driver's license, and I'm afraid she must be tiring you out with a very rough ride."

"Not at all. She drives very safely, and she knows how to take good care of this old man."

The coffee arrived, interrupting the conversation. Katsura handled her spoon with refinement and took dainty sips of coffee. Both her hairdo and her dress were quite casual, and her make-up was light, which pleased him. Yet she seemed to emanate a zest for life which Taki had never had, so perhaps there was no connection after all. Still, Tachibana was not ready to give up the idea completely.

"Yuko told me that you know something about my family background," he said.

"Oh dear! Did she tell you that?" Katsura looked a little embarrassed. "It's really only your name that I had heard, I'm afraid."

"But may I ask how you knew about the title of viscount in my family?"

"I heard that from my grandmother, when I was in junior high school, I believe. During spring cleaning once, I happened to open an English dictionary I noticed on the bookshelf in my father's room, and I saw the name Tomohiro Tachibana inside the cover. My grandmother was right beside me at the time, and I asked her who he was. She said he was the young master of a viscount's family, who had given the dictionary to my father when my father was a student. But the dictionary was an old one, and I already had a newer one, and then my grandmother died shortly after that, and I forgot all about the old dictionary until around ten years ago when Yuko found it somewhere or other and asked me the same question I had asked my grandmother. Wasn't it funny how history repeated itself, I thought, and I gave Yuko the same answer my grandmother had given me."

Tachibana suddenly remembered the circumstances. Having heard that Keijiro's son, about a year older than himself, was working his way through school in Nagoya or Osaka, and having himself received a big new dictionary from his own father, he had presented his old concise dictionary to Keijiro to give to his son.

"Do you still have the dictionary?" he asked.

"No. Yuko used it for a little while, but as soon as my father saw her with it, he bought her a new one and locked the old one away somewhere. For some reason, he got terribly angry. Oh! I don't think I should be telling you this. But when Yuko was in her third year of junior high school, I believe, she came home one day and showed me a supplementary-reading book that had been written by you, Professor Tachibana, and I asked her not to mention it to her grandfather. That's why it seems so strange that I should be meeting you now. But somehow or other, I had the feeling that some day I would." Katsura's cheeks were flushed. She had been speaking with the eagerness of a young girl.

"Er, what became of Keijiro, your grandfather?"

"He died about the time I was born. Did you know him well, Professor?"

"Yes. He was very kind to me when I was young," said Tachibana, wondering how he was going to answer if she wanted to know more.

"Oh really?" She let it drop with that.

"Er, I do hope you'll forgive me for prying," he said, "but could you tell me about your mother?"

"My mother?" Katsura was obviously embarrassed. "I'm afraid I don't know anything at all about her except that she died when I was born. I'm sure you'll think it strange, but I don't even know her name."

"I see. Your daughter told me much the same thing. But couldn't you find out by checking the family register?"

"That's what I thought, so I tried it. But I found I was registered as the oldest daughter of Keijiro and Mitsu Noya, my paternal grandparents. They must have had some awfully good reason for not recording my real mother's name. I asked my father about it, but he absolutely refused to tell me anything. It bothered me a lot when I was younger, especially when I got married, but I just don't let it get to me anymore."

"Let's see, if I remember correctly, your father's name is . . ."

"Keiichi."

"Oh yes. He should be about sixty-one, I believe. He's in good health, I trust?"

"Excellent health, thank you."

"I'm very glad to hear that. Please tell him I'd like to see him again."

Whether or not Keiichi had married Taki, Tachibana should at least be able to find out from him what had become of her. He supposed that she must have died an untimely death, and he flinched at the thought of hearing about it, but he felt he had to know.

Having finished loading the laundry, Yuko returned, beads of perspiration on her forehead, ready to take her mother along to the next stop on her route.

"Professor," she said, "there's a place I'd like to take you tonight."

"Oh? Where?"

"Do you remember the study circle I mentioned? Well, they're going to be discussing the Demoness Legend tonight, so I'd really like you to come."

"Well, I certainly wouldn't mind, but I really don't see how I could contribute anything. I'm sure you and the local people must know far more about the Demoness than I."

"Actually, the reason I want you to come is so you can hear what they have to say. You see, my little talk at the class party wasn't really my own, and I'd like you to get it from the horse's mouth."

"Oh, I see," laughed Tachibana. "As a matter of fact, I did have the feeling that your opinions were a little too sophisticated for a freshman. Okay, fine, I'll just have to let you take me, then," he said, like a doting grandfather.

Arriving to pick Tachibana up in a tiny subcompact at an hour she judged he would have finished supper, Yuko filled him in about the study circle on the way there. Its hangout was the Ochi Inn, located on the slope in the Middle Shrine village. The members collected folk tales and legends of Togakushi and published various interpretations and discussions in booklets. She had read one of their booklets when she was in high school and been so impressed that, ever since, she had taken part in their activities whenever she had a chance. The circle's leader was the master of the inn, a middle-aged man named Fusao Ochi, who in his university days was said to have been the champion protest leader of the student union, but whose mild manners today made that hard to believe. He now often chuckled about being afraid to face his wife because he devoted all his time to the circle instead of to business.

"We're honored to have a university professor here tonight," he welcomed Tachibana without affectation. There were ten-odd people present, more than half of them local, but there were five who, like Yuko, were from farther away.

When Ochi introduced Tachibana, one of the women

asked, "Are you the Professor Tomohiro Tachibana who wrote *In Support of a New Interpretation of the Classics?*"

"Yes, he is," Yuko answered for him. "It was reading that book that made me choose the university that Professor Tachibana teaches at. Have you read it too, Mrs. Murata?"

"Oh yes," replied the woman addressed as Murata, her eyes sparkling. "But I never dreamed I would actually be meeting the famous Professor Tachibana!"

Tachibana was greatly embarrassed, but the woman's enthusiastic praise served to put the group in an excellent mood. It turned out that his method in that book—the method of giving not merely a simple interpretation of the classics themselves, but rather of relating them to other works and to historical events—had been adopted as the fundamental method of the study circle.

"This year our theme is the Demoness Legend, actually a big jumble of theories, none really well established. So I thought we should try simply to put together a collection of traditional things, such as the Noh drama, 'Maple-Viewing,'" said Ochi, in a tone that sounded like a carryover from his student days. "I was born around here, so I've been hearing stories about the Demoness Maple since my childhood. Mainly, though, the stories have been the old moral tales about good rewarded and evil punished. In other words, stories about a demoness named Maple who lived in Kinasa and used a cave on Mt. Arakura as a base from which to plunder the surrounding area, until a general was sent from the capital to subdue her.

"But one day, on my way home from college, I happened to get into a conversation with the person sitting next to me on the train, and he told me that Maple had really existed, and that the term 'demon' had been widely applied to someone who symbolized the terror and hatred of the original inhabitants of a place for the conquerors who came to subjugate them—in this case, the Yamato Court. After that conversation, my attitude changed completely, and I became captivated by the Demoness. I began to think of her as a kind of Joan of Arc, a heroine defending the masses against the oppression of the state. Young and naive as I was then, I had to relate everything to some ideology or other, and I was intoxicated with the lurid fantasy of a beautiful woman turning into a demoness over the hatred and despair she felt as a result of oppression."

So Fusao Ochi's original motive in taking up the study of the Demoness Legend had been to develop a new theory which placed Maple on the side of the masses and emphasized the injustice of the state. He had been trying to turn against the state a story it had once used to pacify troublesome natives.

"But with long years of research, that tainted motive was replaced by a purer attachment to Maple and her legend," continued Ochi. "I acquired a real feeling for the days she spent living in Kinasa. I dropped my thoughts of ideologies and resistance movements and began to think only about the passionate world of Maple herself, living among villagers who were our ancestors and expressing her longing for the capital and the man she loved in the only way she could: by fighting."

Tachibana could see where Yuko had gotten her sympathy for the Demoness Maple. The members of the group familiarized themselves with the legend by listening to Ochi's talks, exchanged information about literary records they had found, and sometimes made field trips together. They divided up the subjects for research, and later each reported on his own. It was truly a society based on friendship and a common interest in the study of local history, untainted by any ideological intent.

"All of this is far from the goal I originally had in mind," Ochi went on, "but I am well satisfied. The only other wish I have is to develop some local patriotism through our activities, so that we may stand up against the wave of reckless building that could destroy the natural environment of Togakushi."

"I guess you mean the building of the golf course they're talking about now," said Tachibana with a pang.

"Exactly. That's going to be trouble," frowned Ochi. "Fundamentally, the tourist industry depends on a proper balance between natural resources and development, so we have to tolerate a certain amount of destruction of nature, but not this. If we permit such an outrage, it will mean the destruction of Togakushi. But I don't think that's going to happen. There's a lot of national forest land around here, so I think the plans for the golf course are going to collapse. If they ever do really get started, the whole town will be up in arms against them."

That was probably true, thought Tachibana with a touch of uneasiness.

The presence of the unexpected guest turned the study circle meeting into a lively conversation party. Tachibana listened rather than talked, but came away well satisfied. Yuko was overjoyed to hear that on the way home in the car.

"I'm off tomorrow afternoon," she said, "and I'd like to show you the Shogan Temple in Kinasa and the Daisho Temple in Shigarami. Maple's spirit is enshrined at the Shogan Temple, and at the Daisho Temple, there's a scroll painting that tells the Maple-Viewing story, and a Buddhist mortuary tablet on which the names of Maple and Taira no Koremochi are written together. Then I've got to show you Maple's grave, called Demon's Mound. You'll join me, please, won't you?"

"I'll be glad to."

She let him out in front of the hotel, and was about to start off, when suddenly she stuck her head out the window and said, "Did you notice the resemblance, Professor?"

"Pardon?"

"To my mother!"

He didn't know what she was talking about. She could hardly have known he thought her mother looked like someone. "Who is it you think resembles your mother?"

"Why, you, of course, Professor! I noticed it the first time I saw you!"

"Eh?" He felt like he had been slapped into awareness. So that was why he thought he had seen Katsura Noya before! She looked like his mother! As a child, he had always been told that he looked like his mother. To Yuko, who had never met his mother, Katsura must look like him.

After managing a wave goodbye, he put his hands to his head, trying to collect himself, wondering what it all meant. Could the resemblance be mere coincidence? Such things did happen. It had delighted Yuko, but she didn't seem to attach any special significance to it. He, however, knowing the possible implications, could not help but take it very seriously.

Assuming that Keiichi, son of Keijiro and his wife, had been demobilized right at the end of the war in 1945 and gotten married immediately, the earliest Katsura could have been born would have been the summer of 1946. That would make her thirty-seven. To have a daughter of university age, she would have had to get married at eighteen and give birth at nineteen. Young, to be sure, but not impossibly so.

Unless Keiichi had returned to Japan immediately after

the war, though, Katsura could not be even that old. Sorry
though he was that he had not asked Yuko her mother's
age, he was afraid of what he might have learned. If Keiichi
had been legitimately married, it would hardly have been
necessary to register Katsura's parents as Keijiro and his
wife. There had to be some good reason for that. Perhaps it
was that Katsura had in fact been born before Keiichi
came home from the war, and that her mother—Tachibana
was almost sure that was Taki—had died at childbirth?

If that were the case, then Katsura's real father must be
. . . Tachibana stood in shock, his chest so tight he could
hardly breathe. He was seized by a chill, and beads of
perspiration came out on his forehead.

2 The early morning drums were sounding from the
Hoko Shrine. The sounds infiltrated the tops of
the giant cedars, drank their fill of the mountain
air, and resounded with a deep, mellow boom. Tachibana
was climbing the long stone staircase for the first time in
nearly forty years, aware of his age and feeling his legs get
heavier with each step, as he thought of the years that
had passed. Yet the steps were still as he remembered
them. Even the mossy areas and bare spots where the slope
was too steep looked familiar. Neither did he notice any
change in the cedars which lined the stairs. If they had
gotten thicker or older, he couldn't tell. On his first
arrival in Togakushi, he had been told by Keijiro that these
trees were eight hundred years old. Then they must be
going on eight hundred and fifty now, he thought, amused.
Amused, but melancholy.

He made it to the top in time for the climax of the shrine
dance, where the god Tajikarao stamped on stage postur-

ing fiercely, then took the Rock Door of the Heavens under his arm and carried it off, while turning his grim red face from side to side. The door was replaced by the divine mirror which represented the Sun Goddess, and Shinto music of rejoicing and thanksgiving began. The production had never changed, Tachibana felt keenly, only the actors and dancers were different.

After the dance, the ceremony ended with the members of the Togakushi Religious Association, which had paid for the offering, passing around the ritual libation. Tachibana had been standing some distance away, gazing at the activities on stage with the illusion that time had turned backward. Sorry he had missed the Dance of Urayasu, the dance of the shrine maidens, his favorite, he hoped at least to see the little girls in their lovely shrine maiden costumes, so he went over to the office entrance, from which they ought soon to be emerging.

The lattice door opened, and a middle-aged woman came out. From behind her, a young shrine maiden dancer called, "You'll come get me, won't you, granny?"

"Yes, I'll be here, but you be sure to eat all of that lunch, now," cautioned the woman addressed as "granny," as she closed the lattice door.

"Er, excuse me, could I ask you something?" Tachibana stopped her.

She turned toward him with inquiring eyes. Tachibana did not notice the flash of surprise in them. Going up to her, he saw she was a number of years older than himself. Her work pants gathered at the ankles and her youthful movements must have made her look younger from a distance.

"Will there be more dancing today?" he asked.

"Yes," she replied. "There are reservations for two more

performances. The next one should be beginning pretty soon, I think."

"Oh, that's wonderful. It's still thriving. Hasn't changed since so many years ago."

"No, actually, I'm afraid today is very unusual." She looked at Tachibana searchingly. "Uh, how many years ago do you mean?"

"Well, it's been nearly forty years."

"Excuse me, but you weren't by any chance staying with the Tendoh family then, were you?"

"What?" exclaimed Tachibana in astonishment. "How did you know?"

"From Tokyo? A nobleman's son, I believe you were?"

"Uh, well . . . my name is Tachibana, but . . ."

"Oh yes, Tachibana, that was it! Then I'm right!" Her eyes got bigger. "I'm Haru Kusumoto. I lived just down the road. I was very close to Taki."

"Ah, Haru Kusumoto. I remember!"

"But I'm just an old granny now. You never would have known me, eh?"

"Well, I'm afraid we've both gotten old."

"No, Mr. Tachibana, I knew you right off. You really haven't changed."

Suddenly, Haru began to cry. The sight of Tachibana must have brought back too many memories. Those had been hard times.

"May I accompany you down?" he said, putting a hand on her back. They headed down the seldom-used Women's Slope, so they wouldn't have to worry about meeting anyone.

"I'm sorry. I've made a spectacle of myself," said Haru with an embarrassed smile, hastily wiping her eyes with her cuff.

"The country is a great place, isn't it? You run into friends from so long ago," said Tachibana with feeling. "But I'm afraid I never knew exactly which house was yours."

"I'm not surprised. To us, the young master Tachibana was way up above the clouds."

"Enough!" laughed Tachibana. "I'd prefer to forget that old stuff."

The Women's Slope rejoined the stone staircase at a level area near the bottom. From there, Haru pointed through a gap in the trees and said, "That roof over there, that's the roof of my house." It was a big house at the foot of the peak.

"Then that big fire didn't get your house, did it?"

"No. It was touch and go for a while, but we were awfully lucky. If our house had caught fire, I think the whole peak would have gone up, shrine and all. I never believed in the gods until that day. But Mr. Tachibana, you knew about that fire?"

"Yes, I came back here once in 1947. I believe it was Mrs. Otomo I spoke to, from the house across the street from the Tendohs'. I asked her about Taki."

"You did?"

"Yes. She told me Taki was dead."

"Oh my!" Haru stopped in her tracks and looked up at Tachibana with a sympathetic gaze. After a moment's hesitation, she said, in the tone of someone whose mind was made up, "Won't you come with me to my house? There are some things I'd like to tell you."

Tachibana did not need asking. There was a mountain of things he wanted to find out about Taki.

The Kusumoto house itself still looked as it had in the days when it served as a priest's residence, but it had been completely reborn as the Kusumoto Inn, as indicated by a sign outside and a microbus in front for transporting guests to and from the station. With a melancholy smile, Haru told Tachibana that all such priests' residences had been turned into either inns or restaurants. The prosperous days before and during the war when the government used to make offerings to shrines like the Togakushi ones were gone forever. Most visitors today were students, who used the place as a base to hike across the mountains from the Togakushi Plateau. Young voices were calling back and forth all over the building, inside and out.

She led him into a vacant room that would serve instead of a parlor, made him comfortable, and brought him some cola. Not having put his legs to such use for a long time, he heartily enjoyed the cold drink. She waited for him to finish it, and then began to speak deliberately.

"Taki is alive."

"What?" exclaimed Tachibana, caught unprepared. It took some seconds for the words to sink in. "Alive? What do you mean?"

"She didn't die. You were lied to."

"Lied to?"

"All the villagers had agreed to give that story to anyone from outside the village."

"But why? What happened to her?"

"She became a demoness."

"A demoness?" He had just finished the cola, but his throat felt dry again. "What do you mean, she became a demoness?" he shouted, his eyes wide.

Haru lowered her eyes and took a deep breath. "After that thing happened to her, she went mad."

Tachibana was near choking. With a pain like a dagger thrust, he realized what Haru meant by "that thing."

"The police brought Taki home because of her madness," continued Haru, "but they put Keijiro and his wife in prison. Taki went on living alone in her house. Those of us who were close to her tried to take care of her, but the whole thing was just too sad for words. And to make matters worse, we hadn't noticed it at first, but she was pregnant."

"Pregnant?"

"Yes. She gave birth to a baby girl right in the middle of the great fire."

"I see," said Tachibana, hanging his head. It was pointless now, but a feeling of shame settled heavily on him. He knew that the great fire around the Hoko Shrine had occurred on August 20, 1945. That would mean that the baby Taki gave birth to on that day had to be his. Haru obviously knew that, too. She had not spoken accusingly, but that was small consolation to him. "Where is Taki now?" he finally managed.

"That's not for me to tell."

"Why not?"

"She's had an awful time of it, but now she's finally managing to live in her own way. If you go to her, you'll just stir up sad memories." Haru went on, speaking as one trying to placate a child, and he could make no reply. "But her daughter was raised with loving care by Keijiro's wife. Keijiro's health was ruined in prison, but his wife showed up here alone two days after the fire. Taki and the baby were staying with us. Keijiro's wife waited for her to recuperate and then took both of them home with her. But they finally had to put Taki in the hospital."

"You mean, in a mental hospital?"

She nodded.

Imagining the misery of Taki's madness from Haru's vivid description that she had become "a demoness," Tachibana sank into a deep gloom that continued to torment him after he got back to the hotel. Knowing Taki was alive

could do him no good. Even the confirmation that Katsura
and Yuko were his daughter and granddaughter, which
should have been such good news for him, felt like retribution instead.

He wrote a note to Yuko, a simple note to the effect that
he had suddenly been called back to Tokyo on urgent
business. He thanked her for her kindness and sent his
regards to her mother. The note struck him as too abrupt,
but he was afraid to write more.

It was almost noon. He canceled the reservation for the
remainder of his stay, left the note at the front desk, had a
taxi called, and headed down the hill in it. The weather
was going to turn bad. Clouds were moving across the sky,
and an almost wintry blast of wind began to blow. Feeling
chased, he sank deep into the seat, wishing the driver
would go faster.

He stayed in a hotel in Nagano City that night, and the
next day, with heavy feelings, made the rounds of mental
hospitals in the city and suburbs. From the first, he knew
that the exercise would most likely prove futile, but he also
knew he would never be able to rest until he tried it.

As he had expected, he was treated with coolness everywhere. There was no reason for anyone to divulge a
patient's secrets to him. Besides, he was asking about a
patient who would have entered the hospital more than
thirty years ago, and that in itself earned him a laugh at a
number of places. At one, he was told not very politely that
the hospital itself had only been there for fifteen years, and
was looked at with a suggestion that he ought to consider
having himself committed.

All his efforts proved in vain. He found no record
anywhere of a patient named Taki Tendoh. Physically and
emotionally exhausted, he headed for Tokyo on the last
express of the day, feeling ten years older.

3 It was two days after his chance meeting with Tachibana in Togakushi that Takemura received the order to conduct a thorough investigation of the man.

"May I ask why?" he said. "Did we get something new on him?"

"No, not really," said Miyazaki with a sullen look. "This comes from higher up. I mean, a certain person apparently believes there's some deep significance in the fact that Takeda was having Tachibana investigated."

"That's pretty strange, don't you think? That business is the only thing we found on Tachibana at all, and I can't see the point in going into it again unless something new has come up."

"Neither can I. But I'm asking you to do it anyway."

"Who exactly does this come from? If I'm going to change the whole course of my investigation for someone, I'd at least like to know who it is."

"You're really putting me in a spot," grumbled Miyazaki. Then he counterattacked. "Now look, you aren't getting anywhere anyway. You're hardly in a position to refuse." He finished with a look of triumph.

"Yes, I know," said Takemura with a rueful smile. "I'm not refusing. But I at least want to do the best job I can, and for that I need to know what this guy is really after. And how am I supposed to find that out unless you tell me who he is?"

"Damn you're stubborn!" Miyazaki spread his arms in exasperation. "But look here, Takemura, if any of this gets back to him, it's my ass. If I have your word you won't let that happen, I'll tell you who he is."

"Right," laughed Takemura. "So who is this earthshaker?"

"Hirofumi Shishido."

"What? Well, well, what do you know about that! All right, sir, I'm ready to re-investigate Tachibana as ordered," said Takemura obediently, and then withdrew, thinking it very peculiar that Hirofumi Shishido should still be bothered by Tomohiro Tachibana. He wondered if there was some connection between the two. That was what interested him.

Leaving word that he would be somewhere in the city, Takemura headed for the door. Kinoshita got up to follow, but Takemura stopped him. He was not going far enough to need a car, and he judged that it would be better to do this alone. His destination was Kisuke Takeda's mansion.

It had been almost a month since Takeda's murder, and public interest in the case was waning in favor of the prefectural eliminations for the nationwide high school baseball tournament—a welcome circumstance for the police. Takemura had not needed Miyazaki to tell him he was at a dead end. No helpful clues had been discovered to either the Takeda murder or the subsequent Ishihara murders. The period between the Ishiharas' departure from Nagoya and the discovery of their bodies the next morning at Arrowstand was still a total blank. The visit to the Hall of Heavenly Wisdom, the only lead they had, had not helped at all. Public aside, the police themselves were getting impatient, and high-level administrators were beginning to fume.

Takemura was calmer than the rest, because his view of things was a little different. He could not deny, of course, that the investigation was at a standstill, but that did not bother him excessively, for he had found himself at such dead ends often enough before. To go through everything available on a case without finding a single clue was not rare, and the effect of being blocked in every direction was often a sudden inspiration. He was sure one was coming. What he was suffering now were labor pains. Stuffed to the bursting point with information as he was, the slightest inspiration would serve as a needle to pop everything loose. Only the time was not ripe.

*　*　*

Takeda's widow, Sachie, must have been in a good mood, for Takemura was shown immediately to the parlor. From outside, the house looked purely Japanese, but inside, various concessions had been made to Western style. The parlor had sliding doors and Japanese walls, but a carpeted floor and a rococo reception set made it look like a movie scene depicting Japan's 19th-century opening to the West.

He was kept waiting only long enough for a sip of tea before she entered wearing a pale lavender dress of medio-cre design that made her look even thinner than she was. Knowing nothing of fashion, he assumed the dress must be elegant and decided it was not bad.

"If this is about your investigation, I believe I told you that Izawa was handling such matters," she began, with a mild, but not disagreeable reminder.

"Yes, I haven't forgotten. But I would like very much to get your own ideas on a few matters."

"I'm afraid I'm short of those."

"But as his wife, I should think your view of him must have been different from other people's."

"His wife?" she said with a scornful smile. "Oh, never mind. What do you want to know?"

"Anything you can tell me about Tomohiro Tachibara. As you know, your husband was having him investigated, but we still don't know why. Mr. Takeda made the request from the Koshimizu Plateau Hotel, and it so happens that Professor Tachibana was staying at the same hotel on the same day. It appears that they met there and your husband contacted the detective agency right away. We know he asked them to get back to him as soon as possible, so he must have been very worried and in an awful hurry. But for the life of us, we couldn't come up with a single reason—business or private—for the urgency, so we eliminated Tachibana as a suspect. But now we've been urged by a certain person to reopen that line of investigation, and that's why I'm here."

"What person?"

"I'm afraid I'm not at liberty to tell you that, but anyhow, we're stuck. So I'd like to check once more to see whether you might remember anything, or whether there might be some mention of Tachibana in Mr. Takeda's diaries or other papers."

"I've never heard of this Tachibana. I may be getting senile in my old age, but of that much I'm sure. And Kisuke didn't leave any diaries around here. He was always so afraid I might find out something about his private affairs that he just never would have left anything like that in the house. If there are any such things, they would be in his office. That's why you'd do better to talk to Izawa."

Her antipathy for her husband came through in the way she spoke of him, using his first name to a stranger. Takemura could guess how she must feel. They might not even have had any physical relations, let alone spiritual intimacy. Maybe that was why they had no children. Of course, the superfluous thought did occur to Takemura that he and his wife, who were not lacking in physical relations, did not have any children either.

"But instead of looking for something new on this Tachibana," said Mrs. Takeda, raising her voice, "hadn't you better be questioning this 'certain person' you mention? It sounds to me as though he must know something."

"You're right about that," said Takemura, impressed with her acumen. "That's exactly what I think. But that's the trouble with working for the government. I'm under orders from on high not to go near him, and I can't disobey."

She glanced at Takemura with a sarcastic laugh. "It must be *that* guy, then. The one who came up through the military police . . ." She stopped, scorning to let the name pass her lips.

"Came up through the military police? Who do you mean?"

"You can drop that innocent pose."

"It's no pose "

"What? You mean you really don't know? No, I guess maybe you don't. You are pretty young, aren't you?"

"I'm much obliged to you for that," said Takemura with a smile, it being rare nowadays for him to be called young.

"Well, I guess I'll just have to tell you. I mean Hirofumi Shishido, the Diet Representative."

"Oh really? Was he in the military police?"

"That he was! I forget his rank—second or first lieutenant—but he was a rotten bastard who used the influence of his superiors to throw his own weight around. He wormed his way into my father's good graces and then got the best of him. I've heard about an awful lot of other nasty things he's done too. It *is* him, isn't it?"

"Well . . ." Takemura scratched his head. "I'm afraid I can't confirm your guess."

"Then it is him! Well, what do you know? If he's worried about this Tachibana, you can bet it's because he's got a guilty conscience. You just go question him and see! I bet you'll find he did something to the man."

Though the conversation had taken quite an unexpected turn, Takemura had a feeling there might be a lot in what she said.

"Can you tell me when your husband and Representative Shishido got to know each other, and how?"

"Well, I don't know too much about that, but it was through Shishido's patronage that Kisuke met my father, so they must have known each other for some time at least before that."

"And when was that?"

"Around 1948 or 1949, I believe. Anyway, it was a couple of years before the Korean War. As a matter of fact, it was in the midst of all the confusion over that war that my father's business and our family finances recovered. Shishido did a neat job of setting himself up in the world, too. It's a wonder he wasn't tried as a war criminal! But I suppose he weaseled out of that just by being what he is. Anyway, he got rich and then got into politics and became a Diet member. There are an awful lot of things wrong with this world, I'll tell you."

"What had your husband been doing before he got to know your family?"

"I'm not sure, but I think he was some sort of broker, times being what they were. There were a lot of black marketeers in those days. Shall we say that he was one of the higher-class ones?"

It did not seem to be merely that she enjoyed revealing her husband's evils. She must have had a genuine, heartfelt antipathy for him. If so, it was natural that he should have been drawn to another woman. The Takedas' marriage must have been one strictly of convenience.

"I have one more question. Where was your husband from?"

"Togakushi."

"Really?"

"That's right. A place called Hoko Shrine. His family name was Tokuoka. The place used to have houses that lodged pilgrims to the shrine—though they've all been turned into inns now—and Kisuke gave himself out to my father as the second son of a family that owned one of the houses. But I found out long after that they were nothing but peasants."

"So he was from Togakushi?" mumbled Takemura, still trying to absorb the information.

"Yes, Togakushi. That's why Shishido made him help with the golf course. He figured Kisuke would be a good persuader in his own hometown. But Kisuke didn't like the idea. For some reason, he hated going to Togakushi. He never used to go back there before. Anyway, his family doesn't live there anymore. There was a big fire the year the war ended, and they were burned out and had to leave. Maybe it was that memory which made him not like to go back. But Shishido had him over a barrel, and from the beginning of this spring, he had been going there almost every day. Now we've seen the upshot."

"You have suffered a grievous loss."

"Not really. Anyway, he died in his hometown. Maybe he died happy."

What a terrible thing to say, thought Takemura.

＊ ＊ ＊

Though Takemura had gotten tired of Sachie Takeda's disagreeable tongue, he could not deny that she had helped him to understand a lot of things. Back at headquarters, he called the Ishihara home in Nagoya. The phone was answered by Shizu Kasai, whose guarded voice relaxed and warmed up as soon as he identified himself. With his help,

Hisako Hirai had eased up in her determination to treat Shizu badly, and Shizu was full of endless thank yous.

"I'd like to ask you something," interrupted Takemura, as soon as he could get a word in. "That villa in Togakushi, I believe I remember being told that Mr. Ishihara bought it this spring. Am I right about that?"

"That's right. It was this spring."

"Okay. Now, I'm afraid this may seem like a prying question, but he bought it because Kayo—Mrs. Ishihara— wanted it so badly, right?"

"Yes, that's right."

"And Mr. Ishihara himself was strongly against it, right?"

"Yes."

"You do know why she wanted to buy it, don't you?"

"Pardon? Well, uh, I . . ."

"Wasn't it exactly because she knew Mr. Ishihara didn't like Togakushi?"

Takemura could almost see her hesitating at the other end of the line. He continued, "Isn't it true that after all the trouble and expense of buying the villa, he never once visited it? He must really have hated Togakushi, don't you think?"

"Yes, he did. He had no objection to a villa; he just didn't want it there. But she insisted, and since he wouldn't tell her what it was he had against the place, he wasn't in a good position to refuse."

"But isn't it true that she wanted that villa in Togakushi exactly because she knew he objected to it?"

Shizu did not reply.

"Now, look, this is very important, and I need an honest answer. Didn't Kayo figure that if the villa was in Togakushi, Mr. Ishihara probably wouldn't visit it?"

"Yes, I think that was her idea."

"And of course, it was because she wanted to meet Mr. Takeda there, wasn't it?"

"Yes. I tried my best to stop her, but . . ."

"Okay. Now, that villa wasn't new. They must have bought it from someone. Do you know who? I mean, do you know who brought it to their attention?"

"Yes."

"His name was Shishido, wasn't it? Hirofumi Shishido, the Diet representative?"

"Yes, it was Representative Shishido. If that man hadn't meddled, none of this would ever have happened."

"What was Shishido's connection with Kayo?"

"It wasn't with her. He was an old acquaintance of Mr. Ishihara's. And nobody asked him, either. He just popped up with an offer to sell the villa cheap, and forced it on them. If he hadn't . . ."

"I see. Well, thank you very much. I'll be in touch with you." She was starting to grumble, and he hung up a little abruptly.

"Sergeant Yoshii," he called, choosing a man more suited than Kinoshita for the job he had in mind, "there's something I'd like you to check out for me at the Legal Affairs Bureau. You know the Ishihara villa on the Koshimizu Plateau in Togakushi? Well, I want you to find out from whom Mr. Ishihara bought it, when, and for how much, and then find out when and from whom the former owner bought it."

Yoshii came back with pretty much what Takemura had expected. The previous owner had been Hirofumi Shishido, but he had purchased it only a month before selling it to Ishihara. Considering the time necessary for negotiations and registering the sale, the villa could not have been in Shishido's hands for more than two weeks or so. Moreover, he had sold it for about half of its true value, according to the real estate agent that Yoshii spoke to. Of course, he had bought it for approximately the same amount, so it must have been the owner before him who took the loss.

"Shishido bought it from one of the directors of a big construction company in Tokyo," said Yoshii. "The lot had been purchased ten years before and the villa put up almost immediately. The whole cost in those days would have been about twenty percent less than what he sold it to Shishido for, so I suppose you could say he didn't take any loss, but on the other hand, considering today's prices, he sold it for a lot less than he could have gotten for it. The real estate agent I talked to thinks Shishido must have put some kind of pressure on the guy."

With Shishido's reputation, Takemura would not have put that past him. Still, he had not profited financially, so why the big hurry to buy and sell the villa? Of course, he might have found himself suddenly strapped for funds just after buying it, though that was not likely. Much more likely was that he had been using Kayo as bait to lure Takeda to Togakushi. He had probably first mentioned the villa to the Ishiharas, and Kayo, for love of Takeda, had jumped at the offer. That was how the love-nest had come into being. The villa had made it possible for Takeda to escape the prying eyes of his secretary Izawa, who might have told Mrs. Takeda. Thus, Takeda had finally agreed to go to Togakushi to help Shishido with the golf course project.

With that as his theory, Takemura paid another visit to Fukami, the head of Investigative Section Two.

"I'd like to ask you about something, just for my information," said Takemura, "but first, I guess you already know that Kisuke Takeda was one of the original sponsors of the Togakushi golf course project, don't you?"

"Oh yes, I know that," replied Fukami. "But I believe we already agreed that his murder doesn't seem to have had anything to do with the project."

"Yes, I know, but what I'd like to ask you is this: if a project like that is carried out, the sponsors stand to profit considerably, don't they?"

"That depends on the circumstances, but in the case of Togakushi, I think you might say that the circumstances would seem quite attractive. What I mean is that most of the land around there is government owned, so whether it's sold off or only leased out, the concessions would be worth an awful lot. That in itself would turn the heads of a lot of entrepreneurs."

"In the selling off of government land, isn't there a strong likelihood of meddling by politicians?"

"Yes, it's possible."

"Like for instance, Hirofumi Shishido?"

"Now hold on there, Takemura! Let's not mention any names! I was only talking generalities."

"Okay, then I'll ask generalities," said Takemura, quickly reminded that he couldn't talk to the head of Section Two as easily as he might chat with a detective in his own section. "Isn't there an awfully good chance that there's a politician somewhere behind the project?"

"Since you put it that way, I can't say that there isn't. But you could only find out for sure by coming up with some likely information," said Fukami, hinting that the answer was affirmative.

"Can we assume that such a politician would try to avoid publicity, perhaps by using a businessman that he could trust as front man?"

"Yes, of course. That's a common way of doing things."

"By the way, I hear it was quite some time after the talk about the golf course got started that Takeda moved in on Togakushi. Do you have any idea why a shrewd fellow like him would have waited so long to get moving?"

"Well, I'll have to admit that bothered me a little, but it's possible he might have considered it some sort of a matter of timing."

Takemura realized that Section Two had not learned of Takeda's aversion to Togakushi. But it seemed evident, at least, that he had been strangely slow to get into the project. Apparently, he had wanted to avoid Togakushi so much that it was not until Shishido waved Kayo in front of him as bait that he reluctantly let himself be lured there. What could it have been that had made him dislike the place so much?

Leaving Section Two, Takemura fell into thought. In addition to Kisuke Takeda, there was Ryuji Ishihara, who had wanted so much to avoid Togakushi that he would not even visit the villa he had taken all the trouble of buying there. Something more than just the scenery of Togakushi must have disagreed with both men. The proof was that they had both ended up murdered as soon as they over-came their aversion to visiting the place. There must have been something in Togakushi that both of them were afraid of.

The Hall of Heavenly Wisdom

天
智
院

"Summer didn't really seem like summer at all this year, did it? It was autumn before a person even turned on an air conditioner," said Fusae Nakayama, as she put the mail down on the table. "My son says the earth is cooling off. He says there's an Ice Age or something coming. I told him that at that rate we'd be having to keep our winter things ready in summertime, and he laughed at me."

Tachibana had been stretched out on the sofa in the living room, absentmindedly gazing out the window, but with Fusae making such a commotion, he decided he might as well get up and look at his mail. Among the routine notices from various academic societies and late-summer greeting cards was a postcard from Yuko Noya, who wrote how happy it had made her mother to meet him, and how disappointed she herself had been to find him gone when she arrived at the hotel looking forward to taking him to Kinasa.

He scrutinized her card with complex feelings. How would she react if she learned she was his granddaughter?

A child of modern times, she might accept it more easily than he thought. But it was not likely that her mother would take it so easily. And Tachibana was not at all sure that he could handle it himself. It was that uncertainty that had made him flee in such a panic, afraid to face mother and daughter.

Flee as he might from Togakushi and Yuko, though, he could not flee from himself. His thoughts of Yuko and Katsura—and beyond them of Taki—were getting stronger every day, depressing him more and more. Guilt tormented him with the feeling that he was the one who had destroyed Taki and driven her to madness. How miserable and lonely she must be! To think that she did not even know she had a daughter still alive and a granddaughter as well gave him unbearable pain.

Should he leave well enough alone, or not? He went over and over that question in his mind, finally deciding that he at least had to see Taki once. He would even settle for a secret glimpse, to avoid giving her the emotional shock that Haru Kusumoto feared. He felt that if he did not get that much, he would never again have any peace of mind.

* * *

On August 17, Takemura and Kinoshita paid another visit to Tachibana. Although the chance meeting in Togakushi had created a certain intimacy, making their preliminaries much less reserved than on their first visit, neither side had forgotten their relationship.

"Well, what can I do for you today?" said Tachibana, smiling, but obviously on guard.

"Actually, I'm afraid we're here about pretty much the same thing again," replied Takemura, somewhat embarrassed. "We asked you last time about Kisuke Takeda, but

then we learned he had married into the Takeda family and
changed his name from Tokuoka. So now we'd like to ask
you whether the name Tokuoka rings a bell."

"Tokuoka?. . . Let's see . . . It does sound vaguely
familiar, but I can't remember just where I've heard it
before."

"He was from the Hoko Shrine village in Togakushi."

"The Hoko Shrine?"

Takemura did not miss the shadow that crossed
Tachibana's face. "You knew him then?"

"I know the Hoko Shrine, of course, but I don't remember whether anybody named Tokuoka lived around it or
not."

"Er, you sound like you must have spent some time
there, Professor. Did you?"

"Oh yes."

"When?"

"A long time ago. 'Way back during the war. Before
either of you were born, I imagine. I spent almost two
years there, recuperating from tuberculosis. Of course,
even before that, when I was a little boy, my family used to
spend the summer there, the way people visit the seashore
nowadays, you know."

"Could you have met Mr. Tokuoka then?"

"I suppose so, but I'm afraid I have no recollection of it.
It was such a long time ago, and besides, I really didn't
have too much to do with the villagers."

"But it seems rather hard to believe that he was having
you investigated, while you say you don't even know him."

"Be that as it may, I still don't remember him," said
Tachibana, with a sour smile.

"Could it be he remembered something you don't?"

"That could very well be. It was rare for the local people
to have anyone from out of town like that. Why, just the

other day, I ran into an old woman there who remembered me. I didn't remember her until she told me her name, but she said she had recognized me immediately."

"Really? Well then, I guess it's quite possible that Mr. Takeda could have remembered your being in Togakushi. And then when he saw you at the party on July 3rd, he recognized you. Sounds reasonable enough up to that point, but I'm damned if I can understand what he did after that. I mean, why in the world would he have wanted to have you investigated?"

"Yes, that certainly is strange, isn't it?"

Takemura could not tell whether he was lying or not.

"By the way, Professor Tachibana, do you know any-thing about a man named Ryuji Ishihara?"

"Oh yes. Wasn't he murdered in Togakushi too? I read about him in the newspaper. I've never been in the habit of reading the crime news and such very carefully, but I have been keeping up with that case. An awfully strange case, isn't it, what with those arrows sticking out of the bodies and all."

"That it is. Not only that, but the bodies were left at a shrine called Arrowstand Hachiman, in a place called West Arrow."

"West Arrow? Arrowstand Hachiman? I say, those are places associated with the Demoness Legend."

"You must know the legend well."

"Oh, that well, anyway. Hah! Maybe the murders are a manifestation of the Curse of the Demoness."

Tachibana's own words gave him a start, reminding him of Haru Kusumoto saying Taki had become a demon-ess. He recovered almost instantly. Though Takemura had not missed it, he had no way of knowing what had caused it.

"So it brings the Curse of the Demoness to your mind,

too, Professor? Actually, some of the local people said the same thing."

"I would imagine so. Togakushi is that kind of place."

"But I'm afraid the police can't write the murders off as a curse," said Takemura, looking as serious as he could. "So I'm terribly sorry about this, but I'm afraid I do have to ask where you were on the night of July 10th."

"What? Me? You want an alibi?"

"No, no. I wouldn't want you to take it so formally as that."

"Still, it isn't something that wouldn't bother a person," rejoined Tachibana, though still smiling.

"So how about it? July 10th," insisted Takemura.

"Well, let's see. July 10th was a Saturday, wasn't it? I believe I stayed home all day. If I remember correctly, it was a sunny day, and awfully hot. I don't usually go out on days like that."

"You didn't go out in the evening either?"

"No, I hate even more to go out at night."

"Were you alone all the time?"

"You mean, is there anyone who can support my alibi? No, I'm afraid not, except for a neighborhood woman who stopped in during the day to do some housekeeping."

"Do you drive?"

"No."

"Okay, thank you. By the way, I started to ask you before, but do you have any recollection of personally ever having had anything to do with Ryuji Ishihara?"

"No, none at all. He was from Nagoya, wasn't he?"

"Yes, but he owned a villa in Togakushi."

"Oh did he? Nevertheless, I'm afraid I really didn't know him."

"Then how about a man named Shishido, Hirofumi Shishido?"

"Has he been murdered too?"

"No."

"Wait a minute! Hirofumi Shishido? Isn't there a member of the Diet by that name?"

"Yes, that's right. That's who I mean. Then you know him?"

"Not me. I hate politicians!"

"Not as a politician. I mean personally."

"Oh. No, that would be even less likely. Why? Does he know me too?"

"Well, he does seem to know something about you."

"Well, well! That's quite an honor! I must be getting famous. But I confess it bewilders me to find myself known by so many people. And if it makes me the target of a police investigation besides, then frankly, it's rather hard to take." For the first time that day, Tachibana frowned.

"I'm terribly sorry. But I can tell you at least that we have no particular reason to suspect you. This is merely a procedural matter."

"I should hope so, because if you do suspect me, I can tell you that you're way off the track. But if you're having to go around talking to people like me, I guess you must be having a pretty hard time with your case."

"You are right about that," said Takemura with a smile, scratching his head. "A case as bad as this one, and we still haven't got the slightest idea who we might be looking for. I'm not kidding! I'm almost ready to believe that it is the Curse of the Demoness!"

"It must be awfully rough on you, having to run around to places as far away as Tokyo and Nagoya."

"No, no, that's part of our job. We don't mind. But I'm sorry to have broken in on you like this, when you're so busy."

That was true, and Tachibana made no attempt at polite

denial. "I guess you must make a lot of visits that prove useless," he said.

"Yes, of course. We just have to be prepared for that."

"How did you do in Togakushi that day we ran into each other there? Did that visit prove useless?"

"Well, pretty much so. We were there to see an old woman who tells fortunes. Mr. Ishihara's wife was one of her followers, so we thought the Ishiharas might have visited her the day they were murdered. But it proved pretty well useless."

"I guess you might have done better to have her tell your own fortunes."

"You said it!" replied Takemura with an unaffected laugh. "Joking aside, though, Detective Kinoshita here thought she was an insolent old hag, but I was downright impressed with her myself. She could read people's minds just like that. The proof is in all the followers she seems to have."

"What is she called?"

"Her place is called the Hall of Heavenly Wisdom."

"Oh yes, I remember. That's the place you were asking directions to. That's quite an elegant name, isn't it?" said Tachibana with an untroubled laugh.

Takemura joined in. Whatever anyone might say, he did not think Tachibana was going to make much of a suspect. He could not help feeling anger at Shishido's perversity and the police authorities who had given in to it.

✳ ✳ ✳

As they emerged from the building, Kinoshita turned and looked up at Tachibana's corner of the third floor. "Do you think he's completely innocent, then?" he asked, with a dissatisfied air.

"Oh yes, he's innocent."

"You seem awfully sure."

"Oh, I can tell that much. Why? Do you see some reason to suspect him?"

"No."

"Well?"

Takemura started out walking briskly. Kinoshita hurried to catch up with him.

Coming toward them along the quiet, narrow residential street was an old man. Looking back and forth between a paper in his hand and the information on the gateposts, he was apparently trying to find someone's house.

"Excuse me, but can you tell me if there's a man named Tachibana living around here?" he asked with a bow when he reached them.

Takemura and Kinoshita glanced at each other.

"Yes, on the top floor of that three-story apartment building over there," answered Takemura, pointing.

The old man, who had an honest face under a head of white hair parted on the side, thanked him with profuse bows and started off.

"He's from Nagano," muttered Takemura, recognizing the accent. "Come on, let's get out of sight for a minute."

He pulled Kinoshita into an alley, from which they peeked around the corner to watch the old man walking on toward the apartment building, stoop-shouldered but briskly.

"What?" exclaimed Takemura, leaning forward. The man passed the building without so much as a change of pace. He could hardly have missed it. He even glanced up at the third floor as he passed. But he just kept on going and turned the next corner.

"What's the matter with him? You pointed right to the place!" said Kinoshita, bewildered, starting to leave the alley. Takemura jerked him back just in time, as the man reappeared, coming toward them again at the same pace. He obviously knew the building was there, but he walked right past the entrance again.

"Uh-oh!" said Takemura, and dashed further into the alley. Though younger, Kinoshita was less agile. He came clumping along behind Takemura, managing to get around the corner at the end of the alley just before the man turned in right where they had been standing.

"He's coming in here!" exclaimed Kinoshita. There was a dead end just ahead of them, making them feel quite like trapped fugitives.

Luckily, the man took only five or six steps into the alley. Soon, his mind apparently made up, he headed out toward the apartment house again. Takemura dashed back to the corner of the alley, reaching it in time to see the man's back disappearing through the entrance.

"He sure took a long time to make up his mind," he said.

"Who do you suppose he is?" asked Kinoshita.

They stood there at the corner of the empty street, motionless as a part of the scenery.

2 Tachibana knew instantly who the old man was. "You're Keijiro's . . ."

"Yes, I'm Keiichi Noya," he replied, making a deep bow.

Keiichi looked so much like his father that Tachibana felt he was seeing Keijiro again. Even the polite manner was the same. When Tachibana commented on the resemblance, the embarrassed Keiichi quickly passed the palm of his hand across his face, another gesture of Keijiro's. Tachibana had to smile.

Clumsily preparing tea for them himself, Tachibana apologized, mentioning his wife's recent death. Keiichi was so embarrassed that he bowed almost with servility.

Their conversation began with polite superficialities, an awkward time passing before either of them managed to get to the point, both being too aware of a past that neither liked to talk about.

"I'm afraid I have a particular reason for imposing on you today," Keiichi finally began, after taking a long time over his tea.

Tachibana instinctively went on guard, but there was no escape.

"It concerns my daughter and granddaughter," said Keiichi, his eyes resolutely fixed on Tachibana, every trace of the geniality of a moment ago gone. "I would prefer that you do not speak to or go near either of them again."

"What do you mean?" said Tachibana, almost losing control. "What reason can you have for that?"

"I think you know the reason, Professor Tachibana."

"Then it's true that Katsura and Yuko are . . ."

"You need not continue," interrupted Keiichi, holding up his rough hands, palms outward. "Neither of them knows a thing about any of it."

"I see," said Tachibana, lowering his head meekly. "I don't know how I can ever thank you enough for what you have done."

"There is no need. It all happened such a long time ago."

"There is just one thing I would like to ask you. Do you mind?"

"No. What about?"

"About Taki."

"Oh, yes. It was a terrible shame about her. She passed away right after the war."

"I'm afraid there's no use trying to hide it. I know she's alive."

"What?" Keiichi's expression darkened, and he took a deep breath. "You do? You know?"

"Actually, I visited the Hoko Shrine shortly after the war, trying to find out about her. I was told then that she was dead, and I gave up all hope. But just recently I found out from a woman who was close to her that she was still alive after all. It was a tremendous shock to me. The woman said that the villagers had agreed among themselves to keep what had happened to Taki a secret."

"That's right. As a matter of fact, it was my mother who asked them to do it. She was dreadfully afraid, even after the war was over, that the military police might come after Taki again. That may sound ridiculous today, but everyone was frightened in those days. Just look what those bastards did to Taki! It drove her insane!"

"Yes, I found out about that, too. But I'm the one who can never be forgiven. It was I who led her into it. I should have died defending her rather than lived on with that shame."

"No, you needn't blame yourself. Taki doesn't blame you. She loves you even now. And my parents wished you well until the day they died. They were very relieved when they learned you had returned safely from the war."

"Then, you mean, they knew I had come back?" said Tachibana, astounded.

"Yes, of course."

"But why didn't they get in touch with me? My family never moved, and your parents must have known our address."

"In hindsight, perhaps they should have. But at the time, it was quite impossible. My mother felt she could not let you see Taki in the condition she was in."

Tachibana was speechless. The attack that night on Taki and himself came back to him afresh. He had never been able to gloss it over. His remorse at not having defended her to the death had colored his whole life. He had spent the forty years since then running away. On the battlefield, he had run from death, but fear of his superiors had caused him to abandon his principles and fire a gun to kill enemy soldiers. Off the battlefield, he had never been able to endure the struggle for position. He had run from all worldly problems. Ever since that night he had fled a situation he had no right to flee, he had found no pride in anything. He had sought the ivory tower of the academic world as a refuge from his sorrow. His self-esteem was so low that he believed he was such a coward as to even feel relief when told that Taki was dead.

"I was demobilized in the spring of 1946," said Keiichi, averting his eyes from the sight of Tachibana's remorse. "My mother was alone in Yashiro, caring for Taki's baby, not yet a year old. My father had died shortly after the war ended. My mother said the police had beaten him horribly and released him a living corpse. Taki's madness was so uncontrollable that my mother and the Kusumotos had had to commit her. That's when my parents had her baby, Katsura, registered as theirs. So the family register makes Katsura my sister, twenty-four years younger than I. Actually, though, I raised her as my daughter. I never told her about you and Taki. Instead, I told her that I was her real father, and her mother was a beautiful woman who died when she was born. I told her that we hadn't had time to be formally married because of the war, and since there was no guarantee either that I would return alive, she had been registered as her grandparents' child, so that she would not be illegitimate in the eyes of the world. I told her she was the gem that had come out of her parents' love . . ."

Here, Keiichi's voice broke slightly, and Tachibana suddenly realized that he, too, must be in love with Taki.

"In 1963, a lot of things happened," continued Keiichi. "That was the year that Taki got out of the hospital, and also the year that her granddaughter Yuko was born, in March. I had told Katsura that when she got out of middle school, I would be happy to send her on to college, but she had insisted that she wanted to stay and help around the house. At the time, I had a small cleaning business near Yashiro Station, and I think she must have known that college would have been a strain on my finances. She was always such a considerate girl. Then, before I knew it, she brought home a boy she said she wanted to marry, a boy she said wanted to be adopted into the family and take the family name. He was the third son of a rich family in the neighborhood, six years older than she. If I wanted to put it vulgarly, I'd say she trapped him, but she knew exactly what she was doing. With the money his family settled on him when he married her, we started the chain of stores we've got now, and gradually expanded into a large-scale operation. Katsura must have been born with the power to see the future. Everything she does works out well. Her husband, Masao, is a fine worker—even if he is something of a social climber. We've expanded into a chain of more than ten stores that stretch all the way from Nagano City to near Ueda. With a high-sounding name, too: Hokushin (Northern Alps) Laundry. Our cleaning plant is in Kawa-nakashima, and . . ."

"Er," Tachibana had been listening intently, but he couldn't wait any longer. "Where is Taki now?"

"Pardon?" Keiichi's expression turned in a flash to one of embarrassment. "You mean you don't know where she is?"

"No. When I heard she had been in a mental hospital, I

checked every one I could find in Nagano. But from what you say, she was released a good twenty years ago, right?"

"Yes, but . . ."

"Then is she living with you now?"

"How could she be? Her daughter and granddaughter don't even know she exists."

"Then where is she?"

"What will you do if I tell you?"

"Go and see her, of course."

"That would not be quite convenient."

"Not convenient!" For the first time since Keiichi's arrival, there was anger in Tachibana's tone. "What do you mean, not convenient? Is my meeting her going to cause you some kind of trouble? All I want to do is apologize for everything I've done to her."

"I understand that very well, but it would not be convenient for you to do that at the moment."

"Is it Taki who doesn't want to see me? Or is it you who don't want her to—because you're in love with her?"

"That's ridiculous!" Keiichi paled, clearly shaken by the direct challenge. "You mistake me badly. Haven't I told you that Taki still loves you? I don't believe her heart has changed or she has grown up at all in the thirty-eight years since you were last together. When she got out of the hospital, she wanted to go right back to the Hoko Shrine. You know why? To wait for you! When I tried to tell her you were dead, she just laughed and said there was no use lying to her. She wanted to go back to the place where her old family home had stood, but unfortunately the land had been sold, so she had to move into a nearby . . ." Keiichi stopped, realizing he had made a slip.

"So she's back in Togakushi?" said Tachibana, excited.

"Well, er, yes, but . . ."

"Living alone?"

"Yes, alone. On rare occasions I make a few house repairs for her, or clean something big, since that's my line, but mostly she does for herself."

"Then she isn't sick anymore, right? She's completely recovered, so I can't see why I shouldn't visit her," said Tachibana with an accusing look.

"No, she isn't really well," Keiichi said hastily, with a wave of the hand. "She may appear calm, but she sometimes says or does things that are not ordinary."

"But that's just her nature. Maybe you don't know, but she's always been like that, ever since she was a little girl. I'm sorry, but unless it's Taki herself who is trying to avoid me, I want to have a look at her just once, at least from a distance."

Keiichi sighed, knowing that continued refusal would be interpreted as being for his own personal reasons. "All right. Since you feel that strongly about it, I won't try to stop you. But I do ask that you not visit her before the beginning of September. In fact, I insist on it."

"I'll agree to that, but why?"

"I'm afraid I can't tell you, but I would greatly appreciate it if you do not go near Togakushi again until then. Do you mind?"

Though Keiichi was being as polite as possible, Tachibana could see he would brook no refusal. Overpowered, Tachibana nodded assent. Only then did Keiichi relax and take another sip of tea, which by now was thoroughly cold.

"Oh, let me make some more hot tea," said Tachibana. "I'm afraid I'm not a very considerate host."

"No, no, that's all right. I've got to be going. But it must be inconvenient for you, living alone like this."

"No, actually, some things are easier. Besides, there's a neighbor who's been taking care of things around the house for me. But I'm afraid I'm not very well equipped to entertain guests. Here you've come all the way from Nagano, and I can't serve you anything but tea. Oh yes, I just had a couple of other visitors—I can't call them guests—from Nagano. Maybe you ran into them outside. A hard-faced pair, they were."

"Why yes, now that you mention it, I did. In fact, I asked them directions to your apartment. But I don't know if I'd call their faces so hard," laughed Keiichi.

"Well, maybe not their faces, but their expressions at least. They were detectives."

"Detectives?" said Keiichi with a bewildered look. "Detectives from Nagano?"

"That's right," replied Tachibana, smiling. "This was the second time they've been here."

"What would detectives be wanting with you?"

"Well, it seems I'm a suspect in a murder case. Those serial murders in Togakushi."

"What?"

"I may not look it," laughed Tachibana, but I'm a dangerous criminal. You'd better not get too close to me. Since you asked them directions to my apartment, they'll be on your tail next, I bet."

"But that's no laughing matter! What possible reason could they have for suspecting you?"

"Apparently, this fellow Takeda who was murdered had employed a detective agency to investigate me. They said his real name was Tokuoka, and his family had lived near the Hoko Shrine a long time ago, when I was there. I don't recall the name, but he must have recognized me. I can't imagine, though, why he would have wanted me investigated."

"You mean the name Tokuoka doesn't mean anything to you?" asked Keiichi curiously, looking hard at Tachibana.

"Not a thing! Good grief! You mean, you suspect me

too?" Tachibana raised his hands in front of his face, as if to hide himself from Keiichi's gaze.

* * *

Emerging from the building, Keiichi took a seemingly casual look around him. Something moved two blocks away in the shade of a telephone pole, but he couldn't tell what it was. Out on the main street, he hailed a cab. After he had gotten in and the cab started moving, he looked back to see two men hailing another cab. Not surprised, he smiled sourly, knowing how suspicious his behavior had been, walking back and forth in front of the building like an infatuated youth.

He got to Ueno Station in plenty of time to catch Asama #11 for Nagano. Buying a luxury-car ticket, he passed through the gate. He did not need to look back to know the two detectives had gone to the ticket window right behind him to ask his destination.

On the train a little way out of Ueno, they came sauntering toward him from the front of the car. He stood up while they were still some distance away.

"Thank you for your directions," he said. "Are you headed for Nagano, too?"

They did a poor job of pretending they were just recognizing him. With nearby passengers eyeing them, they seemed slightly embarrassed.

"Mind if I join you?" said Takemura, sitting down next to him. Flashing his badge, he softly identified himself.

"Police, are you?" said Keiichi, likewise softly.

Takemura smiled pleasantly. "Actually, I'm afraid we've been following you."

"Good heavens! Why?"

"What is your connection with Professor Tachibana?"

"I have none, really. My granddaughter is a student of

his. He's been very kind to her, and I just thought I'd pay him a visit to thank him."

"You mean, you came all the way from Nagano just for that?"

"No, no, that was just incidental. I happened to be in Tokyo for some sightseeing."

"You came to Tokyo today?"

"Yes."

"What train did you take?"

"Uh, let's see. . . . It left Nagano a few minutes after eight, I think."

"Oh, that must have been the next train after the one we took. You must have gotten to Ueno Station at just twelve o'clock."

"Yes, you're right."

"Then did you give up the idea of sightseeing?"

"Pardon?" Keiichi looked dismayed for an instant, then chuckled. "You're on the ball, aren't you? Well, I guess you've got me. I confess, I did come to Tokyo today just to see Professor Tachibana. It's true that my granddaughter is a student of his, a freshman, and I was worried because he's been paying too much attention to her. I went there to warn him. You get all kinds these days, you know."

Takemura recalled the girl he had run into in Togakushi with Tachibana. "You wouldn't by any chance be connected with the Hokushin Laundry, would you?"

This time Keiichi really looked dismayed. "How did you know that?"

"We happened to see your station wagon in Togakushi. There was a young woman driving it, and Professor Tachibana was sitting beside her."

"Hah! That must have been my granddaughter! So she was with him!"

"Yes, but I didn't get the feeling there was anything you need to be worrying about."

"You never can tell."

"Excuse me," said Takemura, picking his time, "but may I ask your name, please?"

"I'm Keiichi Noya, from Yashiro, Koshoku City," said Keiichi. "I own the Hokushin Laundry," he added, rather proudly.

3 "So this is the best you can do, Superintendent? This puny report that you 'can find no substantial basis for suspecting Tomohiro Tachibana'?" said Hirofumi Shishido sarcastically, tapping the report on the desk with his finger.

The man he was addressing as "Superintendent" was Chief Nagakura of the prefectural police. Shishido, just arrived this morning from Tokyo for a visit to his constituency, had dropped in at headquarters without warning. Although the Chief had known Shishido would soon be beginning his reelection campaign, he had hardly expected the first step would be to get the endorsement of the prefectural police, so he was flustered by this untimely visit from an important Diet representative.

"You told me you were putting your best man in charge of the case, Superintendent," continued Shishido, "so I had great expectations for the results. But if this is all you can come up with—well, I don't see how any good citizen can stand for it!"

The use of "Superintendent" instead of the less formal "Chief" was intentional, to put Nagakura in his place as a mere civil servant in a long line of others.

"But Inspector Takemura is one of our most reliable

men," said Nagakura. "The media call him a master detective."

"I don't give a damn what they call him! All I see in the media is that the investigation is going poorly and that they're already referring to it as an unsolved mystery. He doesn't sound so reliable to me! Why don't you replace him, or better yet, get the help of the metropolitan police in Tokyo?"

"The situation has not come to that," said Nagakura, somewhat embarrassed, giving the obvious answer with exaggerated politeness. "Inspector Takemura reached his conclusion after a most thorough investigation, and I can assure you that Tomohiro Tachibana has nothing to do with the case."

"You see what I mean? There must be something wrong with this Takemura fellow! What do you think I am, a crackpot? I have damned good reasons for suspecting Tachibana. I can't tell you what they are right now, but that I should put you onto him and you not be able to pick up a thing—that's totally incredible! There've already been two victims—no, three. You've got to prevent a fourth murder. I'm warning you!"

"Oh? Then you think there's going to be another murder, too, Representative Shishido?"

"Pardon? Well, er, I'm just afraid there might be, that's all. But what do you mean, 'too'? Is there someone else who thinks so?"

"Exactly."

"Well he must be a clever fellow. Who is he?"

"Takemura."

Shishido gave Nagakura a funny look. "What makes him think so?"

"We really don't know. Miyazaki, his superior, says he's just got kind of a sixth sense. By the way, he keeps insisting that he needs to see the person who wants Tachibana investigated."

"You didn't tell him it was . . .?"

"No, of course we didn't tell him it was you. But with his powers of deduction, I would bet he's guessed," said Nagakura, rather sarcastically.

With a sharp glance at him, Shishido got up and went over to the window. He stood looking out at the Zenko Temple, backed by mountains covered with evergreen trees, their green especially fresh at this season. The scene, however, did nothing to calm him. He had his hands clasped behind him and Nagakura could see that his fingers were moving restlessly.

"I suppose I should see him," Shishido finally mumbled.

"I beg your pardon?"

"I said, I guess I should see this Takemura or whatever his name is. Tell him I want a private meeting, with him alone. Let's see . . . why don't we make it at the Moon-Viewing Pavilion?"

Hirofumi Shishido had named the restaurant with the finest cuisine anywhere in the vicinity.

* * *

Inspector Takemura's customary attire was not suited to the formalities of the place. The girl who received him was heard to whisper to her comrades that she had almost taken him for a tramp. With his poorly knotted tie, dark blue trousers with no crease, and wrinkled jacket, it was indeed hard to believe that he was the ace inspector of the powerful prefectural police.

When the bodyguard showed Takemura into the private room, Shishido could not hide a slight frown. The rustic countenance was hardly the bright, talented face that he appreciated.

Takemura remained standing as he introduced himself. Shishido had a cushion placed on the other side of the low Japanese table and invited him to sit down.

"I'm Hirofumi Shishido. Terribly sorry to have dragged you out like this." Shishido was absurdly poor at first meetings such as this one. "Well, how about a drink?"

He nodded to the girl who had brought the saké holders. She picked up Takemura's cup, which had been placed upside down on the table, and offered the saké in a sugary voice.

"No thank you, I'm on duty."

"Oh, I wouldn't worry about that," said Shishido.

"Regulations, I'm afraid. Besides, my wife is expecting me home," said Takemura, flatly refusing.

There was no mistaking Shishido's displeasure.

"But we have a feast prepared for you," said the girl, trying to save the situation.

"Never mind! Leave us alone!" snarled Shishido.

His secretary and bodyguard left with the waitress. Shishido and Takemura were alone in the big room looking out on a garden. Shishido helped himself to several cups of saké, one after another, wondering whether or not he should talk, however briefly, to this low-life.

"Nagakura told me," he finally began, intentionally omitting the chief's title, just to be sure Takemura understood the difference in their social positions, "that you are expecting a third—I mean, a fourth—victim in the Togakushi case."

"That's right, I am."

"On what basis?"

"My intuition, mainly."

"Your intuition?"

"Yes. My intuition just tells me it's going to happen."

With a forced smile, Shishido concealed his indiscreet

desire to explode. "Well, intuition aside, I'd like to hear your reasoning."

"I'm afraid I rely more on my intuition in a case like this," said Takemura reluctantly, "but if I've got to be logical, it's the unusual way the victims were killed. I mean rather, the way their bodies were left on display. If the object had been only to kill them, then why take the time and trouble and risk for the rest of it? I think the displays were a warning to the next victim."

"Hmm. Then the displays must mean something in particular, right?"

"I'm sure they do. Maybe you already know that everything in them has been taken from the legend of the demoness Maple. I'd say the motive for the murders must be some deep grudge connected with the legend itself, or with Togakushi or Kinasa. Unfortunately, we can't put our finger on anything concrete. All we've found out so far is that Kisuke Takeda's original family name was Tokuoka, and he's from the Hoko Shrine village in Togakushi. As for the Ishiharas—especially Mr. Ishihara—we can't find any connection with Togakushi, except that he seems to have had a peculiar dislike for the place. A negative connection, you might say. Oh yes, for that matter, there are indications that Kisuke Takeda disliked Togakushi, too. Pretty strange, since he was born there. I hear he was quite reluctant to get involved in that golf course project. In fact, the information I have is that somebody got him into it only by dangling a certain woman in front of him."

Takemura had been speaking with his impertinent detective's eyes fixed on Shishido. Shishido averted his own eyes in annoyance and looked through the glass doors at the darkness outside.

"That doesn't particularly interest me," he said. "Tell me, just how much of an investigation did you do on

Tomohiro Tachibana before you decided he was inno-cent?"

"We did everything we thought we should."

"That's what Nagakura said. May I ask, you checked for any connection he might have with Togakushi, didn't you?"

"Of course. We learned that he spent some time in the Hoko Shrine village during the war, recuperating from an illness."

"So doesn't that point to a connection with Takeda? Besides, Tachibana was staying at the Koshimizu Plateau Hotel the night Takeda was murdered, right?"

"So you're suggesting that the two of them must have had some kind of fight nearly forty years ago, and Tachibana decided to take that opportunity for revenge?"

"I'm saying it's possible."

"Are you going on any particular knowledge, sir?"

"Hmh? Er, no, of course not. But in view of the murder, it seems like a natural assumption."

"Well, of course, if Tachibana should prove to be the murderer, that might be a good place to look for the motive, but at present, I can only say that we have no reason at all to suspect him. I'm sorry if I sound rude, sir, but your own suspicions do seem quite unusual to me. Are you sure you don't have any concrete basis for them?"

"I told you I didn't! Look, weren't you just talking about intuition? Are you trying to tell me that the intuition of a police officer is something great, but the intuition of a member of the Diet is useless?"

"Of course not," said Takemura, forcing a smile. "With all your experience, sir, I'm sure you must be many times more capable than I. Besides, since you yourself were once a military policeman . . ."

"Where did you hear that?" interrupted Shishido, changing color. "Oh yes, you've been talking to that old Takeda bitch, haven't you? Well let me tell you, if you're trying to threaten me . . ."

"Threaten you, sir?"

"Don't you know what will happen if you raise ghosts like that just before an election?"

"I'm not trying to do anything of the sort."

"You'd damn well better not be! Not for my sake, for your own!"

Diet member and police inspector sat glaring at each other across the table. This time, however, it was Takemura who looked away first.

"All right, sir," he said. "I'll be careful."

"You'd better be! Okay, now that we understand each other, you can get back to work. And see to it that you do a good job!"

"You mean, continue investigating Tachibana?"

"Yes, of course. Without mentioning the reason, I can tell you at least that the man did have quite enough motive for murder. Look, Takeda was killed right after he employed a detective agency to investigate Tachibana. Doesn't that alone make him thoroughly suspicious? Why, in the old days, I'd have had your head for dropping him like you did!" Shishido did a powerful imitation of chopping off a head.

"All right," said Takemura, almost feeling his head fall, "I'll go back and really get down to work again on Tachibana. But you must understand, sir, that I'll have to go wherever the investigation leads me."

"Certainly. But I don't see what that has to do with me."

"For instance, I'll have to ask you what part you played in the purchase of that villa for the Ishiharas."

This Takemura was a hard case. Leaning forward on the arms of his backrest, chest thrown out, Shishido looked at him sharply. "What do you want to stick your nose into that for? Who the hell do you think you're investigating, anyway? If you're not careful, you know, your head really will roll!"

"All right then, would you at least tell me this? How did the connection get started between you, Mr. Takeda, and Ryuji Ishihara?"

"That does it!" Shishido sprang to his feet with a speed that belied his age. Kicking the backrest out of his way, he stormed out of the room yelling, "Hey, we're leaving!" His secretary and bodyguard came running up to protect him front and back.

Takemura, still seated, bowed to Shishido's receding back. As the noise faded from the entryway, one of the waitresses looked into the room.

"Oh, you're alone! Why, it doesn't look like you've touched a thing. Please, you must have a drink!" She sat down, picked up a saké holder, and held out a cup.

"You won't catch me touching his saké!" said Takemura.

"Pardon?" She looked at him in wonder.

＊　＊　＊

The next morning, Hirofumi Shishido paid another visit to prefectural police headquarters.

"I want Takemura off the case," he said bluntly, to Nagakura and his chief of detectives, Tsukamoto.

"You want me to replace Takemura?" The request seemed so absurd that Nagakura had to repeat it for confirmation.

"That's right," scowled Shishido. "He's an ill-mannered son-of-a-bitch."

"Oh?" Nagakura looked with concern at Shishido, then exchanged glances with Tsukamoto. "Was he rude to you?"

"You're damned right! He's got no manners at all. And he obviously has something against our governing party."

"What happened, exactly?"

Shishido moved his eyes restlessly back and forth from end to end of the table in front of him. "Let's just say that he has lost sight of what he's supposed to be investigating."

"I'm not sure I understand. Do you mean that he wouldn't take your suggestion that he further investigate Tachibana?"

"Yes, that's about it. An investigating officer with his obsessions will never solve this case."

"Oh really? I always thought he was quite flexible."

"Then maybe he's taking me for an amateur."

"Oh, I hardly think he could be doing that," said Nagakura, appalled at the realization that he was dealing with a spoiled child, though unsure how serious Shishido was, because the man was so cunning.

But Shishido was totally serious. Annoyed at Nagakura for trying to defend Takemura, he said with an angry glare, "Well? Will you do it or not?"

"Since you feel so strongly about it," said Nagakura, realizing it was a serious ultimatum, "I will of course honor your request."

"Good," said Shishido, straightening up and taking from his inner jacket pocket a folded sheet of paper. "Actually, I'm a little nervous, because of this."

Shishido unfolded the paper on the table for Nagakura and Tsukamoto to see. It contained one line in blue ink, in a poor hand obviously disguised to avoid identification.

"THE GENERAL DIES LAST."

"What is this?" asked Nagakura, staring at Shishido in amazement.

"I don't know. Anyway, there it is, and under the circumstances, it seems natural to take it as a death threat."

"A death threat? Then you think the word 'general' means you?"

"Well, 'general' sounds a little silly, but taken in relation to Takeda and Ishihara, it may be stretching things a little, but I was a low-ranking commissioned officer during the war. That's probably why the murderer uses 'general.'"

"But why use anything at all?"

"Don't you know? In the Demoness Legend, the last person to die is the general."

"Oh?"

"Where are you from?"

"Chiba Prefecture."

"Ah, then I guess you wouldn't know. But I suppose you do know at least that these Togakushi murders have all had something in them to suggest the legend, don't you?"

"Yes, Tsukamoto here told me that. I believe he heard it from Takemura. Is that right?"

"Yes, that's right," replied Tsukamoto.

In disgust, Shishido waved his hand in front of his eyes. "I'm sick and tired of hearing about Takemura! I guess you just haven't got anybody with any talent around here."

"We damned well do!" blurted Tsukamoto, knowing he should have let that pass, but unable to help it.

"Oh, you do? Well, then, I offer my humble apology. With that assurance, I can rest easy that you'll put a good man on the case." Shishido returned Tsukamoto's scowl with a sweet smile.

As soon as Shishido left, Nagakura called in Miyazaki. On hearing the request, Miyazaki became as indignant as if it were his own replacement being requested. Nagakura left the work of persuasion to Tsukamoto, while he himself merely looked on. In the end, Tsukamoto lost his temper and shouted, "Takemura, Takemura, all I ever hear is Takemura! Are you trying to tell me that in the whole damned force, there's nobody with any talent besides Takemura?"

Nagakura was appalled to hear him repeating Shishido's words, while Miyazaki was silent, knowing nothing of what had passed earlier.

Back in his office, Miyazaki called in Takemura right away, and with a transparent smile, offered him a cigarette, saying, "It sounds like you had a rough time of it last night."

"No, it wasn't so bad," replied Takemura. "Why? Have you seen Representative Shishido?"

"No, but I heard about it from the chief," said Miyazaki with an awkward look. Then, stubbing out the cigarette he had just lit, he continued. "It's difficult for me to say this, but I want you to take a little rest."

He stared at the ceiling, with a great frown.

Takemura was not especially surprised. After last night's incident, he had expected something like this. But he wasn't going to take it calmly. "Pressure, is it?" He practically spit the words out.

"Yeah, that's about it."

"Are you going to stand for it?"

"Mhm. Not much I can do about it. It's not just me, of course. A couple of people above me tried to protect you, but there's just no way. We're replacing you, effective immediately, until the situation changes."

"Were you told why he wants me replaced?"

"Why he . . ." Miyazaki stopped, and Takemura could tell he was every bit as enraged as himself.

"What do you mean, 'until the situation changes'? What kind of change are you waiting for?"

"Don't put me on the spot like that. Let's just say, until there's some new development in the investigation."

"Like another murder?"

"We don't need that!" joked Miyazaki, smiling. He had been afraid Takemura would put up more resistance.

"But it isn't normal to replace the officer in charge of a case when not even two months have passed. What are you going to tell the press?"

"That you're sick. That's only for the press, though. As far as I'm concerned, you're working. I guess a week's sick leave should do, and I promise nobody will ask how you spend it." Miyazaki smiled, then added, "For instance, you could go sightseeing in Tokyo, or you could go to recuperate in Togakushi."

Miyazaki was trying to make the best of an unavoidable situation, and perhaps he was succeeding, but Takemura could not accept it, and was badly offended.

Political meddling might be common enough in cases of graft, but in a murder case it was extremely rare. Why had Shishido suspected Tachibana strongly enough to go so far? Takemura could not help but believe that therein must lie the key to the mystery. Exactly who was Tomohiro Tachibana? Takemura was finally beset by doubts. On the surface, he appeared to be just a timid college professor, but could it be that he held some power to rock the political and financial worlds? Takemura was filled with a new interest in Tachibana.

✳ ✳ ✳

Getting off the bus at the top of the steep slope which effectively split the Hoko Shrine village in two, Takemura entered the gift shop right by the bus stop. The shop was simple, but the woman tending it seemed refined. She welcomed him with a pleasant smile.

"Mind if I ask you something?" he said, showing her his badge.

Her expression immediately turned tense. "Yes?"

"Would there be anyone in the neighborhood old enough to remember things here during the war?"

"You mean, the Pacific war?" she asked Takemura dubiously.

"That's right. The Pacific war. Before I was born."

"Same here. My mother might be able to tell you a few things, but I'm afraid she's out at the moment. You could talk to Grandma Kusumoto. She's lived here all her life."

"Oh, that's great. Can you direct me to her house?"

"Right over there," she said, pointing to a building on a slight rise across the road. "The Kusumoto Inn."

Takemura looked over and saw the sign. Thanking her, he quickly crossed the road. In the open space in front of the inn were parked its microbus and three cars probably belonging to guests. Just as he was about to push the doorbell beside the entrance, four boys of college age emerged. One of them turned and shouted inside that there was someone at the door. The boys went on, and shortly after, a woman in her middle or late forties came to the door. Figuring she could not be Grandma Kusumoto, he showed her his badge and asked for the grandmother of the house. Asking him to wait, the woman hurried back inside. After some time, she returned, practically dragging along a reluctant old woman.

"I'm Takemura, prefectural police," he said, automatically raising his voice, because the woman was so old. "I'm sorry to disturb you, but I hear you're familiar with things around here during the war, and I wonder if you'd mind my asking you a few questions?"

"Lower your voice, young man. My ears are fine," she said, not in the least amused.

"Excuse me, but I wonder if I may ask your name?" said Takemura, scratching his head.

"My name is Haru, Haru Kusumoto," she said, and peered at the page in his notebook as he wrote it down. "No, no, I don't write it like that!" She corrected him.

"Okay, so what do you want to ask me about? I'm kind of busy, you know."

The old woman was so snappish that Takemura decided she must have something against the police. She reminded him of Takeda's widow, which led him to wonder if perhaps she too had been a shrew whose parents had had to find a husband for her.

"It's about something that happened a long time ago, probably during the war, I think. Did you know a man named Tachibana who was here from Tokyo?"

"Tachibana?" Her expression changed. "You mean, Viscount Tachibana?"

"Viscount?" It was Takemura's turn to be surprised. "Was Tachibana a viscount? Tomohiro Tachibana, a man of about sixty now?"

"You bet he was! Of course, he was only a boy back then. They called him 'young master.' Uh, what has he done?"

"Not a thing. But there seems to have been some sort of connection between him and a recent murder victim, and we've been going around talking to people, trying to find out about it."

"Well, this is no place to talk," she said, after scrutinizing his face for a while. She invited him in, leading him through a corridor to the left into an empty dining hall in the back which faced north toward the mountainside. Though the windows were closed, it was so cool as to feel almost chilly.

As soon as they had sat down facing each other across a table, she asked with an uneasy look, "Are you talking about the Tokuoka murder?"

"Tokuoka? Oh yes, he was known as Tokuoka around here, wasn't he? Yes, that's right. He had changed his name to Takeda, but that's who I'm talking about."

"And what does Viscount Tachibana have to do with the murder?"

"Nothing, but it's our job as police to investigate everybody." Seeing her relief, Takemura decided she must know something. "Anyway, may I ask you, what exactly was the connection between Professor Tachibana and Mr. Takeda—I mean, Tokuoka?"

"The connection?" There was obviously something she hesitated to say.

"Were they friends, for instance?"

"Hah! Just the opposite!" said Haru violently. "Viscount Tachibana friends with a man like him? Why, that Tokuoka . . ." She spoke as though she could hardly bear to say the name.

"Was there some trouble between them, then?"

With that question, she seemed to decide that she had better be careful what she said. She clamped shut her mouth full of false teeth and looked like she was not going to say another word.

Takemura was up against the stubbornness of age. He changed his approach. "Tokuoka seems to have known quite well who Professor Tachibana was, but the professor says he didn't know Tokuoka. Why would he lie about a thing like that?"

"I don't expect he was lying. If he says he didn't know him, he probably didn't. To the villagers back then, the viscount was someone above the clouds. What reason would he have had to know some kid named Tokuoka?"

"You mean, their social positions were different?"

"That they were!"

"So there couldn't have been any trouble because they didn't even have anything to do with each other, right?"

With a sharp glance at Takemura, Haru Kusumoto clammed up again.

"Okay then, would you just tell me this?" he said. "Where was Tachibana staying at the time?"

"At the Tendohs'."

"The Tendohs'? Where would that be?"

"On the slope. But their house burned down in the great fire the year the war ended. It's not there anymore."

"You mean, they moved?"

"Yes."

"Do you know where they moved to?"

"No."

This time she clammed up for good, obviously anxious for him to leave. Forcing a smile, he thanked her and got up.

Leaving the Kusumoto Inn, Takemura returned to the gift shop to ask directions to the town hall. He was told it was ten minutes by bus back down the road toward Nagano City. The next bus not being due for a while, he strolled up the road toward the shrine.

The Hoko Shrine, the most impressive of the three Togakushi Shrines, perfectly satisfies the condition that a shrine be majestic. Just a glance at the long staircase going up to it was sufficient to impress Takemura with its majesty—and to rid him of any desire whatsoever to climb up to it. Instead, he washed his hands and face with holy water from the trough at the bottom, then bowed in apology toward the top. He knew the gesture was rather silly, but the mood of the place was such that he just felt like doing it.

* * *

The Togakushi Town Hall was located on a stretch of tableland near the southern foot of the Togakushi Mountains, with the school, the post office, the agricultural cooperative and so on clustered around it, the area more or less forming the central part of Togakushi.

Flustered by Takemura's badge, the young woman at the family-register window quickly called over a village official. The official sported a small mustache, which did serve to impress Takemura with the man's officialdom.

"I'd like to ask you about the Tendoh family of the Hoko Shrine village," began Takemura.

"Tendoh? You mean the Tendohs who were Shinto priests?"

"Oh? Were they Shinto priests?"

"Yes, but they aren't there anymore."

"I know. Can you tell me where they've moved to?"

"There's one of them still living midway between the Hoko Shrine and the Middle Shrine, at a place called the Hall of Heavenly Wisdom."

"What? Is that woman's name Tendoh?"

"That's right. Taki Tendoh. She's the last survivor of eight hundred years of Tendohs."

The information was so unexpected that Takemura found himself at a loss for a moment. If that was Taki Tendoh at the Hall of Heavenly Wisdom, he might suddenly have latched on to the thread that would make the intricate connection between people he had not so far been able to connect.

"Has she done something again?" asked the official, looking suddenly worried.

"Oh no . . . well, well, so that shrine maiden was Taki Tendoh. But you say she's the last surviving member of her family? She's pretty old, isn't she?"

"Yes, she was born December 25, 1926."

"Really?" Takemura was once again surprised. "You must have an awfully good memory!"

"No, but that was the first day of the Showa Emperor's reign. You see that birth date once, you aren't likely to forget it."

"Oh really? It was? What a strange coincidence! I've heard the shrine maiden is pretty strange, too."

"Yes, she isn't exactly ordinary," said the official, pointing to his head.

"You mean she has some sort of mental problem?"

"Yes. The story is that she was raped by the military police during the war, and it drove her crazy," whispered the official.

"The military police!" Takemura practically shouted, making the official's whisper useless.

"Sshh, not so loud."

"Oh, I'm sorry!" Takemura apologized meekly. "But what did she have to do with the military police?"

"The family was hiding a college student who was trying to evade the draft. Times being what they were, that must have been an awfully serious offense, which got her into a lot of trouble. But what I'm telling you is rumor, and it happened a long, long time ago. So who knows?"

"But what happened to the rest of the family? Was nobody left?"

"No. She was already an orphan before that. I believe her parents had died a year or so earlier. So she was living with the draft evader and an elderly couple who took care of the house, I think."

"What happened to them?"

"I imagine they're long dead."

"Do you know their names?"

"I'm afraid not. They weren't from around these parts. If you want any more information along those lines, I would suggest you talk to Haru Kusumoto, at the Hoko Shrine."

The official's expression indicated that he assumed the

interview was over. Takemura, however, did not mind. He was already thoroughly satisfied that the hidden background of the case had all just come to the surface.

Leaving the town hall, he sat down on a bench at the bus stop and opened his notebook. This new information about Taki Tendoh at the Hall of Heavenly Wisdom enabled him to connect everyone in a line diagram, with Hirofumi Shishido, Ryuji Ishihara, and Kisuke Takeda on one side, Kayo Ishihara in the middle, and Taki Tendoh and Tomohiro Tachibana on the other side. Then, crossing out the names of the three murder victims, he was left with Hirofumi Shishido on the one side, and Taki Tendoh and Tachibana on the other. With that, it became quite clear why Shishido was so afraid of Tachibana. To him, Tachibana had to be the murderer.

But if Takemura could still trust his own senses, Tachibana was no murderer. On the other hand, the woman at the Hall of Heavenly Wisdom could hardly have brought off such an operation alone. She would have needed an accomplice. Could she and Tachibana be in it together, after all? He shook his head and stood up. The bus for Nagano was coming down the road between the fields of buckwheat, backed by the Togakushi Mountains.

Death of the General

将軍の死

In the open space in front of the entrance to the Koshimizu Plateau Hotel, more than thirty people were lined up in rows, those in front holding a long banner that read, "Oppose Golf Course Construction!" and the rest signs with various other slogans. Low clouds directly overhead threatened a downpour at any moment, but the demonstrators stood there silently, looking every bit as ominous as the sky.

From his hotel window, though, Hirofumi Shishido could hardly read even the large writing on the banner, and there were not enough demonstrators to seem threatening. Nevertheless, he frowned. "Damn! I hate demonstrations like that!" he said, nodding down at the crowd through the window. "They only make me want to win even more."

Quietly enduring Shishido's contempt, Fusao Ochi was sitting on the sofa behind him as he stood at the window. On the table in front of Ochi was a document entitled, "Please Do Not Construct the Golf Course," which Ochi had presented to Shishido and which Shishido had simply flung down on the table.

"Blast it," said Shishido, finally turning around and sitting down deep in the chair facing Ochi, "if you wanted to ask me for something, you shouldn't have brought a mob like that along with you." He leaned his head backward over the back of the chair and glared at Ochi through the lower part of eyes open to slits.

There were two other people in the room, two men named Suzuki and Shirai, who served as both secretaries and bodyguards to Shishido. Both were wearing the same kind of well-tailored dark-blue summer suit, and both were standing there without a word.

"This is the first time the people of Togakushi have ever done anything like this," said Ochi. "That in itself should let you know how strongly they feel."

"Strongly? Look, that's just a handful of people! Most of the people around here are in favor of development."

Ochi, with the objection common among writers to using the same phrase too often, had done his best to reword his attempts at persuasion as frequently as possible. Shishido, on the other hand, well endowed with the audacity, obstinacy, and coerciveness so necessary to a politician, had no such qualms. Filled to overflowing with the kind of confidence that made him care not a fig for such a puny protest, he had used those same words over and over again.

Having found out that the real ringleader behind the golf course proposal was Representative Hirofumi Shishido, Ochi knew he was facing a real crisis. The promoters might already have gotten the government to sell off to private ownership the national forest land Ochi had believed would present an impenetrable wall to developers. Shishido might be right that the situation had already progressed beyond the powers of any protest Ochi could organize to stop it.

"Or perhaps you'd like to have a village referendum or something?" With Ochi's silence, Shishido became even more overbearing. "Then we could really find out which side most of the people are on, couldn't we?"

* * *

The pep rally for Representative Hirofumi Shishido was such a success that the banquet room of the Koshimizu Plateau Hotel was filled to overflowing with Shishido supporters from Nagano City and every other city, town, and village in his constituency. There were far too many overnight guests to be accommodated in the same hotel, and the overflow turned into a boon for the neighboring hotels and inns, whose operators had been somewhat unhappy with the ill effect of such a cool summer on their business.

Many important people were present besides Shishido, and the police had provided a fair number of guards. There was, however, no real trouble—only the tiny demonstration of the golf course protest group, and that broke up before evening. The party took place without incident and ended as scheduled, shortly before 9 P.M. Everyone left except those guests spending the night at the hotel, and quiet returned to the plateau.

In high spirits, Shishido was relaxing in his room over a few drinks with Izawa, who had assumed control of the Takeda Firm. Kisuke Takeda's death had made it even easier for Shishido to exert power over the firm, which served as the main source of his political funds. It was true that Takeda's widow, Sachie, hated him, but she would have employed the devil himself to save the firm. And Izawa made the perfect puppet for Shishido.

They drank until 11 P.M., at which time Izawa left the room along with Shishido's two secretaries.

"Breakfast is at 8:00 tomorrow," said the secretary named Suzuki.

Shishido nodded, shaking hands with Izawa. "You've worked hard," he said. "Things look real good. Well, good night."

"Good night," said Izawa, bowing politely.

Shishido closed the door, and they heard him lock it. Suzuki took the precaution of trying the knob. Then the two secretaries and Izawa said their goodnights outside the door, and went each to his own room.

That was the last time any of them saw Hirofumi Shishido alive.

✳ ✳ ✳

Just before eight the next morning, Suzuki knocked on Shishido's door. There was no answer. He tried the knob. It turned, and the door opened. The living room was empty, so he called into the bedroom, but got no answer from there either. He stood waiting for some time, thinking Shishido might be in the toilet, but he heard no sound. Timidly, he opened the doors to both the toilet and the bath, but both were vacant. Wondering if they could have missed each other, he rushed down to check the second-floor restaurant.

Shirai, the other secretary, was leaning anxiously out of the restaurant door. "What's wrong?" he asked.

"Is he here?"

"What do you mean? Didn't you just go to get him?"

"Yes, but he wasn't in the room."

"He wasn't? That's strange." Shirai looked at his watch. It was nearly 8:30. Guests were emerging from their rooms up and down the hall and coming over to say good morning to the two secretaries. They greeted the guests one after another with gathering impatience.

"Is something the matter?" asked Izawa, coming over to them.

Suzuki told him.

"Just like it," muttered Izawa, immediately worried.

"Just like what?"

"Just like Mr. Takeda's disappearance."

"That's a hell of a thing to say!" said Suzuki, turning pale and getting angry. "The way I heard it, Mr. Takeda had gone out somewhere the night before. The Representative was right there in his own room all night."

"Sorry, you're right. Still, I'm worried. I do think you'd better find him quick."

The lobby was crowded with people, all of them in a big hurry. With everyone wanting to check out right after breakfast, the front desk looked like a battlefield. The departing guests felt bad about leaving without saying goodbye to Representative Shishido, but they were forced to say their respectful farewells instead to his secretaries and ask that their apologies be conveyed. Forced to take Shishido's place in seeing all the guests off, the secretaries could not begin the work of looking for him.

When they finally got hold of the manager and told him the situation, the manager turned white, apparently thinking of the same thing that had occurred to Izawa. But he had to avoid any hint of commotion. At any rate, he decided at least to have a look around Shishido's room.

It was already after nine. Hardly any guests were left in the hotel. Room doors were standing half open, and the women making the beds looked at the group in considerable surprise as it passed.

Shishido's suite looked much as it had the night before when Izawa was there. The saké bottles and cups were still on the table. But when Suzuki went into the bedroom and opened the wardrobe, he exclaimed, "His suit's still here!"

He turned to look at the bed. Shishido's bathrobe was gone. He must have left the room in it.

"Then he must be somewhere in the hotel!" said Shirai, a simple man, with some relief.

"All the same, though, we don't know where he is," said Izawa, "and if he's still in the hotel, then I'd say we have even more to worry about. He may have gotten sick and collapsed somewhere."

"His key's not here," put in the manager.

"But when I went in, the door wasn't locked," said Suzuki. "Why would he take the key and not lock the room?"

"Anyway, let's split up and look around the building," decided Shirai, rushing out of the room ahead of everyone.

Finally the manager summoned the desk clerks, who were no longer busy, and instructed them to search the building on the chance that Representative Shishido had been taken ill and collapsed somewhere inside. Before long, one of them found Shishido's room key on the floor beneath a ladder positioned to reach a small hatch to the roof.

Everyone rushed to the ladder. The desk clerk climbed it and opened the hatch, letting in a breath of fresh air.

"But I hardly think he would have gone out that way," commented someone.

"Then why was his key here?" Shirai lashed out.

"Who knows?" said Izawa bluntly. "Anyway, we have to assume he was here."

"But what could he have been doing?" said the manager, looking around uncomfortably at the others. Nobody had any answer to that.

"And where did he go from here?" Shirai began to shake nervously. They were only wasting time, and nobody knew what to do.

"What was next on his schedule?" asked Izawa.

"A luncheon meeting at twelve in Nagano," replied Suzuki without looking at his memo book.

"That's in less than two hours," said Izawa, glancing at his watch. "I hate to say it again, but this certainly does remind me of Mr. Takeda's disappearance. We weren't able to do anything ourselves then, and I really do think that the sooner we report this to the police, the better."

Suzuki and Shirai looked at each other, unwilling to admit the worst possibility.

"I know Inspector Takemura, who is handling the murders of Mr. Takeda and the Ishiharas," said Izawa. "Why don't we get his advice?"

"No, no, we can't do that!" said Suzuki hastily.

"But it would certainly be better than just calling the police emergency number. He might think of something."

"No. We can't do it."

"Why not?"

"Because he's off the case."

"Off the case? Why?"

"He wouldn't do what the Representative wanted, so the Representative asked that he be replaced."

"Oh? Such a good detective, too," mused Izawa.

* * *

Large numbers of men from several departments were dispatched to Togakushi. Moreover, though the report had just been received, Superintendent Tsukamoto, the chief of detectives, rushed to the scene as well. That was something rare for a mere disappearance, and there was fear it would alert the press. But Chief Nagakura had decided they must assume the worst and take the chance. After all, it was a Diet representative who had disappeared, and the police had to do all they could.

"I suppose Takemura is already on his way?" Tsukamoto asked Miyazaki, who was riding with him.

"No."

"What? How could you not send him?"

"He's on vacation."

"Vacation!" said Tsukamoto, with a look of disgust.

Miyazaki pretended to be enjoying the scenery. After all, it was Tsukamoto who had ordered him to replace Takemura.

"So where is he now?" asked Tsukamoto.

"I'm afraid I don't know. I told him to do whatever he wanted for a week."

"That wasn't very smart."

"I should think it would be even less so to use him in a search for Shishido."

"Only if we were to find Shishido alive."

"What?" exclaimed Miyazaki, turning to look at Tsukamoto. This was the first official prediction he had heard that the representative was dead. "You think he isn't?"

"You ought to know that," said Tsukamoto, turning away with a scowl.

Miyazaki reached for the transmitter microphone.

* * *

As soon as Takemura turned the corner off the main street, he noticed. At the corner of the same alley where he and Kinoshita had concealed themselves to watch Keiichi Noya, there was a man standing in the shade of a telephone pole, watching Tachibana's apartment. Takemura walked straight up behind him, tapped him on the back, and said, "Hey, what are you doing?"

The man jumped and spun around, instantly on guard. "Oh! Inspector!"

"What are you doing in a place like this?" asked Takemura, recognizing him as a detective named Hirayama, from the same section, but on a different team.

"We're staking out Tachibana. Motomura is over there on the other side."

"Oh." Shishido certainly was afraid of Tachibana, thought Takemura, a little bewildered. "Well, do a good job."

"Where are you going, Inspector?"

"To visit Tachibana."

"What?" With a funny look, Hirayama watched Takemura move on.

As Takemura approached the apartment, he caught a glimpse of the other man, in a sport shirt, moving slightly in the distance on the other side of the building. Mischievously, Takemura waved to him.

Tomohiro Tachibana welcomed the Inspector almost like an old friend. Interested in learning how the investigation had developed, he cheerfully began to prepare coffee with a siphon.

"I've been kicked off the case," said Takemura, in the casual tone of polite conversation.

Tachibana turned toward him in surprise, the match he had just used to light the alcohol lamp still burning in his hand. "That doesn't sound very pleasant. Exactly what do you mean?"

"Watch out! The match!" warned Takemura.

Tachibana quickly blew it out. "You mean you've been relieved of your position in charge of the investigation?"

"If that were all, it wouldn't be so bad. No, I mean somebody just had to have his own way. Outside pressure, that is. A certain person found it inconvenient to have me on the case."

"Why, that's outrageous! Who? Some politician?"

"Hirofumi Shishido."

"The Diet representative?"

"That's right. But the strange thing is that he seems terribly worried about you, Professor. He seems to have gotten it into his head that you're the murderer we're looking for, and he's been pressuring the police to investigate you."

"What a nuisance! What's his basis for that kind of slander?"

"He says it's because Kisuke Takeda was having you investigated, but I don't believe that's all, because as soon as I started digging into the connection between Shishido, Takeda, Ishihara, and yourself, I got canned." Takemura managed a smile.

Tachibana did not. "I don't understand," he said, dubiously. "Did you find some scandalous connection that would hurt Shishido if it were known?"

"That," said Takemura, "is why I'm here. I'd like to ask you a few questions along those lines."

"Me? But I don't . . ."

"I don't know whether you know anything or not, but if Shishido won't tell us anything, the only one left to ask is you."

"That's all very well to say, but as I told you before, I know nothing about any of them."

"Are you sure?" Takemura looked deep into Tachibana's eyes.

The look disconcerted Tachibana. "Well, er, Takeda, I mean Tokuoka—I can't say I didn't know him at all, but I've already told you about that. As for Shishido and Ishihara, though, I've never even met them."

"That's strange. From the way Representative Shishido has been behaving, it's pretty hard to believe."

"Look, what are you trying to say? First of all, have you found out how the three of them were connected?"

"Pretty much."

"Oh? I suppose they're all from Togakushi?"

"No, but it was Shishido who introduced Kisuke Tokuoka to the Takeda family, so they must have known each other since the war. I also learned that Shishido and Ryuji Ishihara were in the military police, Nagano division headquarters."

"The military police?" Tachibana caught his breath.

"How about it? Does anything come back to you now?"

Tachibana was silent.

"I already know what happened to the young master, son of Viscount Tachibana," pressed Takemura, but Tachibana remained speechless with surprise, which Takemura was quite sure was genuine. "Then you really didn't know?"

"So help me, I didn't. Then Shishido was one of those military policemen?" The fierce anger suppressed in Tachibana's tone came through. "That such a man should not only go unpunished, but even become a brazen political power. . . . What do you think of that, Inspector?"

Takemura could only remain silent.

"Ah yes, you're on the side that has to protect people like that. Too bad." Suddenly it came to Tachibana. "Oh! So that's who Tokuoka was!"

"Pardon? You remember him?"

"Oh yes, I do remember him. He must have been the informer. Yes, I believe I saw him once or twice in the Tendoh garden. But he had changed so much that I never would have recognized him. So that's who he was!"

"I see. So Takeda informed on you. Then the motive becomes clear, doesn't it?"

"The motive? Oh, you mean the motive for murder! It does indeed! They were my mortal enemies. I believe if I had had the courage and the strength, I would have done it. Unfortunately, I didn't. Of course, I'm sure the police must already know quite well that it would have been physically impossible for me to have done it, right? Callous of me, but if it were within my power, I would at least thank the person who wielded the devil-quelling sword in my place."

"I don't think you would have been able to do it by yourself, anyway, Professor. But you probably weren't the only one with a motive."

"Oh?"

"Isn't there someone else, who would want revenge even more than you do?"

Tachibana was silent.

"Why did you conceal the matter of the Hall of Heavenly Wisdom, Professor?"

"The Hall of Heavenly Wisdom?"

"Surprised, are you? Don't try to tell me you didn't know about that either."

"What are you talking about? What about the Hall of Heavenly Wisdom?"

It was Takemura's turn to be surprised. "Then you really didn't know? You're on the level? The Hall of Heavenly Wisdom is Taki Tendoh's place."

"Taki's place?" Tachibana stared at him, pupils dilated, wondering why he hadn't realized it before. The Chinese character for "heavenly" was the first character in Taki's family name, and the character for "wisdom" was the first character in his own given name! He was greatly stirred at the depth of her feeling for him revealed in the name she had given her home.

Keiichi Noya had told him that her heart had ceased to change or mature from that time on, her feelings never taking a step away from the Togakushi of that day at the end of 1944. She had simply been waiting all this time. Just waiting, thought Tachibana. But waiting for what? With a shiver, he remembered Haru Kusumoto's words that Taki had become a demoness, recalling at the same time the terrible wild dance of the Demoness Maple in the Noh drama.

The loud ring of the telephone brought him back. The caller was a woman whose voice he did not know. She asked for Takemura.

"It's for you," he told Takemura. "Your wife, I guess."

"My wife?" Takemura took the receiver with foreboding. He had told Yoko not to let anyone know where he was, and she would not be calling him herself unless there were some extreme emergency.

It was Yoko. "Oh good, you're there," she said. "Will you hang up and wait just a minute? You'll be getting a call from your boss."

In a moment, he was listening to Miyazaki telling him tensely about Shishido, before ordering him in a hoarse, subdued voice to get back to Nagano as fast as he could. After Miyazaki hung up, Takemura stood there for a while, the receiver still pressed to his ear.

"What's wrong?" asked Tachibana, concerned.

"Something quite serious," said Takemura, and he meant not only the probable death of Hirofumi Shishido, but also the loss of an important clue to the case.

"What?" asked Tachibana.

"Representative Shishido has disappeared."

"Disappeared? Like Takeda?"

Both detective and professor were upset, each for his own reasons.

"Professor Tachibana, please tell me just one thing. There was an elderly couple taking care of the Tendoh house when you were attacked by the military police. What were their names?"

"Oh, that was Keijiro and his wife. Mr. and Mrs. Noya."

"What?" exclaimed Takemura, looking at him sharply.

With a gasp, Tachibana realized the implications. For a moment, both men remained frozen. Then Takemura excused himself, got up slowly and departed, leaving Tachibana sitting there.

Outside again, Takemura beckoned to the detectives on the stake-out. With looks of displeasure, they came over to him.

"Tell me, how long have you been watching Tachibana?" asked Takemura.

"Since yesterday," replied one of them.

"I don't suppose he's gone anywhere, has he?

"No."

"Then you can stop watching him. Why don't we go back together?"

"Huh?" The two men looked at each other.

"It looks like the big boss who had you sent here is dead," said Takemura, walking off at a brisk pace.

* * *

For a while after the Inspector left, Tachibana remained slumped in his chair, incapable of motion, choked by the fear that something terrible was happening. Again he heard the voice of Keiichi Noya, telling him not to go near Togakushi until September.

September began tomorrow.

2 Bessho Hot Springs of Nagano Prefecture has a history so long that legend has it it was first used by the god Yamato-Takeru on the first emperor's Eastern Expedition. In any case, the evidence that it has been used for a very long time is indisputable. On the southwestern edge of the Ueda Basin, it is reached in about half an hour by a rustic two-car train from Ueda Station on the JR Shin'etsu Line. Just below the station, the Aizome River flows from the confluence of two tributaries, and the road from Ueda forks to follow both of them. Both forks are lined with hot-spring inns and souvenir shops. The surrounding mountainsides are dotted with so many old temples that the place is called the Kamakura of the Japan Alps.

Bessho is most famous for the Kitamuki Kuan-yin Temple, on whose grounds is the Aizome cinnamon tree. It is known also, however, for another historic site: the burial mound of General Taira no Koremochi. After winning fame by subduing the Demoness of Togakushi, the General spent his last days here and is buried in a pyramid-shaped mound covered with ancient cherry trees, on a plot of ground contained in the V formed by the fork of the road from Ueda.

At about 6:30 on the morning of September 1st, an elderly couple taking the hot-spring cure were passing the General's Mound on a stroll. Almost everyone in the rows of inns being still asleep, there were few cars on the street, and no other pedestrians. Steam rising from the many hot springs dissolved quickly in the morning air, and it was so quiet that they were aware of the sound of their wooden clogs.

They paused in front of the sign giving the history of the mound, the elderly husband beginning to read it aloud for the benefit of his wife. Suddenly, he stopped, having seen an old man in a bathrobe collapsed across the exposed roots of a cherry tree, in a position suggesting he had tripped while walking from the side of the road onto the mound. Going up to him, the elderly couple realized he was dead. It was easy to imagine that he had had a stroke or a heart attack and died on the spot. Since he was wearing a bathrobe, they assumed he had been a guest at one of the inns. That was too close to home for them.

They flagged down a passing car and explained the situation. In a short while, two patrolmen from the police station in the center of town reached the scene. Neither of them had been around long enough to be accustomed to handling dead bodies, otherwise they would have known at a glance that the man had been dead for some time.

The site being practically at the entrance to town, it would not do to leave the body on display for long. Throwing a sheet over it, they waited for the doctor and the morgue squad, who were far from speedy in arriving. When the doctor did finally get there, he judged that the man had been dead for twenty-four hours or more, and moreover that there were indications of death by poisoning.

That meant trouble. The body could not have lain there unnoticed for twenty-four hours. It must have been left there. But until they could identify it, they were forced to assume it must be that of a guest at Bessho Hot Springs.

With the first report from the local police to the prefectural police, however, Bessho Hot Springs became the scene of more excitement than had probably been witnessed there since the time of the god Yamato-Takeru. The local assistant inspector found himself talking to the head of Investigative Section One, Miyazaki himself.

"Then you haven't identified the body yet?" Miyazaki confirmed.

"That's right. Not yet."

"And he was about sixty years old?"

"Yes, about that."

"And I'll bet he was wearing a bathrobe, wasn't he?"

"Yes, but how did you know?"

"Never mind. Just get the area roped off right now. Then don't touch a thing until we get there."

"But it's right beside the road."

"I don't care. Set up a detour."

The assistant inspector didn't know what was up, but he had the area blockaded with the greatest precautions his little force was capable of. Since it was right beside a well-traveled public road, they had their hands full just controlling curious passersby. They could not have begun any kind of investigation even had they not been warned not to.

The emergency vehicles following one after another nearly stopped ordinary traffic along the highway from Nagano City to Ueda. From Chief Detective Tsukamoto on down, most of the people in Investigative Section One and in the investigative task force were mobilized. Several tens of cars, both police and private, all rushed to the scene at almost the same time, followed quickly by cars of the mass media, which had been all ready to go ever since the news of Representative Shishido's disappearance.

The focus of all the confusion and excitement, like the eye of a typhoon, was strangely quiet. The General's Mound itself, though slightly more melancholy than usual, was as calm as ever.

Shortly after nine, several men approached the eye of the typhoon. They stopped at the edge of the road while the local police chief left the group, went up to the body, and lifted the corner of the white vinyl sheet from the dead man's face.

"That's him, isn't it?" said Tsukamoto softly.

"Yes, it's him all right," confirmed Takemura. The man from whom he had parted at odds just the other day was lying there, a lifeless mass. The miserable corpse of Hirofumi Shishido, former military-police lieutenant and member of the lower house of the Diet, was on display at the General's Mound.

About twenty minutes later, Chief Nagakura arrived, together with all the heads of the various relevant departments. Before long, Shishido's family, secretaries, close associates, and others with various and sundry connections began to gather. The tiny hot-springs resort was buried under half the people of the Nagano Basin.

The site was inspected with particularly scrupulous care by police well aware that the eyes of the media were upon them. The assumption was that the murderer had come by car, stopped beside the road, and concealed by the car itself, pulled the body out and sent it sprawling onto the General's Mound. Whoever did it had apparently not set foot on the mound at all, and so had left no footprints or any other traces.

Hirofumi Shishido's body was rushed to the University Hospital in Nagano City for autopsy. Family members and associates departed the scene almost at the same time as the body, leaving behind police, reporters, and countless spectators.

Chief Nagakura held a press conference, assuring the media that the prefectural police would make every effort to solve the heinous crime. Although he was showered with questions concerning the connection between this murder and the murders of Kisuke Takeda and the Ishiharas, he avoided giving definite answers.

The death of Hirofumi Shishido made waves incomparably greater than those made by any of the previous deaths. Although Kisuke Takeda had been an important man, he had nevertheless been no more than a local power in Nagano. Shishido, on the other hand, had been not only a respected member of the National Diet but also the leader of an important faction, with a good chance of eventually becoming the head of his party. There had only been one murder ever of an active member of the Diet, long long ago. Conjectures and surmises were flying everywhere, as the mass media tried to find something to use as background.

The first thing most reporters thought of was the recent suicide of an important Diet Representative in Hokkaido, and that made them suspect that something was being concealed for political purposes. To make matters worse, it was clear that Shishido had been murdered, which gave considerable support to the surmise that someone must have wanted him removed for political reasons.

The police, of course, could not afford to ignore that possibility. Using extra staff to make sure they did not miss anything, they made a list of all of Shishido's political opponents, both in his own party and others, and began to check out everyone on the list. They started an investigation as well of Shishido's secretaries, support organizations, business enterprises associated with him in any way, and so on—every person or group which offered the remotest possibility of providing something to go on. Even if they were doing it merely for show, they at least made an excellent start.

The real investigation, however, was taking place in Miyazaki's Section One, because it was believed that the key to the case would be the explanation of how the murder and disposal of the body were actually carried out. Chief Detective Tsukamoto himself was put in charge of a special team and given everything he needed to deal with the case.

Still, it looked unsolvable. Hirofumi Shishido was supposed to have gone to bed in his suite on the third floor of the Koshimizu Plateau Hotel in Togakushi at about 11 P.M. on the night of August 30. This was confirmed by two of Shishido's secretaries and the present de facto head of the Takeda Firm, Izawa. Yet, two days later, on September 1st, Shishido had been found dead at Bessho Hot Springs outside Ueda City, about fifty kilometers away. How to explain the thirty hours and fifty kilometers between when he was last seen alive and when he was found dead?

A little after three, most of the police finally left Bessho Hot Springs and headed for Togakushi. Tsukamoto had Miyazaki and Takemura ride with him in his own car, having quite forgotten shouting at Miyazaki about whether the Nagano prefectural police didn't have any other capable investigating officer besides Takemura.

Driving along, they kept receiving one report after another on the radio from headquarters. Cause of death was cyanide poisoning. Estimated time of death was within two or three hours either way of 2 A.M. the morning of August 31, in other words, within three or four hours of the time Shishido's secretaries and Izawa left him after drinks in Shishido's room following the party. The more details they got, the more they were reminded of Kisuke Takeda's disappearance.

"Even so," said Tsukamoto with a heavy sigh, turning to Miyazaki in the seat next to him, "where in blazes could Shishido have gone? It defies common sense to think he would have left the hotel alone in his bathrobe in the middle of the night."

"It certainly does," acknowledged Miyazaki promptly. "From what we learned yesterday, Shishido was left with his room locked. And then, poof, this man who was supposed to have been asleep in a locked room is gone the next morning. The morning after that, his body is found far away at Bessho—and in a bathrobe, besides. It sure is a mystery."

"I know it's a mystery!" snapped Tsukamoto. "Haven't you gotten any farther than that?"

"Well, I've sure been thinking about it, but it's a pretty difficult problem," said Miyazaki, rubbing his chin. A man who somehow gave the impression of calmness in tense situations, he was always more nervous than he looked. Actually, he was a typical middle-level administrator. If such a man got his job done without any serious errors, it was because he was blessed with men of ability as his subordinates. And Miyazaki was blessed with Takemura. All he needed now was the endurance to hold out against the nagging of superiors and the clamoring of the media until Takemura came up with the brilliant solution to the case.

"How about it, Takemura?" asked Tsukamoto, redirecting his question. "How would you explain Shishido's being found in a bathrobe? Where the devil could he have been going dressed like that?"

"I don't believe he was going anywhere," snapped Takemura, a little annoyed at having his train of thought broken.

Ignoring the tone of the answer, Tsukamoto jumped on the content. "What do you mean you don't believe he was going anywhere?"

"Well, it stands to reason that a Diet representative wouldn't go out in his nightclothes."

"That's true, isn't it?" agreed Miyazaki immediately, earning himself a look of displeasure from Tsukamoto.

"But that's just the problem," said Tsukamoto. "That he did go out. Right?"

"No, not necessarily," said Takemura. "All we know for sure is that his body was found at Bessho. That's no proof at all that he went out of his own accord."

"I see. In other words, you're suggesting that he was taken forcibly from the hotel?"

"Well, I really can't say. I'll have to see the hotel again before I can be sure, but from the way that place is built, I wouldn't think it would be too easy to get somebody out like that. At least the hotel that Kim Dae-jung was kidnapped from had an elevator."

"I don't follow you. If he didn't go out of his own accord and he wasn't kidnapped, then how in the hell did he get out of the hotel?"

"I mean he was taken out already dead, of course."

To Takemura that might be a matter of course, but not to Tsukamoto. "What?" he exclaimed. "Are you trying to tell me that the murderer killed Shishido in the hotel room and then went to all the trouble of taking out the body?"

"That's what I think."

"Why would anybody have done a ridiculous thing like that?"

"Why not? Some pretty ridiculous things were done in the Takeda and Ishihara murders."

"Yeah, I suppose so. But look, what if that really was what the killer wanted to do? How could he have done it? Physically, I mean. Didn't you just say it would be hard to get even a living person out of there?"

"A living person, yes, but dead ones don't resist. Actually, the possibility first occurred to me when Takeda was murdered, but I suspect it even more strongly now."

"Stop right there!" yelled Tsukamoto.

The driver hit the brake.

"No, no, not you! I was talking to them," said Tsukamoto quickly, with a sigh of disgust. "Now you've lost me completely. You mean you suspect that Takeda, too, was killed in his room and then his body was taken out?"

"Yes, but this is still nothing but hypothesis. I can't say any more until we get to the hotel."

"Oh, I don't see why we need to wait that long! It's all pretty clear to me. The desk clerk stated that Takeda never returned to the hotel that night, and if he didn't return to the hotel, how could his body have been taken out of it?"

"I should be able to answer that after we get to the hotel," replied Takemura, a bit annoyed. Something else was bothering him now. Looking back, he saw Kinoshita and Yoshii following in their car a little way behind. "Could you stop the car a minute, please?"

The driver did so. Takemura got out, flagged down Kinoshita, whispered something in his ear, and quickly got in again. As they entered Nagano City, Kinoshita turned off.

"Where's he going?" asked Tsukamoto, still meddling.

"Tokyo," said Takemura.

Tsukamoto wanted to ask why, of course, but finally managed to suppress his curiosity.

They passed prefectural police headquarters without stopping and went straight on toward Togakushi, because Takemura was anxious to have a look at the hotel as soon as possible. About the time they got onto the Birdline, the sky began to look threatening. Thick clouds were spreading out from the Togakushi Mountains, and the wind was picking up. The first drops of rain hit the windshield as they passed through the Hoko Shrine village. Then, before they knew it, they were in the midst of a torrential thunderstorm.

Takano, the hotel manager, looked ready to cry at the sight of more police. This had to be the worst summer of his life. Suzuki, Shishido's secretary, who had been awaiting the police at the hotel, greeted Takemura with an inscrutable look. The death had occurred just after his boss had asked that Takemura be removed from the case, and he could not help thinking that it might have been different otherwise.

Takano led the group to the room in question, telling them it had been left just as it was found the morning Shishido disappeared. Takemura headed for the bedroom, checking the floor carefully as he went. The rest of the group stood in the doorway, watching him at work. Before long, he stuck his head out of the bedroom and called for Inspector Kojima of CID.

"Have a look at this, will you?" requested Takemura, pointing to the pillow in a white pillowcase on the bed. "This little stain. What do you suppose it is?"

There was, sure enough, a circular stain about three centimeters in diameter, though so pale that anyone not looking very carefully would certainly have missed it.

"What stain?" said Kojima. "It's probably just saliva."

"Could you have it analyzed for me?"

"Sure." Kojima sent one of his men off to the laboratory with the pillow.

Next Takemura called the manager over. "I suppose this shirt had been sent out for cleaning?" he asked, pointing to a white shirt on the bed.

"That's right. Representative Shishido had asked us to have it cleaned the night before, and it was delivered here the next morning."

"But he was already gone then, right?"

"Yes. The boy brought the shirt to his room at 7:30, but when he knocked on the door there was no answer, so he had to bring it back to the office. He was going to wait for the representative to call and ask for it, but then we had all the excitement. After it was over, he brought the shirt back here and left it."

"I see. So that's it!" said Takemura, pleased.

"Did you figure something out?" asked Tsukamoto.

"Yes. Now I know why he was wearing a bathrobe."

"Oh? Why?"

"Because he had sent his white dress shirt to the laundry, and how can you be dressed in a suit with no shirt?"

"So what?" said Tsukamoto, wondering if Takemura was in his right mind. "That's only common sense."

"Yes, it certainly is—if you know about it. Well, well, well, so he didn't have a white shirt!"

Tsukamoto looked at Miyazaki. Was this the great detective, the pride of Section One? Miyazaki shook his head. He didn't know.

Leaving the room, they went to the ladder leading to the roof, beneath which the key had been found on the morning of Shishido's disappearance. Takano and Suzuki took turns describing the circumstances.

"It was a desk clerk who discovered the key?" asked Takemura.

"That's right," answered Takano.

"The same one who was on when Mr. Takeda disappeared? Aihara, I believe his name was?"

"No. It was a man named Mizuno."

"I imagine you were all surprised by the discovery?"

"Oh yes, very. I was down on the first floor myself, and I forgot my age so far as to run up the steps three at a time."

"Then I guess it's safe to say that nearly everyone in the hotel gathered right here?"

"I think so. All of us were looking for Representative Shishido. Besides, most of the guests had left."

"I see," said Takemura. He pointed to the hatch above

the ladder. "If you go out onto the roof that way, can you get down to the ground?"

"With a rope, I suppose, but it's quite some distance, so I hardly think it would be easy."

"Difficult, then, but possible?"

"Yes, I'd say so, but . . ."

"Inspector Kojima, I hate to trouble you, but could you please check the roof and the windows of all the rooms for traces of a rope or something?"

Kojima directed his men to do so.

Takemura went back and examined the third floor all the way from Shishido's suite to the stairs, creeping along with nose to the ground. The rest of the group looked on quietly enough, but even so, he was disgusted with the crowd, which he could see out of the corner of his eye. It was all very well for Tsukamoto to be so enthusiastic about his work, but he moved with such an entourage that he looked like the head of a hospital making his rounds.

Takemura went down the stairs to the first floor and along the corridor beside the office, which led past rooms for live-in help, a laundry room, and a storage area, to a door which led outside.

"I presume this door is locked at night?" he said.

"Yes, of course," said Takano.

"Where is the key kept?"

"In a bunch with other keys, usually in the office, but sometimes at the front desk or in the night-watch room."

Takemura asked to see the bunch. It contained keys to all the hotel entrances and exits as well as all the guest rooms. There were extras for everything in the safe at the front desk and in the manager's home.

"Would you mind if I borrow the keys to all doors that lead outside, and the key to the suite for a little while?" he requested.

"I guess not," said Takano, easily selecting four keys from the bunch and handing them to him.

Placing the keys on his handkerchief, Takemura examined them carefully, then handed them to Inspector Kojima, asking that they be checked to see if a wax impression had been taken of any of them.

"I think that's about it for now," he said finally, seeing by his watch that it was after 6 P.M. "Why don't we have some supper while we wait?"

At Takemura's suggestion, they all went into the restaurant. Guessing that most of them had probably gone without much lunch, the hotel staff was kind enough to prepare them a good supper.

"Well, Takemura, you seem to have figured something out, right?" said Tsukamoto, disinclined to eat.

"If you'll wait just a little longer, an hour or so," said Takemura, "it should all become clear."

As Takemura had predicted, around 7:30, Inspector Kojima was summoned to the telephone. He came back to the table looking excited and whispered a word in Takemura's ear. "So I was right," said Takemura, with a nod.

"What is it? What's up?" asked Tsukamoto, impatient.

Takemura waited for a hotel employee to move away from their table before replying softly, "The stain on that pillow tested positive for cyanide."

Tsukamoto looked at Miyazaki, then asked Takemura, "Then does that mean you were right about Shishido being killed in the room?"

"It looks like it. It's just too bad I didn't think of that after Takeda's murder, until it was too late. I should have had his room examined more thoroughly. I do believe he must have been killed the same way."

"I can't for the life of me see how you can believe Takeda

was killed in his room when he didn't even return to the hotel."

"I'm not at all sure he didn't. Why don't we perform a little experiment?" said Takemura, standing up and inviting Tsukamoto and Miyazaki to come with him down to the front desk on the first floor. On duty were the clerk named Aihara he had spoken to at the time of Takeda's disappearance, and another man.

"Would you mind doing me a favor?" Takemura asked them. "For the next five minutes, I'd like you to watch television on that set back there in the office. Watch it carefully, because when you're finished, I want you to tell me everything you've seen."

The puzzled clerks went somewhat reluctantly into the office behind the partition and turned on the television. As soon as Takemura was sure they were concentrating on the screen, he went out through the front doors, stayed outside for a moment or so, then came back in, walked right past the front desk and up the stairs, turned around and came down again.

When the five minutes were up and the clerks came out of the office, he asked if they had seen the guest who walked by the desk while they were watching television. Neither of them had seen a thing.

Takemura turned to Tsukamoto. "Here's what I think happened. July 3rd was a Saturday, and that's when the two-hour program "The Mystery" comes on, at 9 P.M. Mr. Aihara here likes that program, and I remember he told me he thought that night's mystery was an especially good one. So it would not have been strange at all if Mr. Takeda had returned to the hotel during the program without Mr. Aihara seeing him."

"Hmm. No, I suppose not."

"Actually, that possibility occurred to me at the time,

but I still had the preconceived notion that the killer could have had no reason to get a dead body out of the hotel, so I didn't consider it too seriously. It wasn't until after the Ishiharas were murdered that I realized we were dealing with an abnormal killer, and I couldn't assume normal reasoning. And now, this. The killer must have been set on getting the body out of the hotel at any cost. My guess is that this murder was the last, so I'm not sure why he needed to do that, but I'm beginning to think that his real purpose may not have been merely—as I had believed—to send a message to the next victim. In other words, maybe he had a deeper reason for . . ."

"Hold on a minute!" Tsukamoto almost screamed. "This is all too much for me! I'm not following you at all. Would you mind going back and putting that in a little better order?"

"All right," sighed Takemura. But just then he was called to the phone.

It was Kinoshita, from Tokyo. "I'm in Professor Tachibana's apartment," he said. "The professor isn't here, but as I stood waiting in front of the door a while, his maid arrived. She says he left this morning on a trip."

"Oh really? Where?"

"Nagano."

"What?" Now he'd done it, thought Takemura, biting his lip. He had flippantly told the men watching Tachibana to go home, just when he could have used them.

3 Tachibana asked to be let out a little way past the Hoko Shrine Village.

"You mean right here?" asked the driver. It was the middle of nowhere. To the left was the forested peak of the Hoko Shrine and to the right, a stand of cedar. There was not even a side road.

"Yes," said Tachibana. "I just need a little walk."

There was no room to turn around, so after Tachibana got out, the taxi had to continue for a hundred meters or so to the entrance to the Hall of Heavenly Wisdom. Conscious of the driver's eyes as he passed on his way back, Tachibana went through the motions of exercising his arms as he walked slowly along.

Reaching the break in the cedars where the taxi had made its turn, he saw the small sign with the words "Hall of Heavenly Wisdom," practically buried in the tall grass beside the road. He stood in front of it hesitating, almost turned back, and then finally headed down the little wagon trail. Weeds grew rampant along both sides, and their rank odor assailed his nose. They had invaded the road itself as well, where they had been pressed down into two tire tracks. The bare earth visible at occasional spots in the tracks testified to the considerable number of cars that passed back and forth along them.

But the cottage that the track led him to could not by any stretch of politeness be called very nice, with the weeds growing out of its thatched roof, its soot-blackened eaves, and its crumbling walls. Seeing it, he shrank at the thought of the ghastly life that Taki must be leading.

In the open space in front of the cottage were two cars, parked as if waiting in line, their engines off, their windows and doors all open. In each of them, a man and a woman were just sitting. Fully exposed to the sun, the cars must have been terribly hot inside, but the people couldn't use their coolers because they didn't want to make noise with their engines. Sensing Tachibana's approach, they all turned his way, obviously on guard against anyone cutting in front of them.

Tachibana went up to the car closest to him and asked, in a virtual whisper, "Are you waiting in line?"

"Yeah, we sure are," answered the man. The middle-aged couple appeared to be husband and wife.

"Will you have to wait long?"

"Who knows? She hasn't even opened the door. We've been waiting more than an hour ourselves, so I imagine the people in front of us must have been waiting for a couple of hours at least."

"Do you always have to wait so long?"

"Yes, when there are a lot of people in front of us, but this is the first time she just hasn't opened the door, so I don't know what's going on."

"Could she be out?"

"No, I don't think so. We saw some smoke a little while ago. I think she must be eating. Maybe that's what's taking so long. Still . . . you from Tokyo?"

"Yes."

"Thought so. Terrible, isn't it? So are we. She makes me come here with her," he said, indicating the woman with his thumb.

"Do you come often?"

"Once or twice a month. No getting out of it. My wife won't let me make any business decisions without the oracle of this Hall of Heavenly Wisdom. This your first time?"

"Yes."

"You look like an intellectual. I guess you guys have got your troubles, too. I'll tell you though, this shrine maiden does make some pretty good hits. But you know," he said, lowering his voice and pointing to his head, "she's kind of funny here."

"Cut it out!" scolded his wife. The man chuckled.

"Er, does she live alone?" asked Tachibana.

"Seems to. We heard at one of the inns that she has hardly anything to do with the villagers, and if anybody so much as comes by to make sure she's all right, they get shouted at. Of course, she does such a good business that the tax collector can't just leave her alone. Trouble is, she doesn't know herself how much money she makes. She's got a tangerine crate or something in the corner where people make donations before they leave, and I hear she lets the tax collector check from time to time to see how much is in it and decide how much tax she's got to pay."

"I wonder how she takes care of herself? Housekeeping and all."

"Oh, they say the village tradesmen see to that. Her rice is delivered, her laundry's taken out, and so on."

Tachibana thought of Keiichi Noya and the Hokushin Laundry station wagon.

Another car pulled up, carefully observing Tachibana's place in line. The driver apparently knew the man Tachibana had been talking to, because he got out and went over to say hello.

"We left around dawn, but we sure made lousy time. There was one hell of a traffic jam around Ueda. Took us two hours just to get through the city. You spend the night?"

"Yeah, in Nagano. But you see how much good it did us."

"No, I'd say that was the best thing to do. That was a really terrible tie-up. They say some Diet representative or other was murdered in Bessho. Cops all over the damn place."

So it had been done, thought Tachibana, his knees going weak. He was numbed by the thought that it was all over now. The MP officer who had shoved the rifle into his mouth that fatal night was dead. Revenge or punishment, Taki Tendoh and Keiichi Noya had achieved their goal. Forty years had not sufficed to wash away their grudge. Tachibana felt small and beaten. They had given everything, while he had lived the cowardly life of the puny little person he was. He tottered away from the cars to the shade of a locust tree beside a brook. How could he face her now—he who had not shown her one ten-thousandth of Keiichi Noya's devotion?

Sensing movement among the people behind him, he turned around. The first couple was approaching the cottage door, and there were words of greeting as a woman dressed like a shrine maiden appeared there. He tensed up, hardly aware that he was trying to conceal himself against the trunk of the tree. She stepped out from under the eaves into the sunlight, and he was surprised to see that she was wearing the Noh mask that represented a beautiful woman. The mask with its hint of a smile, along with the white robe over scarlet pantaloons, should have had a comical effect, but somehow it didn't. In fact, it lent her a sort of majesty, testified to by the unconscious retreat of her customers with each step she advanced.

She looked up at the sky, muttered a word or two, and disappeared back inside. The first couple humbly followed her in. Apparently they were going to get their fortunes told after all.

It was a good thirty minutes before they emerged, shoulders drooping. They must have been told of some misfortune to come. Getting into their car, they sat sunk in thought for a while before slowly starting off. After sympathetically watching them go, the second couple entered the cottage. Just afterwards, a third car pulled up.

In another thirty minutes or so, the second couple came

out, looking very happy. The husband was kind enough to call to Tachibana that it was his turn. Tachibana waved thanks, but called back that he would pass.

He could not bring himself to leave, though. Instead, he remained loitering under the locust tree. Around three, the sun began to be hidden behind clouds moving in faster and faster across the sky. Around four, the last customers left. By this time the clouds were quite thick, and the wind was picking up. Above his head, the large branches began to sway, and his skin told him that the temperature was dropping. A squall was on its way.

He became more and more agitated, torn between the desire to leave without seeing her and continue his life as it was, and the fear that if he did so he would never have another chance to see her again. And then he would have to live the rest of his life with the deep remorse of never having been able to do a single thing for her.

He felt a drop of rain strike his cheek. The squall was coming from the mountains to the west. There was a terrific flash of lightning, followed immediately by a peal of thunder, apparently from directly overhead. Drops began to fall faster and the intervals between streaks of lightning shortened. He had no choice but to run for cover under the eaves of the cottage.

The wind was now so strong that sometimes it blew the raindrops horizontally. The predominant wind blew from behind the cottage, so not much rain got under the eaves in front, but even so, it was falling as dense as fog, and he was already soaked. The temperature was steadily dropping, and he was beginning to shiver.

"You out there, come inside," said a woman's voice from behind the wooden door he was leaning against.

He trembled all over, no longer from the cold. Whether the voice was Taki's or not, it seemed to come from somewhere deep beneath the earth, filling him with a nameless fear. He hesitated, then slowly put his hand on the knob and opened the door.

Though at first it was too dark inside to make much out, to his momentary relief at least, he could tell that the shrine maiden was not standing right there. Eyes adjusting to the darkness, he saw that the cottage was quite unfurnished, and the only light came from a small window beside him, dimly illuminating a wooden floor a step up from the earthen entryway. In a corner of the entryway was a tiny washstand into which water, probably from a spring, was trickling through a bamboo pipe. A strange but vaguely familiar odor came to his nostrils.

Across the room he made out a wooden door that looked quite heavy, and he guessed that the shrine maiden was beyond it. He still entertained the slightest of doubts as to her identity, and he half hoped she wasn't Taki after all. Sitting down on the step with hushed breath, he persuaded himself that she had asked him to come in out of the rain simply because she had felt sorry for him. Inside, he could still hear the thunder, but the violent sound of the blowing rain was somewhat muted.

"Come in here," came the woman's voice from beyond the door.

He jumped, feeling her irresistible force. Taking off his soaked shoes, he crossed the room like a murderer going to his execution. Except when he pulled open the heavy wooden door, he did not feel he was using his own power.

It was even darker beyond the door, the only light coming from a sacred taper and cedar sticks burning on two altars, but they dimly illuminated the shrine maiden. He stepped into the room, closed the door behind him, and sat down on the crude straw matting which covered the floor.

At first he kept his eyes lowered, but after he calmed down, he raised them and looked directly at her. Still wearing the Noh mask, she threw some sort of dried grass into the fire on the cedar-stick altar which stood between them. With a sputter, the grass sent up a column of smoke like that from a smudge pot, the smoke at the top of the column quickly dispersing. This was the source of the odor he had been smelling.

She didn't speak, and he couldn't tell whether she was looking at him from behind the mask.

"Are you Taki?" he asked, unable to bear it any longer. He could not see her expression for the mask, but neither could he see any other sign of reaction. "You are Taki Tendoh, aren't you?" he pressed. But she remained silent. Her silence could be interpreted in so many ways that it threw him into confusion.

When she had put all the dried grass she had onto the fire, she picked up an earthen teapot and teacup beside her, poured a cup of what looked like some kind of unrefined saké, and held it out to him to drink. Taking it and raising it to his lips, he could tell the liquid was definitely alcoholic. Without knowing what was in it, he unhesitatingly gulped it down, sending a cold feeling through his empty stomach.

After a time, the air became so dense with smoke that the shrine maiden, though right in front of him, appeared hazy. But the smoke did not bother him in the least. Rather, he felt as though he were enjoying a superb cigar.

All at once, he began to feel himself part of a limitless universe through which he could roam at will, freed of all doubts, fears and inhibitions, his whole being overflowing with a rich, expansive feeling and a mood of exaltation that made him want to laugh for joy.

Slowly, the shrine maiden removed her mask.

"Taki!" he cried, overcome with emotion. Before his eyes was his radiantly beautiful Taki Tendoh. "It's me! Tomohiro!"

"Tomohiro!" She stood up, quivering and swaying.

He stood too, nearly forty years erased from his being. Tachibana the youth embraced and kissed Taki the maiden. The heady fragrance of a young girl tingled in his nostrils.

After a while, she gently pulled away, took his hand and led him to the back of the room, where she opened a door to the left of the second altar. There was a light behind it, and he realized he was looking at their secret room of so long ago. Though dizzy, he followed her into it without question.

On the soft bedding, they embraced again and lay there entwined, Taki overcome with shyness as Tachibana buried his face in the nape of her neck, his lips roving over it. With a presage of supreme bliss, he sank into a world of dreams and visions.

✳ ✳ ✳

Tachibana crawled desperately up out of the darkness, head, arms and legs as heavy as lead, feeling like a squirming, wriggling slug.

Seeming somehow to have made it to the surface, into the burning brightness, he raised himself on both arms. Little by little, the feel of the crude straw matting under his palms reminded him of the world of reality. In front of him was the cedar-stick altar. Beyond it, on the second altar, the sacred taper was burning with a faint sputter, almost consumed.

Taki was not there.

He got up, went over to the altar, took out a new candle and lit it with the old one. Then he slowly pulled open the wooden door to the left of the altar. In a corner of the dark little bedroom, the crude bedding was piled up. There was, of course, no one there.

He no longer knew which was reality and which was a dream. Awake, he found it too ridiculous even to imagine that his beautiful Taki had really been there and that he had behaved as he did with her. But the memory of their embrace was strangely vivid.

Taking the candle, he went out into the front room. The sun had set and he had only the light of the candle to guide him. One step into the room, he saw a woman's face at his feet. It was the Noh mask Taki had been wearing. Its chin was pointing toward him, and from the angle of his gaze, the mask that was supposed to represent a woman smiling seemed to be crying instead. He winced.

There was a white envelope beside the mask, addressed to him. Picking it up and turning it over, he saw that it was from Keiichi Noya. Still holding the candle, he anxiously tried to open it. Suppressing a cry of pain as a drop of melted wax fell on the back of his hand, he looked down, saw the deep wrinkles there, and felt his age all the more keenly.

> Professor Tachibana,
> Having seen the look of supreme happiness on Taki's face, I no longer know whether I was correct or not in keeping you away from her for so long. I sincerely believe that my motives in doing so were, for one thing, the wish to preserve her tranquillity, and for another, the wish to keep you from seeing the pitiful state she was in. I am ashamed to admit, however, that you may also have been right when you said that I harbored certain feelings for her myself.
> When Taki went mad, the people of the village said she had become a demoness. When I first heard of that, I was indignant, but later I realized that it was not really slander, but rather the expression of a kind of fear.

The truth was that she really had become a demoness. I believe that the only feelings she had were her devotion to you and her vicious hatred of the men who had done what they did to you. Though her illness eventually seemed to abate, and I finally had her released from the hospital, I do not think anything had really changed at all.

At the end of May this year, when I came as usual to do a few things for her, I found her in a state of unusual agitation. "The enemy is coming," she told me. It seems that in the course of her conversation with a woman named Kayo Ishihara, who had come to have her fortune told, Taki had figured out that the man named Kisuke Takeda with whom the woman was involved was actually the Kisuke Tokuoka who had informed on you.

"Revenge is mine!" she said. I did try to dissuade her, but she was determined. I am sure that if I had refused to help, she would have tried to accomplish the task herself. You have seen the upshot: I gave in and began planning the deed.

Two main conditions had to be satisfied. First, of course, it had to be done in such a way that no suspicion would fall upon either of us. Second, the villains had to know why they were being killed.

We planned carefully before killing Kisuke Takeda, but the second opportunity for revenge came so quickly that we had no time to plan. On the night of July 10th, when I stopped to see Taki, I found the Ishiharas asleep in this room. I had no idea who they were until she astonished me with the information that this Ryuji Ishihara happened to be one of the hated military policemen. Before we poisoned them, I threatened Ishihara into telling me the name of the other. Imagine my surprise when I learned it was Hirofumi Shishido! I was a member of one of his support groups. What irony!

Now that we have completed our revenge, I find myself filled with a great feeling of satisfaction, not at all with the emptiness I was afraid I would feel. Seeing Taki's happiness, I feel that I have accomplished what I was living for.

Now, though, I have no wish to live much longer, not because I can feel the firm hand of the law reaching out for me, but rather because I can see no further point to life. Besides, Taki is even more ready for death than I, and I must confess I could expect no greater happiness than to be with her at the end.

My only regret is for Katsura and Yuko. Needless to say, they know nothing at all of Taki's existence, let alone of what she and I have done. I pray that parent and daughter will be able to go on living in peace. I humbly beg you will oblige me by offering them the benefit of your advice and counsel.

By the time you awaken, Taki and I will probably have crossed West Peak and be wandering in the direction of Mount Takatsuma through the primeval forests of the Togakushi Mountains. Outside, the storm continues, and we could not have a better opportunity to begin our journey to the next world. I earnestly beg you to let us go quietly, without trying to alert anyone.

Please burn this letter as soon as you have read it, and do me the honor of telling the police simply that Taki and I have committed suicide together for love.

One more thing: Taki tells me that the Noh mask was her favorite, used in the Maple-Viewing play by Maple before she turns into a demoness. She wanted to take it along, but at my humble request, she has left it here for you to keep as a memento of her former self and her feelings for you.

With this, I bid you farewell.

—Keiichi Noya

Finishing the letter, Tachibana was overcome by the feeling that in the end, his love for Taki had not equaled Keiichi's. Tachibana had loved only Taki the beautiful woman, but Keiichi had loved Taki the demoness as well.

It was Taki's understanding of the one-sidedness of Tachibana's love that had made her hide her aged face behind the mask until he had entered the world of illusions. He punished himself with that thought.

As Keiichi's letter burned on the cedar-stick altar, Tachibana looked at the Noh mask and cried Taki's name, begging her forgiveness with copious, uncontrollable tears.

4 Early on the morning of September 2nd, Takemura led a squad of men to the Hall of Heavenly Wisdom in Togakushi. Another squad headed for the home of Keiichi Noya in Yashiro. Neither squad was carrying a warrant, the case being still at the stage of voluntary submission to search and questioning, but since there was some fear of an attempt at escape, a number of men were assigned to each squad.

Both squads, however, struck out. The Hall of Heavenly Wisdom had been vacated, and the only people at home at the Noya house were Keiichi's daughter and her family, who said they had neither seen nor heard from Keiichi since he left the house at 5 P.M. the day before in his Hokushin Laundry station wagon.

Too late, thought Takemura, looking up at the sky. He should have moved the night before. He would not have caught Keiichi Noya at home, but he might at least have been able to stop him and Taki Tendoh at the Hall of Heavenly Wisdom. In truth, however, he had not insisted on going out immediately because he had not really expected them to move so quickly, especially in the storm that had been raging.

He headed straight from the Hall of Heavenly Wisdom to the Koshimizu Plateau Hotel, where he found still quite a few guests in spite of all the trouble and the hotel's having been requested to keep vacant the whole third floor, on which was the suite in question. CID had spent until late the night before carefully examining the premises, with results about as Takemura expected. He had come now to present his view of the case at a ten o'clock conference this morning, which even Chief Nagakura was scheduled to attend.

Before the conference, he asked to see the woman who collected the sheets and robes from vacated rooms. He needed to check on just one more point that bothered him. Looking into the room he was directed to, he saw a stout, robust woman of about fifty.

"Good morning!" she greeted him, loud and amiable.

"Good morning!" said Takemura, forcing himself to sound amiable in return. "Do you do this every day?"

"You bet! Every day!"

"But the last couple of times I was here, I saw another lady doing it. Once at the beginning of July, and then just the other day, August 30th."

"Oh yes, those two days I was asked to let somebody take my place."

"You were asked, you say? By whom?"

"By the boss."

"You mean by the owner of the hotel?"

"No, by my boss at the Hokushin Laundry."

"Ah, Mr. Noya?"

"Oh, you know him?"

"Well, I . . . Then, are the women who work here dispatched from Mr. Noya's company?"

"Dispatched? That's a pretty big word. No, I wouldn't call it that. They're from the village, and besides, they only help out during busy seasons. It's almost autumn, and they'll be off now until the winter ski season begins."

"I see. By the way, do you know who it was that took your place?"

"No, I'm afraid not."

When the woman had finished making up the room, she put the dirty sheets, robes, towels, and so on into the pushcart with the big bag and proceeded to the next room, looking a little annoyed to see Takemura following her.

* * *

Arriving with his entourage a little behind schedule, Chief Nagakura was surrounded by reporters making a terrific commotion. In the entourage, Takemura saw two men he did not recognize. Both looked in their mid-thirties, and neither looked especially important, but Takemura had the instinctive feeling that he had better not drop his guard with either.

The reporters greeted the news that they would not be permitted to enter the hotel with considerable booing, as they retreated to the shade of the gift shop canopies across the street. The day's fierce sunlight belied the storm of the night before.

Spotting Takemura, Miyazaki came over and said, "We missed them, huh? I guess we should have listened to you last night."

"No, I think it would already have been too late," said Takemura, comforting his embarrassed superior. The night before, Takemura had suggested they go after Keiichi Noya and Taki Tendoh right away, but Miyazaki and Tsukamoto had together urged caution.

"Maybe so," said Miyazaki. "Anyway, their having run proves their guilt, right?"

"I suppose so, but I'm just going on theory, and I'm afraid we're going to have a hard time proving anything without them."

"Well, it's probably only a matter of time until we get them. We'll put out a nationwide APB today."

"Will you? Well, it would be nice if we found them," said Takemura, dejected.

"What do you mean, if? You think we may not?"

"I'd rather not think about it, but if I've got the right picture of our murderers, then I don't think we're going to find them alive, at least."

"No?" Miyazaki's eyes widened. "Then you're sure they're the murderers?"

"Well, aren't they? Didn't you just say so yourself?"

"What? Oh, I guess I did. But I'm not as sure as you seem to be. It is a pretty wild story, you know, and I'm not the only one who thinks so. Superintendent Tsukamoto only half believes it. He says he told Chief Nagakura about it this morning, but who knows what the chief will say?" It sounded like Miyazaki was waiting to come down on the same side of the fence as the chief.

The hotel had offered the use of its restaurant for the meeting, arranging the tables in conference-room style. Once inside, Takemura was surprised to discover that he was the only person present of the rank of inspector or below.

Nagakura himself introduced Takemura to the two men he had not recognized. One of them, thin and nervous, was an official of the National Police Agency named Miyamoto. The other, a rather corpulent, affable-looking gentleman, was a Mr. Ishida of the Investigative Committee of the Cabinet. Takemura had never met anyone of such high position before, nor had he heard of any other detective handling crimes of violence who had. He didn't even know what they did. He had heard rumors it was the same sort of thing as the American CIA, but he didn't know what truth was in them. Anyway, since the murder victim was a Diet member, he assumed their job included that, at least.

"Mr. Ishida is here to represent the government," said Nagakura. "When he heard what a detailed view you have of the case, he insisted on hearing it firsthand."

"By 'case,' do you mean only Representative Shishido's murder?" asked Takemura.

"I must confess that is our primary interest," said Ishida, leaning forward. "But I'm told, Inspector Takemura, that you view his murder as inseparable from the others, and have been operating on that assumption. So I'm ready to hear about the whole thing."

"Thank you," said Takemura, and immediately began his presentation. "The case begins with the disappearance of Kisuke Takeda from this hotel on July 3rd. He had arrived here around 2 P.M. that afternoon, and after attending a meeting which began at 3 P.M., retired to his room a little after six on the pretext that he wasn't feeling well. He was last seen leaving the hotel alone, shortly before seven. Four days later, on July 7th, his body was found at a place known as Poison Plain in the Arakura Campground near the village of Imai in Togakushi.

"Our subsequent investigation makes it almost certain that he went from the hotel to a nearby villa owned by Ryuji Ishihara. At the villa that night was Ishihara's wife, Kayo, with whom Takeda was having an affair. Now, his actions from this point on have been our biggest riddle, but according to testimony from an occupant of the villa next door, sometime between 10 P.M. and 11 P.M. that evening a car left the Ishihara villa and returned five or six minutes later. Common sense would tell us that must have been Kayo taking Takeda back to the hotel, but the fact is that the desk clerk did not see him come in, and nothing was heard of him until his body was found four days later, at which time he had been dead for three or four days. Cause of death was poisoning.

"We went on the assumption that Takeda had left the villa and been driven back to the hotel by Kayo late on the evening of the 3rd, been taken captive by someone between the car and the hotel entrance and subsequently poisoned, his body being left on Poison Plain on the 7th.

"There were two important points to be considered. First, how was he taken captive? And second, how and why was his body left on Poison Plain? Now, since discovery of the body, we had been proceeding on the assumption that he had been taken captive before being murdered. I did have some doubts as to the validity of that assumption, but we continued to base our investigation on it, until the murder of Representative Shishido, which convinced me that it was mistaken.

"If Kayo drove Takeda back to the hotel, it is hardly likely she would have dropped him off very far from the entrance. There is reason to believe that he wanted to keep his affair with her a secret from his secretary, Izawa, so she might have dropped him off a short distance away, but still, ten or twenty meters would have been enough. If he had been attacked by someone on his way in, his shouts of struggle or cries for help would have been heard by her or by someone in the hotel. Moreover, when his body was found, there were no external injuries that would have indicated such a struggle.

"Now, here's what I think happened. I think Takeda did, in fact, return to his room in the hotel, and was killed there after taking a bath and getting into bed. To tell you the truth, until the murder of Representative Shishido, I was hung up on the preconceived notion that nobody would have tried something so ridiculous, which is why I couldn't rid myself of the kidnap theory. But if we assume that Takeda was murdered in the hotel, then we no longer have to force everything to fit the unnatural theory that he was kidnapped."

"That may be true," interrupted Ishida, gesturing with his hand, "but now you've got a theory that means the body had to be gotten out of the hotel, and that seems even more dangerous and unnatural, wouldn't you say?"

"It sure does," said Tsukamoto, seeing the opportunity to express his hearty agreement. "That's the first thing that bothers me about it."

"I don't think so," said Takemura, unperturbed. "This way the murderers would have had plenty of time to refine their plan and develop confidence in it. Actually, it enabled them to commit the perfect crime. Besides, they had the added purpose of sending someone a warning, and for that, they needed the body."

"To send someone a warning?" Ishida frowned.

"Exactly. By putting the poisoned body on display on Poison Plain, they made their intention clear. I didn't realize it at the time, of course, but putting it together with the subsequent murders of Mr. and Mrs. Ishihara, it became obvious."

"I see. But before you go on to the Ishihara murders, would you mind explaining just how Takeda was killed and how his body was gotten out of the hotel?"

"I'm afraid we'll never know the exact details of that unless we get to ask the murderers, but we can deduce at least that they must have secretly gotten into his room in the middle of the night and forced the poison down his throat while he was asleep—a comparatively simple method."

"So you mean they had a key to his room?"

"That's right, they did. I believe they must have had a

key to one of the outside doors as well. In other words, they were people in a position to get hold of the keys—one more reason why they had to get the body out of the hotel. After all, who would ever believe that anyone would kill someone in the hotel and then try to carry the body out? It would be much more natural to assume that Takeda had been murdered after leaving the hotel of his own accord. Also, they even had a bit of good luck when he just happened not to be seen re-entering the hotel that night."

"So the only question is, how did they get the body out, right?" asked Ishida, looking thoroughly interested now.

Takemura smiled faintly and nodded. "We have not found any conclusive evidence that the murderers did get into the hotel from outside. But at around 2 A.M.—the estimated time of death—the halls would have been mostly deserted, allowing them to move freely until they got to Takeda's room. If they saw someone in time, they could conceal themselves before being seen. If not, they could pass as hotel guests.

"They could not afford to be seen carrying the body, though. There might not have been much chance of that, but they had to make absolutely sure it did not happen. They most likely did not expect any hotel employees in the halls at that time of night, but they had no guarantee that they might not run into a guest, what with vending machines located at the end of the hallway on each floor and the possibility of a thirsty guest coming out of his room to buy something in the middle of the night. The minimum condition they had to satisfy was that any guest they did happen to meet should not become suspicious. And for that problem, they had the perfect solution.

"As soon as I figured out how they had done it, I knew who we were looking for. But it wasn't until much later, I mean, until after the murder of Representative Shishido, that I did finally figure it out. Permit me, therefore, to discuss his murder before I do those of the Ishiharas.

"Now, we may assume that the murderers intended to use just the same method to kill Representative Shishido that they had used for Takeda. Only this time, something big went wrong: Representative Shishido sent his white dress shirt out for overnight cleaning before he retired. That was totally unexpected, a contingency they had failed to provide for, and a circumstance that has been extremely significant in enabling me to identify them. Until I found out about it, I had been considering the possibility that the murderers were people who worked for the hotel. From this circumstance, though, I realized they must be people from outside, but ones who knew the hotel well and had the opportunity to copy keys. That erased all my doubts about who they were.

"But leaving that aside for a moment, the missing shirt must have presented a dilemma to the murderers. They must not have discovered it was missing until after they had killed Representative Shishido and started to dress the body. They couldn't leave the body in the hotel, so they had to take it out dressed in the hotel robe."

"I see, I see," said Ishida, rubbing his hands together with glee. "And now you're going to tell us how they got the body out, right?"

"As for that," said Takemura, wetting his lips, "during the night, they put the body into the big bag on the laundry cart, and put the cart in the storage room at the west end of the hallway. With the body wrapped up in a sheet and covered by other dirty sheets, they wouldn't have had to worry about anybody noticing it, even if someone passed right by the cart.

"Incidentally, since the suite used by both Takeda and Representative Shishido is on the third floor, the murderers had to use the service elevator to get the cart out. That elevator makes a lot of noise, though, so it wouldn't do to start it up in the middle of the night. Instead, they came back in the morning looking perfectly innocent, put the cart on the elevator, went down to the first floor, dumped the body, sheets and all, into the laundry's station wagon, and drove away with it.

"Two people would have been needed for the operation, one to drive the car, and the other, someone who could go around collecting laundry in the hotel without arousing suspicion. A woman working at the hotel for the laundry would have been perfect. And in fact, I learned from hotel employees yesterday that on the day before and the day of the disappearances of both Takeda and Shishido, they saw a quite elderly cleaning woman they had never seen before arriving at the hotel in the laundry's station wagon. Also, I just spoke to another cleaning woman, who told me that before each of those days, she was asked by the laundry owner, Keiichi Noya, to take the day off."

"I see," said Ishida. "So it seems certain, then, that the murderers were people from the laundry, right? But I hear that this morning a squad was sent to some place called the Hall of Heavenly Wisdom. Who were you after there?"

"An old woman named Taki Tendoh, who lives there alone and tells fortunes. She has quite a following. I believe she is our principal instigator. Since we failed to get her today, I'm afraid I can't back up what I'm telling you, but from what I've learned so far, she does have a definite motive for the murders. I'm convinced also that she was the woman who posed as an employee of the laundry and had a direct part in carrying out the murders."

"Hmm," said Ishida, leaning forward, totally absorbed. "So you're saying that this old woman, Taki Tendoh, is the main killer, and Keiichi Noya is her accomplice. All right, that leaves the question of motive. What was her reason for murder—and four murders, at that?"

"At this point, we can only conjecture about the details. We do know, however, that at the hands of three of the four victims—Kisuke Takeda, Ryuji Ishihara, and Hirofumi Shishido—she had suffered considerable physical and emotional torment. I can only believe that her motive was revenge. To learn any more, though, we would have to get a confession from Taki Tendoh herself, or barring that, information from a Professor Tomohiro Tachibana in Tokyo."

"Tachibana?" interrupted Ishida. "You don't mean Tomohiro Tachibana of T— University?"

"Why yes. Do you know him?"

"As a matter of fact, I do. But what could an ivory-tower scholar like him have to do with all this?"

"I'm just getting to that."

"Oh, I'm sorry. Please, go on."

"I sent a man to Tokyo yesterday to see him, but Tachibana had just left on a trip to Nagano. I had hopes he might be coming here to see us, but it doesn't look like he was. So for the time being, let me tell you about the facts I've picked up so far, and the deductions I've made from them. Before I do so, though, it will be necessary for me to discuss the unusual nature of the murders.

"First, Takeda's body was not disposed of until the fourth day after his death, when it was already in a considerably decomposed condition. I can think of no other reason for that delay than the killers' determination to display the poisoned body on Poison Plain.

"Then, with the next two murders, the maniacal nature of the first one really became clear. The bodies of the Ishiharas were left at the Arrowstand Hachiman Shrine in the village of West Arrow—with arrows stuck in them. The

Ishiharas had visited the Hall of Heavenly Wisdom on July 10th, and were poisoned there, I believe. The reason for their visit was that Ishihara had accused his wife of carrying on an affair with Takeda in Togakushi, while she maintained that the purpose of her trips there was to go to the Hall of Heavenly Wisdom. His insistence on going there with her to check out her story led them into a trap.

"I took the abnormal display of the first three bodies to mean that someone was committing a series of murders for revenge, and wanted to be sure the next victim in the series knew it. As a matter of fact, Representative Shishido did receive a threatening letter, which seemed to me at the time to frighten him somewhat excessively. But his death proved that his fear had not been ungrounded. And this time, the murderers went to the elaborate trouble of hauling the body fifty kilometers to the General's Mound in Bessho Hot Springs."

As Takemura paused for breath, Ishida interrupted once more. "Then does that mean we can expect the murders to continue?"

"No, I don't think so, because the threatening letter said that the general would die last."

"I see. But if that's the case, why did they need to go to all that trouble with the body?"

"Only the murderers themselves know that for sure, but as I mentioned before, one reason was probably to throw the police off the track by getting the body out of the hotel. Another may have been a macabre sort of aesthetic sense of completeness. Perhaps you already know that the manner of each display had something to do with episodes in the legend of the Demoness Maple. Well, the General's Mound is the grave of one protagonist of the legend, Taira no Koremochi. The killers likened Representative Shishido to General Taira, so they probably wanted to leave his body in a fitting place. You see, during the war, Representative Shishido was in the military police, and . . ."

"Just a moment," interrupted Ishida softly. "So your investigation has taken you that far, has it, Inspector Takemura?"

Takemura looked at Ishida, wondering what the matter was. Ishida threw inquiring glances, first at Nagakura, then at Tsukamoto, both of whom looked awkward and remained silent. Miyazaki looked vacant, as if he had heard nothing.

Finally, Ishida seemed to have made up his mind. Turning back to Takemura, he said, "Okay. Go on, please."

"Is there some kind of problem?" asked Takemura, with an inadvertent touch of reproach.

"As a matter of fact, it is an awfully delicate matter, what with the prospect of the lower house of the Diet being dissolved and a general election coming up. A lot of people have got a lot to say about it. But anyway, you go ahead, please. I believe you were saying that Representative Shishido was a first-lieutenant in the military police during the war."

Takemura smiled ruefully. He had not mentioned Shishido's rank. "To continue, then, that fact has an integral bearing on the case, made even more clear by the fact that Ishihara was once Shishido's subordinate. The story goes way back to the end of 1944, at which time a draft-evading student was hiding in the Tendoh house, whose occupants were hereditary priests of the Hoko Shrine. The student was Tomohiro Tachibana. The people sheltering him were Taki Tendoh and an elderly couple of family servants named Noya.

"One night, two military policemen raided the Tendoh house and arrested Tachibana. The informer who led them there was, I believe, a man named Kisuke Tokuoka—later

Kisuke Takeda—who lived in the neighborhood. We can't know exactly what happened that night, but the members of the household, not to mention Tachibana, must have been treated with extreme cruelty, such cruelty that Taki Tendoh's hatred has continued to this day."

"What?" exclaimed Ishida in dismay. "Are you saying that the motive for these murders lies in something that happened forty years ago? That seems a little hard to believe, doesn't it?"

"To tell you the truth, I can't say that I haven't had my own doubts about it. But from the weird nature of the crimes, we have reason to assume the murderer to be abnormal at least in some respect. And if that's the case, isn't it possible that forty years' time has not served to erase the memory of what happened that night? The fact is that after that raid, Taki Tendoh did suffer mental problems, from which she has never fully recovered. Moreover, she secretly cultivated marijuana, which she apparently used in her fortunetelling. Since hemp had been grown in Togakushi for a long time, she probably knew about it from early childhood.

"The extremely elaborate planning of the murders, though, makes it obvious that someone else must have been involved. That person, I believe, was Keiichi Noya, the owner of the Hokushin Laundry, and the son of the Noya couple who took care of the Tendoh household. The Hokushin Laundry serves the Koshimizu Plateau Hotel, and laundry employees have free access practically anywhere inside the hotel, so it would have been a simple matter to take a wax impression of keys. We had all the hotel keys checked yesterday and traces of wax were found on a couple that clearly indicate such impressions were in fact taken.

"Now, I doubt this Keiichi Noya is fundamentally of a

criminal disposition, but he does seem to have quite an aptitude for the job. For instance, in the murder of Representative Shishido, he realized that it might be difficult to get out with too many people on the alert downstairs, so he left the room key on the floor under the hatch to the roof, knowing its discovery would cause a stampede to that spot.

"So what it boils down to is that after an almost perfect series of murders, Keiichi Noya and Taki Tendoh ended up having to flee, all because of a white shirt that had been sent out for cleaning. They knew that would make it obvious the crimes had been a sort of inside job, and sooner or later would lead the police to them." Takemura finished his presentation with a deep sigh of near sympathy for the murderers.

"I see," said Ishida, sounding sympathetic too. "So the erstwhile victim became the oppressor."

No one raised any objections to Takemura's clear reasoning. Even Miyazaki, the proverbial fence-sitter, seemed to go along.

"Well, that's really something! I don't doubt that it must all have happened just as you say, Inspector Takemura," said Ishida, standing up and shaking Takemura's hand.

Miyamoto of the National Police Agency, who had maintained silence throughout, finally smiled and said, "You've done a good job."

But the bigwigs had not quite completed their mission. The last to speak was Chief Nagakura.

"Please don't let anything that has been said here get out of this room," he said, mainly to Takemura.

* * *

A short time later, Keiichi Noya's Hokushin Laundry station wagon was found beside the road near the boundary between Togakushi and Kinasa, about a kilometer west of the village of Upper Kusugawa. The finder, a resident of Kinasa, also told police that he had seen the same car parked at the same spot on the evening of July 6th, the day before Kisuke Takeda's body was discovered. The investigator who called in the report mentioned to Takemura that the spot was located at the entrance to a path going up to a place called Maple's Cave. Takemura quickly spread out a map. Sure enough, at a point where the path reached a ridge after climbing the north slope of Mt. Arakura, there was Maple's Cave, where the Demoness was supposed to have lived so long ago.

He wondered whether the two were headed for the cave. If they were trying to re-enact the whole Demoness Legend, that was a distinct possibility. As he was absent-mindedly tracing the path beyond the cave with the tip of his ballpoint pen, though, he suddenly let out an exclamation. He had just noticed that it continued down the south slope, finally coming out into the Arakura Campground. So that was it! That was how they had gotten Takeda's body there!

He had been had, he thought, biting his lip. The reason his men had been unable to find a single clue as to how Takeda's body had been gotten to Poison Plain was that they had been looking in the wrong place. The murderers had carried the body on foot all the way over the mountain from Upper Kusugawa! Unable to enter the campground the front way by car and leave the body without being seen, they had negotiated the mountain path at night, burdened by a rotting corpse, in a heavy rain that had been continuing for three days! How determined they must have been to leave that body on Poison Plain!

Takemura had to admit he was beginning to sympathize with them. The old woman at the Hall of Heavenly Wisdom might be a murderess, but maybe she was not so very different from the Demoness Maple, who had resisted the authorities of the day from her hide-out in the Togakushi Mountains. He was reminded of Kinoshita's destruction of the doodlebug trap at the Hall of Heavenly Wisdom. Justice, Kinoshita had called it, the same justice the police administered to criminals. To the strong, apparently, might did indeed mean right.

* * *

Although Takemura had expected an APB for Keiichi Noya and Taki Tendoh to be issued that same day, he was left hanging all day with no word whatsoever from the bigwigs at prefectural police headquarters. The next morning, he was summoned by Miyazaki, who took him to Tsukamoto's office. Tsukamoto in turn took them to the chief.

"Ah, thank you for coming," said Nagakura, standing up to greet them with an easy smile, in conspicuous contrast to the tense looks worn by Miyazaki and Tsukamoto. "Well, sit down!"

Takemura realized with surprise that the chief was speaking not to the other two, but directly to him. He sat down obediently on the edge of the sofa. Miyazaki sat down next to him, and Tsukamoto sat down in an armchair facing them.

"Our two visitors of yesterday left this morning, but I must say, they were most impressed with your presentation, Inspector Takemura," said the chief, taking out a cigarette for himself and offering one to Takemura. Takemura accepted it, and the chief quickly extended a lighter and lit it for him. Something extraordinary was obviously up, though Takemura had no idea what. He tried to prepare himself for anything.

"I know you haven't picked up the suspects' trail yet,"

continued Nagakura, "but you just keep trying, and take your time."

"Pardon?" responded Takemura, unaware that he was gazing hard at Nagakura. Take his time?

Avoiding the gaze, Nagakura leaned back and looked at the ceiling, exhaling smoke. "The fact is, you see, that at the request of certain people, we are going to keep to ourselves what we've learned about Representative Shishido's past. Instead we will announce that the murderers were suffering from paranoia and hallucinations under the influence of marijuana. It is true, isn't it, that this Taki Tendoh spent ten-odd years in a mental institution? You said yourself that the murders were quite abnormal. Our official announcement may not be quite the truth, but still, it can't really be too far off."

Takemura could pretty well guess the positions of the "certain people" who had made the request. With an election coming up, it would not be convenient for them to have the information come out that an influential Diet member from their party had begun his career in the military police of the old Imperial Army.

Miyazaki watched anxiously as Takemura scratched his chin. "I know that makes it difficult for you, but it's all right, really," he said, as if comforting a spoiled child.

"I see," said Takemura, looking back at him with an unintentionally bitter smile. "All right."

"Oh good. I'm glad you understand," said Nagakura. A burden had been lifted from his shoulders. He had not expected Takemura to give in so easily and could not hide his relief.

As for Takemura, he could only wonder at himself for having so easily dropped his principles. On other cases, when his colleagues had been willing to compromise or look the other way, he had always been the one to stumble on alone to the bitter end. He never would have expected he could do what he had just done. Strangely, though, he did not even feel angry. In fact, he had the distinct feeling that things were actually better this way, though he would not have wanted to try to explain to himself why.

Epilogue

 Beyond the Togakushi Inner Shrine, the slope suddenly steepened. The other two routes up West Peak were much the same—as soon as they reached its base, they turned sharply upward, clinging to the rocks most of the way. The distance was not so very great, and chains were provided at difficult places, so it was not especially dangerous. Still, one could get the exhilarating feeling that one was now a true alpinist.

Climbing the path once used by ascetic monks seeking the spiritual retreat of the mountains, Tomohiro Tachibana picked his way carefully, step by step, praying as he went. Passing below the huge rock overhang known as Hundred-Room Tenement, he gained altitude steadily, using the chains where provided. By the time he reached Chest-Splitting Rock, a step away from the ridge, he was thoroughly out of breath. He remembered the first time Taki had taken him up into these mountains, forty-odd years ago—how they had gone straight to the top, passing one party after another—and look at him now! He painfully felt his age.

Reaching the ridge, he came to the fifty-centimeter wide, ten-meter long razor's edge called Ant-Gate Crossing, whose sheer cliffs on either side made it the scene of a good many fatal falls. For novices, there was a path around it, which he took without hesitation.

Arms and legs numb, he barely managed to keep going. Finally he made it to the stone marker at the midpoint of the West Peak ridge trail, which commanded an unobstructed view in every direction. Before him, Mount Takatsuma, the highest peak of the Togakushi Range, seemed to soar to the sky like a gigantic anthill. Below him was a great canyon, like a mortar scooped out of the rocks between West Peak and Mount Takatsuma. The bottom was covered with virgin forest growing to the base of the cliffs. Sitting down on a rock, he gazed at the scene. Somewhere in that forest were Taki Tendoh and Keiichi Noya.

A cold wind was blowing across his skin, moist with perspiration. While the world below was still saying a lingering farewell to summer, Togakushi was already signaling the arrival of an early, merciless winter. After the passage of an all too brief autumn, the long season of pure white would settle in. He imagined the two who would be sleeping under that blanket of white, and envied them their long sleep after the fleeting instant of a human life.

Taki and Keiichi seemed to have kept the police on wild goose chases to the very end. Since Keiichi had abandoned his station wagon at Upper Kusugawa, the police had assumed that he and Taki must be headed for the vicinity of Maple's Cave, and therefore had confined their search to that area. The torrential rain of the preceding night had rendered the police dogs' noses useless, and it apparently never once occurred to the human trackers that the fugitives might have gone off in the opposite direction, far to the north, into the virgin forest all the way on the other side of West Peak.

Tachibana had spent two days keeping an eye on police movements from an inn in Kurohime Township, right next to Togakushi, but across the prefectural border into Niigata, where he figured the Nagano police were less likely to get him. They would almost certainly have been looking for him at his apartment in Tokyo. If they did find him, he was not planning to hide anything except his knowledge of Taki and Keiichi's whereabouts. Still, he wanted to be alone for a while.

Several parties of climbers passed behind him as he sat on the rock. Some of them made polite greetings, but he did not respond—until he heard someone come up, stop behind him, and just stand there. Feeling eyes on his back, he finally turned around.

"Miss Noya!" he gulped.

It was indeed Yuko Noya, standing there with slightly flushed, rose-colored cheeks which reminded him of a wax doll. In a sport shirt and knee-length jeans, she was not dressed for mountain climbing. Her black hair blowing in the wind, she made a queer impression on him.

In contrast to his own astonishment, she almost seemed to have been expecting to meet him there. Taking her time, she came around the rock and sat down next to him, so close that he could feel the warmth of her body.

"What are you doing here?!" he exclaimed. And yet, he had the weird feeling he already knew the answer to that all too obvious question.

"Somehow, I just felt the urge to come, the feeling I would find someone here." She fixed her gaze on the same part of the virgin forest he was looking at.

"Did the police come?" he asked, after a pause.

"Yes. An inspector named Takemura or something. He asked about grandfather, and about you, too, Professor."

"Oh yes, the Inspector." He could see Takemura's face. The man might not look like much, but he was not someone to get careless around. Tachibana knew that sooner or later he would have to face Takemura, but the thought actually gave him a queer feeling of nostalgia.

"But it must have been terrible for you and your family, having the police there," he said.

"Oh no, it wasn't so bad. Mother was very businesslike about the whole thing. I guess somebody must have done something pretty terrible, but the police and the news really weren't saying anything too clear about it. I had the feeling everybody was trying to cover something up."

Tachibana had gotten the same feeling. In the reporting of Shishido's murder, neither newspapers nor television had said a thing that approached the heart of the case. They had not even mentioned that there were any suspects. Something must be holding up the works.

"So, do you know where your grandfather is?" he asked.

"No, but . . ." She hesitated. He waited patiently for her to go on. "It wasn't my grandfather I was expecting to find. It was someone else."

"Me, you mean?" asked Tachibana, smiling at her.

"Yes, I guess. But why here? That's what I don't understand." Her lustrous black eyes were fixed on a point in the vast canyon below, as if drawn there.

Tachibana could only wonder. He had good reason for being here, but what could it have been that made her come too? Their meeting could not be explained as coincidence. Could it have something to do with her grandmother? Perhaps Yuko had inherited Taki's uncanny powers. The inspiration of the demoness.

Overwhelmed by a feeling of tenderness, he knew that

his remaining mission in life must be to do everything he could for this girl.

"Well, shall we go?" he said, standing up and holding out his hand to her.

"Yes," she replied, obediently taking hold of his hand, her black eyes smiling at him as he helped her up.

—THE END—